ALL MIXED UP

COMMON THREADS BOOK #8

HEIDI HUTCHINSON

WWW.SMARTYPANTSROMANCE.COM

COPYRIGHT

This book is a work of fiction. Names, characters, places, rants, facts, contrivances, and incidents are either the product of the author's questionable imagination or are used factitiously. Any resemblance to actual persons, living or dead or undead, events, locales is entirely coincidental if not somewhat disturbing/concerning.

Made in the United States of America

Print Edition
ISBN: 978-1-959097-28-0

to Matilda
for showing me that fishnets and glitter
absolutely go together

AUTHOR'S NOTE

Dear Reader,

Up until now I have been exclusively a closed door writer.

The past few books I've written there were moments during the creative process where I was conflicted about closing the door. It felt like I was doing the characters and the story I had built a disservice.

But I was afraid of transitioning to open door. I thought it would be brand suicide.

Still, I couldn't shake the idea that I was harming the depth of my storytelling. That I was pulling my punches so to speak.

And then I told myself I didn't have a right to show up in that space and contribute to romance in *that* way. The subject matter was too important to get wrong.

See, I learned about sex through romance novels. Without certain books and certain brave authors, I wouldn't know what I know. I've spoken to many people over the years that have expressed the same sentiment. Without romance novels with open door scenes, a lot of us would be very different people.

That's when I realized I had a responsibility to be a voice in that space. To contribute to the genre with the talents I've been given. To hopefully be a meaningful and healthy influence. To pass it on.

I believe this is where my writing was always leading me and I'm excited for this next step.

I recognize that not everyone will support this transition. I didn't come to this decision lightly. It has been on my mind and heart for quite some time. I wanted to be sure that I was making this change for the right reasons.

I hope you stick around, but I understand if you can't.

I know this is a big change and I want to make it easy for you to skip the spicy bits if they make you uncomfortable. The chapters with open door scenes will have an asterisk after the chapter number. Just a small symbol to notify readers of what to expect so you're not blindsided, but nothing too harsh to pull you out of the story.

Not every book moving forward will have open door. It will really depend on the story and the characters. I will be upfront in the blurb if there will be open door scenes so you can make an informed decision.

Thank you for reading my stories. Thank you for sticking with me. Thank you for giving me the chance to be a part of something greater than myself.

Love Always,

Heidi

PROLOGUE

CelebX

BREAKING NEWS

The indie rock band Winking Pete has canceled the rest of their tour.

Ticket refunds began showing up in emails late last night before the band had officially announced the cancelation.

Fans had been watching the ongoing antics of the band's lead singer with some trepidation. What started as showing up late to venues culminated in an "allegedly" drunken tirade in the middle of the third song at the Electric Ballroom.

Shelby Mallory mumbled through the first two songs of the set before being pulled aside by her brother and bass player, Asa Young.

The band began the third song, only to have Mallory shove her guitarist, Nikki Harry, and then launch into an incoherent speech that seemed to touch on everything from the government to her parents' divorce a decade earlier.

Winking Pete has seen nominal success over the past year with their breakout hits, "Bread Crumbs" and "I Hope You Lose Me."

Labeled as "the ones to watch" earlier this year by industry insiders, it now seems that the band's short career has come to a dramatic close.

We have not been able to reach the band's publicist for comment.

CHAPTER ONE

RESOLVE

ANDRÉ

He glanced at the map on the screen of his phone even though he knew exactly where he was going.

In more ways than one.

He'd never been inside XY Records, but he'd driven past it more times than was healthy.

It wasn't in the part of town where he lived. He didn't work anywhere nearby. He had almost no reason to be in Avondale.

Except for those times when he'd find himself driving that direction, going past the unmarked brick building, past the row houses, taking a right, going down the short street filled with bungalows and single-family homes, looking for lights on in the upstairs bedroom of a very specific home that he had once spent more time at than his own apartment…

Yeah. He had no reason to be on this side of town.

No reason to turn down the alleyway behind the recording studio where his ex-fiancée worked every single day.

Except today. Today he had the best reason he could have hoped for.

The rush of hope and terror swept through him for the tenth time since he'd answered the phone call from Johnny Enamorado Torres, the owner/operator of XY Records.

Johnny needed someone to renovate a few spaces in the studio. He'd been given André's number by a contractor that André had worked with a few times over the years. They had discussed Johnny's needs and set up a time to meet in person.

Which was now.

André had no reason not to think he'd be able to get the job. He had excellent references and his work spoke for itself. Even if it *was* a little unconventional to hire an archeology professor to do carpentry work.

His emotions had nothing to do with the job itself.

They were all about the woman he'd never gotten out of his heart and mind.

He clenched the steering wheel.

He'd screwed everything up two and a half years ago. And up until last Christmas he'd been convinced that what was over was over forever. Then he'd seen how his sister and her now husband had navigated the rocky waters of their relationship and he'd begun to think something different. That maybe it wasn't as over as he'd thought.

Maybe he could try again.

What followed that night was unknown to all but himself and whoever had answered the phone.

He'd gotten wine drunk and had called her.

Yes, he'd drunk dialed his ex on Christmas Eve like the complete numpty he was.

He didn't have a very clear memory of what he'd said.

She'd answered. He remembered that.

And his phone said the call lasted twelve minutes.

What had he said to her in twelve minutes?

Oh, he could think of a lot of things.

The problem was, he wasn't sure which things he'd *said* and which things he'd managed to keep inside his big mouth.

It could have been anything ranging from "I still love you," to "I miss your tits."

He groaned audibly as he made the left turn.

God, he hoped he hadn't told her he missed her tits.

He did miss her tits. They were glorious. Best tits in the world.

But he hadn't spoken to her in two years and that's not what he'd wanted to say to her the next time they spoke.

What he'd *wanted* to tell her was he was sorry.

He was so damn sorry some days it was all he could focus on.

Hopefully he'd at least managed to apologize. It would make the next part of what he was about to do that much easier.

He turned the car into the alley entrance.

The studio was sandwiched in between a row of walk-up townhouses and an apartment building. It looked like nothing. No signage; no obvious indicators of what happened inside the brick walls.

Most of the people who worked there and the bigger artists used the back entrance because the parking off the alley allowed more privacy.

At least, that's what he'd been told once upon a time.

And Nicole used the front door because her house was across and down the street.

It was late enough in the day that she should already be gone. He wanted to secure the job before seeing her.

His mind swam with vivid potential scenarios of how they'd meet again. He'd impress her with his growth, and they'd laugh about what an idiot he used to be.

"Your destination is on the right," his GPS told him.

This was going to work. He could feel it in his bones.

It had taken him two years to apologize, and another seven months after that for him to have a reckoning in his own soul that came in the middle of the night in the Badlands of South Dakota.

But when Johnny Torres had called him and offered an open door, he knew it as surely as he knew the Jurassic Period was his favorite to teach.

He had a chance.

An opportunity.

Just a small one, but it was there, and he wasn't going to run away from it.

Not this time.

Never again.

He turned the car into the parking lot, excitement buzzing in his veins.

Every decision in his life had brought him to this moment and he felt good about it.

He was finally ready to embrace life and stop being afraid to be happy.

It was going to be good from here on out—great even.

He hit the brakes as a flash of color and limbs hit his windshield with a loud *thud.* The car came to a hard stop and the colors rolled off the hood of the car and hit the ground.

"Oh God." He slammed the car into park and undid his seat belt.

How had that happened?

"Please don't be a person. Please don't be a person." His stomach turned and his hands shook as he shoved the door open.

The hot, sticky July heat engulfed him immediately as he ran around the front of his car.

It was a person.

He dropped to his knees, hands trembling.

He'd hit a person!

With his car!

"Are you okay?" he asked, not sure where to put his hands.

It was a woman in a bright dress. The fabric tangled around her legs, both of her shoes had come off, her arms were tucked under her body at an odd angle.

And the hair…her hair was blonde.

And she was utterly still.

He reached for her, knowing it was Nicole and still hoping it wasn't.

Footsteps came racing toward him, but he didn't glance up.

"Call an ambulance," he said to whoever had joined them and he felt her neck for a pulse.

A flutter under his fingertips let him know she was alive.

Of course, she was alive. The car had barely been moving. It couldn't possibly be that bad.

Please don't be that bad.

He pressed his face to the ground to get level with hers and brushed her hair out of her eyes. She was unconscious. Or at least, she appeared to be unconscious. He didn't want to move her, but he also wanted to be sure she could breathe.

He looked up to see that they were surrounded by some people he knew and some he didn't.

A dark-haired man in a light blue Henley was on the phone with emergency services.

Sabine joined him on the ground.

Sabine?

He did a double take on his younger sister. Why was she there?

"What happened?" she asked.

"She got hit by a car."

Sabine's head jerked around as she looked from André to his car and back again.

Nicole made a noise and they both looked down to her before Sabine could state the obvious.

"Ow," Nicole whimpered. She tried to move and cried out.

"Don't move. Where does it hurt?" André placed a hand gently between her shoulder blades and lifted it again.

Nicole ignored his instruction to not move and rolled onto her back. She cradled her right elbow with her left hand, face contorted in pain. Water started leaking from her eyes.

"I'm okay," she lied through her tears.

André skimmed his fingers along her hairline, brushing away flecks of dirt and gravel. He scanned the scrapes and marks on her face and arms and legs. His stomach twisted with guilt and fear.

"Please stop moving," he whispered.

If he'd injured her to a point—

No.

He couldn't go there. She was fine.

Her blue eyes flashed as they raked over his face. Like she was just now realizing who he was.

"What…?" she started to ask and struggled to sit up.

He sucked in a breath and held his hands out, palms facing her. "Stay there."

She narrowed her eyes at him and all those fantasies that he'd had about seeing her again crumbled into dust like the guy from *Indiana Jones and the Last Crusade* who chose the grail that wasn't so holy.

Sirens grew closer and relief began to prickle in the back of his mind. "It's okay," he said, trying to reassure her (and himself). "The paramedics are almost here."

He couldn't stop looking at her.

It had been years since he'd seen her, and somehow, she was even more beautiful than he remembered.

Her hair was longer than she used to keep it but not by much. Just past her shoulders. And still blonde. No pink or blue tips like when they'd first met. And she had bangs, which was new.

Her pale complexion was tanned from summer sun, and she smelled like coconut and vanilla.

His gaze landed on her narrowed eyes, and he felt an involuntary smile tug his lips.

Fucking hell, André! Now's not the time!

"André?" she asked. "What are you doing here?"

"I like your hair," he blurted and then shook his head. "I'm sorry. Does anything hurt?"

She took a deep breath and closed her eyes. "My arm hurts."

She was still holding it against her chest. Hopefully it wouldn't be anything serious. He would never forgive himself.

She was speaking clearly though, so hopefully that meant no concussion.

"I'm going to be late for my date," she said.

André swallowed the tightness in his throat.

Date?

In all of his various fantasies of them reconnecting, her dating someone else hadn't factored into it.

But it had been two and a half years.

Of course she'd be dating someone!

"I'll let him know," Sabine said.

André glanced at his sister who had retrieved Nicole's shoes, purse, and phone.

What the hell was Sabine even doing here?

"Thanks." Nicole opened her eyes and looked from André to Sabine and back again. "Did you hit me with your car? Did that really happen?"

"You have a date?"

He hadn't meant to ask that out loud. He regretted it instantly. He regretted it a second time when Sabine swatted him in the arm with the back of her hand.

And regret piled on top of regret when Nicole rolled her eyes and then didn't look at him again.

Like she was dismissing him from her thoughts entirely.

This was not how he'd wanted any of this to go.

The EMTs and police arrived and he was shuffled out of the way.

He watched from a distance as the first responders examined Nicole.

How had this happened?

She'd come out of nowhere.

That's what he said to the officer who'd come over to take his statement. He answered all the questions put to him and provided his identification and insurance information all while trying to watch what was happening with Nicole.

When she climbed into the back of the ambulance with only a little assistance from the EMT, some of his worry drained away. She seemed to be moving fine on her own and she even laughed at something Sabine said right before they closed the doors and drove away with her.

After his adrenaline began to ease off, he remembered that Sabine sometimes worked out of the studio with one of her students. He wasn't sure about the details. She was a tutor for celebrity children.

That was an oversimplification, but it covered the basics.

And now that he wasn't freaking out anymore, her presence made sense.

She was definitely going to have questions about why *he* was there though.

Much the same way the police officer did.

The look the officer gave him when he said he was the victim's ex-boyfriend was noteworthy.

Especially when he tried to explain that he wasn't trying to see Nicole at all and, in fact, was using the alley entrance to avoid her entirely.

"Is she okay?" André asked for the tenth time.

The officer sighed and flipped his notebook closed.

Sabine, also finished answering questions, approached him. "Please tell me you didn't hit her on purpose."

André growled under his breath and forced a smile at the officer who'd narrowed his eyes. He grabbed Sabine by the elbow and turned her away.

"Thank you for that vote of confidence, dear sister," he replied tightly.

Sabine rolled her eyes.

"Do you know where they're taking her?"

Sabine started to answer and stopped. She narrowed her eyes suspiciously. "Why?"

"Oh my God. Sabine." He leveled a look at her. "Do you honestly think I did that on purpose?"

Her expression relaxed a bit. "No. Obviously. But you haven't had contact with her in so long..." Her eyes sharpened on him. "What are you doing here anyway?"

André raked his fingers through his hair and paced away. He returned and planted his hands on his hips. "I was here for a job."

Not that he'd be getting that job now. He doubted very much that Johnny Torres would want to hire the person who maimed his number one producer.

Assuming of course that Nicole had pursued her lifelong dream and was indeed producing award-winning albums for the biggest names in the industry.

Fuck, this could not have gone any worse.

"A job?" Sabine's chin jerked back. "Wait. Are you tutoring? Am I being fired?" She shook her head. "No. That's ridiculous. Are you replacing me?"

"Not a teaching job." André started to explain.

At that moment the man wearing the blue Henley and formidable frown approached them.

"Johnny," Sabine greeted him. André closed his eyes and wished none of this was happening. "This is my brother, André."

Johnny's frown turned more perplexed and he let out a beleaguered sigh.

"André Debois?" Johnny guessed.

André nodded once, grinding his teeth together.

If the earth would open up and swallow him whole now, that would be great.

Johnny made a short humming sound as he glanced between André and Sabine. "I never put it together that you both have the same last name."

"Well, why would you?" Sabine forced a weird laugh and then sobered instantly. "Is he replacing me?" she asked.

"No, Sabine," André said before she could confuse Johnny any further. "I do carpentry work in the summers when I'm not doing field work. I was here to talk about doing some renovations."

"Ohhh." Sabine rocked back on her heels. "That makes more sense."

André faced Johnny and prepared to be told his services were no longer needed. "I'm very sorry about what happened just now."

Johnny's eyebrows lifted and he let out a soft chuckle. "Yeah, that was scary. But Nikki seems to be okay. She agreed to go to the hospital just to make sure nothing major is wrong." He nodded as he added, "And just to have it on record for insurance in case something comes up in the future."

"That's smart," Sabine agreed.

André still couldn't believe that he'd hit her with his own damn car. He'd never had a driving infraction in his life. What a way to make an entrance.

"If you're up for it, we can still have that meeting," Johnny offered. "But if you'd rather reschedule, we can do that too."

Sabine eyed André and he could almost hear her thoughts.

Are you going to tell him about your past with Nikki? Are you sure this is a good idea? Maybe you should rethink this.

But he ignored her. "If I haven't already ruined the opportunity, I'd still like to talk about what you need done."

André glanced at Sabine who flattened her lips with disapproval.

He'd be hearing about this later.

Johnny headed back into the building. André went to follow but Sabine grabbed his arm.

"What are you doing?" she whispered.

"I need the job," André mostly lied. He didn't need the job for financial reasons. It would be too hard to explain to Sabine what else he'd been hoping to achieve. "Can you text me if you find out where they took her?" he asked.

Sabine growled and let him go.

Oh yeah. He was definitely going to hear about this later.

CHAPTER TWO

I BET YOU THINK ABOUT ME

NIKKI

"What the hell happened to you?"

Nikki kicked the drum kit out of the way so she could get the front door all the way open. She didn't actually kick it. She pushed it. With her foot. And it wasn't an entire drum kit, just a bass drum in its hard-side case.

"What I want to know, is why the drums can't live with the drummer," she grumbled. It was a common question that never really got answered. At least not in a way that changed the situation.

And yes, technically Nikki had paid for the drums. But they were Des's drums. The drums bought specifically for Des so Des could play the drums.

Why did they live in Nikki's entryway?

Asa leaped across the living room and over the back of the couch like a gazelle. He grabbed the bass drum and moved it further out of the way.

"Al and Steiny got home a couple hours ago and unloaded before going to bed." He planted one hand on his hip and pushed his glasses up the bridge of his nose. "I'm sure they'll move it when they get up."

"Yeah, in thirty-eight hours." Nikki tossed her shoes to the side and came around the couch into the living room. She collapsed into the old recliner and smiled grimly at her roommate. "Today has been awesome."

"Uh-oh." Asa sat down on the couch and leaned toward her, elbows on his knees. His dark eyes kept darting to the sling around her right hand and she could almost hear the panic squealing like old brakes in his mind.

"It's not broken," she said, before he let his mind go all the way to a worst-case scenario. "It's just sprained. This is mostly a precaution."

He inhaled and nodded slowly.

The last time she'd wound up in a cast it had been because of his sister. And that had changed the trajectory of all of their collective lives.

All things considered he was handling the sight of the sling better than she'd thought he would.

But this was the part where she had to tell Asa—her best friend, her confidant, the one who picked up all of her broken pieces and helped glue her back together—who had caused this current injury.

She squeezed her non-injured hand into a fist.

At least it hadn't been Shelby. It being her ex was actually better.

She told herself hopefully.

"So I was leaving for my date with Ryan—"

"Did he do this?" Asa broke in, his voice raised. He stood up, eyes wide, like he was going to rain down hell on Ryan.

Which—yes, sweet. But also, the exact reason she didn't want to say it had been André.

Since they were kids, Asa had always been a little protective of her.

Again, Shelby's fault.

"No, I got hit by a car crossing the alley," she rushed out.

"What?" he asked, voice clipped.

"Honestly, it could have been so much worse. It's just a small sprain from how I landed." She took a breath and lifted her eyebrows, ready to regale him with how she'd noticed the car at the last second and sprang into the air like the majestic creature she was.

Maybe if she could make the story exciting enough, she could leave out the part involving André.

The doorbell rang and both their heads swiveled that direction.

Their friends didn't ring the doorbell. They knew to just come inside. And also, the doorbell was working?

"Who is it?" Asa held a finger to his lips and his other hand extended toward her with the palm out to keep her quiet. She glared at his palm.

"Ryan. Ryan Malcom," came the reply.

Asa gagged silently and rolled his eyes. Nikki kicked him in the shin.

"Ow." Asa moved out of her range. "You can come in."

Ryan opened the door and Nikki tried to feel something more than indifference for the guy she'd almost been on a third date with.

He was…fine.

Ostensibly there was nothing *wrong* with him. He was tall, athletic, had a steady paycheck, objectively good looking. But they really had nothing in common. And not to sound mean, but he just didn't seem that bright.

Okay, yes, that was sort of mean.

Maybe she was being too snobby about it.

But she could only explain her job so many times. Either he didn't get it, or he didn't care to remember it.

Which was worse?

In her mind, not caring to remember was way worse. Not understanding wasn't something you could really control. But paying attention? That was a choice.

But she was giving it an honest shot—the dating thing.

If only to get Al off her back.

Al was her other bestie. The one currently snoozing away in her upstairs bedroom having just returned from another club tour.

She was living the dream. Or her version of it anyway.

And while Asa was protective, Allison "Al" King was proactive. She believed in getting right back on the horse.

In this case, dating was the horse.

Just because one guy broke her heart and shattered her expectations didn't mean Nikki was supposed to give up.

But it wasn't as easy as Al wanted to make it seem.

Nikki had been "all in" with André in a way that sort of felt like she'd never gotten "all out."

Nikki wasn't interested in casual dating.

Her standards had always been high because her parents' relationship had been so great.

She had no doubt that she'd put her own unreasonable expectations on her relationship with André. Which she'd blamed as the main reason he'd fled.

And just when she'd accepted that love like her parents' was rare and unusual, Johnny and Hannah had fallen in love right before her eyes. And then Sunshine and Sabine.

Maybe she'd just been allowed to witness magic unfold as a way of keeping her hoping.

Whatever the reason, it had worked.

She went on dates because Al had begged her to give it a chance. But inwardly she knew, lukewarm love wasn't enough for her. She wanted what she saw in her parents and her friends' relationships—depth and consistency and peace.

And if she couldn't have that, then she'd just surround herself with good friends and good music. Sort of like a punker's version of "crazy cat lady." She could be a crazy guitar amp lady.

She glanced through her disaster of a front room.

Or a crazy drum kit lady.

The weird aunt that showed up to BBQs wearing fishnets and taught all the kiddies how to make liberty spikes with egg whites and gelatin.

And the dating wasn't so bad. It was nice to go out and have someone buy her dinner every once in a while. If only to say she'd tried.

But she'd put some rules down right away with Al. Four dates was the limit. If she wasn't stupid in love with the guy by date four, she would call it off.

Which meant Ryan still had two more dates before she had to give him "the talk."

She was actually pretty proud of "the talk." She'd perfected it after a night of tequila shots and Mario Kart with Steinhoff and Asa. They had given her tips on how to let guys down without them even realizing it.

It went something like, "You're too amazing a person to be held back by me." Details customized for the man involved.

One thing she had decided to do when she'd started dating again was to never leave them wondering what had happened. Ghosting was unacceptable.

Wonder where she'd gotten that idea.

Anyway, back to Ryan.

He was really into baseball.

She was pretty sure that was the main reason they weren't going to fall in love. That, and he couldn't remember what she did for a living.

"What's…?" Ryan pointed at the bass drum and then the other various musical equipment that littered the wood floors of the formal dining room, living room, and entryway.

She waited for him to finish his question.

He shook himself out of it and faced Nikki. "Are you okay?"

And this was why she had given him more than one date. He was actually very kind.

"Yes, just a sprain."

"Is that going to be hard for your job?"

Oh. Maybe he had been paying attention.

"You're an auto mechanic, right?"

Never mind.

"Audio engineer," she corrected him.

He narrowed his eyes suspiciously. "Then why did you say you worked at that autobody place?"

"Recording studio," she said withholding a sigh.

"But you said you mix auto paint."

"I mix audio." She waved a hand at him. "It doesn't matter."

She was cut off by the doorbell.

Seriously, who had fixed the doorbell?

Ryan opened the door.

Asa opened his mouth to scold him (because who answers another person's door?) but Ryan stepped back as the next person entered the room.

André.

Nikki felt a lot of things all at once.

Confusion, anger, sorrow, frustration, dread.

But none of them were indifference.

André's hazel eyes flicked through the silent audience and landed on Nikki. He swallowed.

"How are you?" he asked.

"Fine," she replied automatically, her throat dry.

"What the *shit?*"

Nikki flinched at Asa's outburst.

Asa looked back and forth between André and Nikki, eyes wide and wild.

And all Nikki could think was, *this was not how I wanted this to happen.*

Maybe that wasn't the most logical line of thinking. If Asa had been in charge of her brain, she would have been enraged at André's presence.

But it had been more than two years since she'd been in the same room with him and she had wanted it to go a specific way.

She'd envisioned this day numerous times. Usually in bed as she fell asleep. She'd be in a tight, cleavage-baring dress, and have a perfect, sun-kissed tan. Her hair would be long and the roots freshly done. Her makeup would be subtle and airbrushed in the way that made her look both glamorous and effortless at once.

She wouldn't even see André.

No.

She'd be busy laughing at the joke of someone important and André would see her from across the room. His breath would catch and his heart would stop.

Because how had he ever let the perfect woman get away?

And then he'd beg her to come back.

And she'd smile and say, "Who are you?"

THAT HAD BEEN THE PLAN.

But no.

She wasn't that fortunate.

Instead, he hadn't seen her at all before he'd hit her with his car.

And now he was standing in her living room, in her safe space, while she was covered in pavement, her hair doing that thing where it curled at her temple but only on one side. Her feet were dirty and her dress was in tatters.

She looked like My Little Pony roadkill.

And André…

He looked how he always looked.

Handsome. Put together. His dark brown hair just a touch too long on top but still flawless.

His white dress shirt was tucked into his slacks with nary a wrinkle.

And did she mention the suspenders?

André didn't wear belts.

He wore *suspenders.* Different colors and threading and loops and clips and some with leather and some without. He collected suspenders the way some people collected shoes. He had a different pair for every outfit, for every event.

Why did he look so hot with suspenders?

It was stupid.

"Why are you here?" Asa asked, interrupting her thoughts.

"I, um. Hi, Asa." André clenched his fists at his sides and took a step closer to Nikki, his eyes never leaving her face.

Asa intercepted. "What. Are. You. Doing. Here?" Asa repeated slowly.

André finally looked at Asa. Really looked at him. And he sucked in a breath like he realized where he was.

"I wanted to be sure she was okay. The hospital wouldn't give me any information."

Asa scratched his cheek and planted both hands on his hips. He pivoted to look down at Nikki. "Hospital?"

"She was in a car accident." Ryan decided to enter the conversation.

Asa threw his hands out to the side. "What is even happening?"

Nikki opened her mouth to speak but André got there first.

"I was at the studio for an appointment—"

She narrowed her eyes at him.

Appointment, huh?

He swallowed. "And I accidentally—"

"He hit me with his car," Nikki finished for him.

"WHAT?" Asa yelled.

Nikki held André's gaze and just barely managed to hold back the smug smile that wanted to curl her lips. He deserved so much worse than Asa yelling at him and he knew it.

André dipped his chin and faced Asa fully. "I didn't see her. It wasn't intentional," he said quietly. Resigned.

Nikki rolled her eyes.

Oh, he could be so very proper when it suited him.

"I just wanted to make sure—"

"I'm fine." Nikki stood up. "It's barely a sprain. You've done your duty; you can go now." And she was going to take some ibuprofen because not only did her arm hurt from her elbow to her wrist, but she was now getting a headache.

She stepped gingerly around the furniture and the three grown men in the room, and headed for the small kitchen at the back of the house.

"If you're feeling better, we can still make it to the game," Ryan said trailing after her.

She groaned.

"Game? What game?" André asked, *like it was any of his business*.

They'd followed her into the kitchen. She got a glass out of the cupboard and filled it with water. She turned to the cabinet that housed their vitamins and medicines, but Asa was already there. He dropped two ibuprofen into her palm.

"A ballgame. We had a date tonight. We'll have to skip dinner, but we can get hot dogs at the stadium," Ryan suggested eagerly.

"Date? Are you...?" André asked.

"I'm her boyfriend. Ryan Malcom." He stuck out his hand.

Nikki choked, almost spitting the pills back out. She shook her head as she finished swallowing. "You are not my boyfriend, Ryan," she said.

He frowned at her and she could tell she'd wounded him. Which hadn't been her intention, but she wasn't going to let him believe something that just wasn't true. He had two dates left in the queue and that was it.

"Don't feel bad, I'm her fiancé," André decided to add.

Nikki shot him a look and he arched an eyebrow.

"What? Too soon?" André asked with a playful smirk.

And she was done.

She grimaced and waved her one good hand in the air, indicating all of Ryan and André. "It's time for you to leave."

Asa herded Ryan and André back the way they'd come. "You heard the lady."

Ryan craned his neck to catch Nikki's eye. "But what about…?"

"I'll call you when I'm feeling up to it, Ryan. I promise. Go to the game, have a hot dog for me." She forced a smile.

"Okay!" Ryan agreed and left without further comment.

André stopped at the door. The smirk was gone and he was back to being apologetic.

"I shouldn't have—"

"No. You shouldn't have," she agreed. "And as usual, you have brought your very special brand of chaos and calamity into my life. I had a truly horrible time. I hope I never see you again." She didn't wait for him to reply because she didn't care what he had to say.

Two and a half years ago she had wanted an explanation.

Two and a half years ago, she would have been thrilled to have him show up at her door.

But it was two and a half years too late.

She closed the door behind him and locked it.

"I am going to bed," she said to Asa on her way to her room in the back of the house.

"Are you sure you're okay?" he asked.

She stopped and turned back to him. He was asking about more than her arm, obviously. Asa had been there when she'd first met André. And he'd been there when André didn't show up. And he'd been there when Nikki had figured out, too late, that André was never going to be there.

"Yeah," she said honestly with a soft smile. "I really am."

He relaxed and nodded his head once. "Because I can go out there and kick his ass if it'll help."

She smiled fully at him. "Not necessary. He has to live with his choices. There's no worse punishment for him."

One thing she had learned in those two and a half years? André Debois was a speed bump. He was nothing and no one to her life.

He'd been a lesson and she'd learned it.

CHAPTER THREE

FEEL IT ALL (AND NOTHING)

NIKKI

She had thought about taking the day off. It wasn't too often you could use "hit by a car" to get out of work.

But after her hardy breakfast of yogurt and Advil, she wasn't feeling too bad.

And besides, if she stayed home, she'd just get bored and buy things she didn't need online.

Also, she had the unusual benefit of liking her job.

Actually, she *loved* her job.

Especially these days.

It was safe to say that XY Records was having a moment.

She'd been making music since she was a child but she'd been *working* in music for more than a decade. She'd started as a runner at XY Records and worked her way up to mixing engineer. She had been working on mastering in her spare time, but mastering wasn't as exciting as the tracking and mixing was.

She'd been able to learn from some of the best in the industry. She'd gone from admiring them, referring to them as peers, and finally, to calling them friends.

Some days were still too wild to describe. When she'd be asked to fly out to

LA or New York for a week to mix something for someone who could afford the best—and they'd chosen her.

While the old-fashioned aspect of recording music was fading into obscurity, there were still those who subscribed to tradition.

Nikki had kept up on the tech of the industry and she could do it all. From using the old-school analog Neve board and recording to tape, to doing it all digital, and everything in between.

If anyone asked, she didn't have a preference.

But if they weren't asking and she was talking to friends she trusted not to judge her unfairly, she'd admit to loving the practice of the old ways.

There was just something about the rawness of recording to tape. She loved the art of imperfection. It was part of the artist's voice. Digital tended to erase that.

It was a conversation she'd gotten into with Zara Lorna just before the holidays.

Eight months ago, Sunshine Capone had invited the world's biggest pop star to "stop by" XY Records to record a remix.

No one could have foreseen what happened over the next few days. Least of all Nikki.

Zara had started with asking simple questions about what switches did what and how to change this thing into that thing. Pretty soon, Nikki was teaching her how to track and the basics of mixing.

And all of that led to her and Zara spending Christmas Eve getting drunk and writing music together.

If she thought about it too much, she'd probably talk herself into believing it hadn't really happened.

Because it was *that* unbelievable.

She hobbled her way across the street a half hour later than she'd wanted to be. But getting dressed had taken more effort than she'd anticipated. While her wrist had been the only injury to report, her entire body was sore.

The keys fumbled in her left hand as she tried to fiddle the correct key front and center.

Her right hand twitched in the sling, trying to be helpful in its own way.

For all of the shenanigans she'd gotten into in her twenty-nine years on earth, this was her second major injury.

And it couldn't even be described as major.

Yes, she was aware she'd lived a charmed life.

In a few ways.

Not in love.

Bleck.

No. She wasn't going to think about André.

Not today.

She slid the key in the lock just as it opened from the other side. She lurched forward and Johnny steadied her with a hand on her good shoulder.

"You know you could have taken today off," he said, locking the door again once she was inside.

"Yeah, but I didn't want to." She shrugged and the muscles in her back told her to fuck off.

She shuffled down the hall to her office and tossed her keys on the desk before gingerly sitting in her swivel chair.

"You all right?" Johnny asked, making a face like he thought she might keel over at any second.

"Turns out getting hit by a car hurts like hell the day after."

Johnny grimaced. He crossed his arms and sat on the corner of her desk.

"Did they give you anything at the hospital?"

She stuck out her tongue and curled a lip. "Yeah. But I don't like how foggy they make me." That was true. But she didn't take anything stronger than over the counter anyway. "Don't look at me like that."

"Like what?"

"Like you're worried." Nikki rolled her eyes. "I'm fine."

Johnny's lips twitched and he stood up. "I'll let you get settled but come find me in a few. Or text me and I'll come to you. I have something to discuss. Also, if you have to go home early, just let me know." He paused at the door.

"Hey."

She glanced up into Johnny's soft expression and sniffed.

He dipped his chin and arched his eyebrows. "Whatever you need, yeah?"

She nodded tightly. "Yeah."

He held her gaze for a beat. Probably trying to decide if he should force the issue or not. Finally, he gave a sharp nod and left her in her "office."

It was an office and workspace and storage room all in one. It was littered with gutted equipment, unopened boxes, instruments that needed to be tested, and various other diversions.

It was a headache and a half to keep track of.

She needed to get it organized.

From down the hall came the distant sounds of male voices and heavy objects being moved.

Huh.

Johnny must've gotten a contractor to finally come in and work on the main-floor lounge.

It was about time.

She moved her wireless mouse to the other side of her computer so she could try to use it with her left hand. Did they have a left-handed mouse around here? Of all the useless boxes of wires and connectors Johnny brought in like they were precious resources, she didn't remember ever seeing something as useful as a mouse in one.

She tried to open her email and missed the icon several times.

Blerg.

This sucked.

Stupid André and his stupid car.

In her email was a small video from Zara that had her smiling.

The pop star was on tour in Europe and so their schedules barely ever coincided. An email in the middle of the night was pretty normal.

The video loaded and Zara's face filled the screen. "So, I've been working on that thing we started on at Christmas. By the way, tell your ma I need that sugar cookie recipe still." She tugged on the eyelashes of one eye and removed the falsey. "So listen…" And she launched into a melody without words, her head bobbing along to keep time. "And nah nah nah, like that. Like he's thinking about calling but at the last minute she calls him instead. And we can double back the chorus on the last round." She pulled off the second lash and leaned into the screen so all Nikki could see was her nose and top lip. "What do you think?" Zara yelled.

End of video.

Nikki chuckled and saved it to her special "Project Z" folder.

She wanted to play it again and take some notes but that would have to wait until tomorrow.

The next email from Zara had come in a few minutes after the first. This one was just text though. It was some of the lyrics they had written that fateful night with more added to it.

Oh what a night that had been.

Unexpected phone calls, confessions, and so many sugar cookies.

She flexed her hurt hand in its brace and growled.

She couldn't take notes.

But she could listen to it again.

She played the video and hummed along to the song that was taking shape. She knew exactly what beat she wanted to use and cued up the sound file.

After some wrestling with the video file using her left hand, she played it on top of the beat.

Yeah.

That would be cool.

She typed out a quick message to Zara and attached the beat file.

But she hesitated before hitting send.

It was a lot—this next step.

So much more than recording a track for someone, or giving a few pointers to an artist, or mixing an already complete song.

Sending this file would be saying, "Yeah, I'm ready for the next step, win or lose."

And she wasn't sure she actually *was* ready for that step.

Especially the win.

The lose was easier to anticipate.

But what if she got everything she ever wanted?

Overwhelmed, she saved the message to her drafts and sat back in her chair.

After a couple hours of struggling to text and email with her non-dominant hand, she got up to go find more ibuprofen and check with Justin to see if Chase had called in.

As far as she could tell, the young audio engineer hadn't shown up for work.

Again.

She left her office and turned down the hall that went deeper into the studio. The control room for Studio X was empty, which was where Justin usually worked during the day.

She wound her way through the halls to the downstairs lounge where loud voices leaked out.

Ugh. She should have found the ibuprofen first.

Why did the skin around her ears hurt? What was that about?

Memo to self: don't get hit by cars anymore.

She turned the corner and stopped in the open doorway of the lounge. Her gaze skated over the backs of those she didn't recognize and landed on Justin. He was sweaty and grunting as he hauled an amp out of the storage closet at the far end of the room.

The lounge was normally a disaster.

But this was so much more.

Guilt sliced through her momentarily before she shoved that aside.

Yeah, maybe she could have gotten to this sooner and then Johnny wouldn't have had to pay someone else to do it.

But that would mean having a lighter workload, and she was excited about the studio's full calendar.

Guilt be damned.

"Justin, have you seen Chase?" she asked.

Justin set the amp down and wiped his forehead with the back of his hand. "Nah. He didn't call either."

"Hm."

They exchanged similar arched eyebrows.

Justin was the head engineer and house manager on the weekends. He handled the commercial clients—like TV spots and jingles. And up until Sunshine Capone had walked in eighteen months ago, that had been their main source of income.

Chase did a lot of the mixing for Justin's clients.

It bothered her that he hadn't come in again today.

Or most of last week.

He'd called out sick quite a few times the last couple of months and it hadn't felt like the truth. But she couldn't just run around accusing people of lying about being sick.

One of the cool things about where they worked was the flexibility. They'd all had to shuffle calendars for each other when opportunities arose that took them out of the studio. Like that time she tried to be in a band. Or when she had to go on location for VIP clients.

"I saw him a few days ago at Cassandra's house show. He spotted me and disappeared." Justin crossed his arms over his chest.

Conversations like this always made everyone uncomfortable.

No one wanted to gossip about their friend and co-worker. But sometimes information had to be shared to get the job done.

"How was the show?" Nikki asked. She'd wanted to go but it had been the second date with Ryan and he'd taken her to a movie.

Actually, it had been a documentary.

Which, at the time, she'd thought he was doing to impress her.

But it wasn't until she got there that she found out it was a documentary on baseball.

Again, nothing against baseball.

She just wasn't into it.

And now she knew a lot more about it than she ever cared to. Still didn't make her love it.

"It was good." Justin wagged his head back and forth. "They're still rough around the edges but they got the spirit."

Her lips quirked up on the side. "Sometimes that's all you need."

"I'll let you know if I hear from Chase." Justin gestured at the pile of equipment they'd made in the middle of the room. "Can we put this stuff in your office for a minute?" he asked.

She heaved a loud sigh. "I don't really have a choice. Yeah. But I might need some help making room in there first."

"I can help with that," a familiar male voice said.

Goose bumps immediately broke out along her forearms and her gaze darted to one of the workmen in the room.

She jerked her chin back and a muscle in her neck cried out in pain.

"What? Ow!" She grabbed the back of her neck. "What?" she repeated.

André rubbed his gloved hands together and took a step her direction. "I can help make room in your office." He frowned at her expression. "Are you okay?"

"What? No. What?" She knew she wasn't being clear in her questions because *what?*

André took another step towards her, concern furrowing his brow further. She retreated and winced when her stiff body protested at the sudden movement.

"Fuck," she hissed.

"Nicole?" André came closer.

"Why are you here?" she asked, her eyes darting around the room, taking in all the work that had been done since the last time she'd been there. She tried not to look at André but he was looming too large in front of her and she really couldn't avoid it.

He was in jeans and a stained red t-shirt that was downright scandalous in the way it clung to every single muscle in his upper body—from his chest to his biceps. Work boots, gloves, sweaty hair pushed back from his forehead, fucking suspenders that only accentuated every curve of his pecs and shoulders.

He was speaking but she hadn't heard a word he'd said.

"And who's that guy?" she gestured to the other man in the lounge she didn't recognize. This one was older, shorter, with dark complexion and black hair.

"Javier," he introduced himself and then folded the knife in his hand. To André he said, "It looks like maple but we'd need to pull all the carpet to see what kind of shape it's in."

What carpet? This carpet?

She looked down at the floor beneath her and then back to André, then to Justin.

Justin had that perplexed look on his face that he used when he was getting ready to play stupid.

"Johnny!" she hollered, backing (slowly) toward the door. When she reached the hallway, she turned toward Studio Y and propelled her aching body as fast as it would go. "Johnny!"

He met her in the hall, his expression puzzled. When his eyes bounced over Nikki's shoulder, she knew she'd been followed.

"What's *he* doing here?" She jerked a thumb over her shoulder.

Johnny frowned at her tone. "He's here to do some measurements. I hadn't decided on hiring him yet."

She narrowed her gaze at her longtime friend and boss. "Uh, he ran me over last night. Or did you forget?"

Johnny opened his mouth, closed it, blinked a few times. "I was going to talk to you before making—"

"You think?" she cut him off.

"Nicole," André said softly behind her. Like a warning.

But she was not amused.

"After the fit you threw when *your* ex started working here, I'd think you'd be more sensitive—"

"Wait." Johnny planted his hands on his hips. "Your ex?"

Nikki's mouth was still open, but no sound came out. She pivoted in the hall so she could see both Johnny and André.

André shook his head at her. "I didn't tell him."

Nikki blinked and looked between the two men as her stomach curled in on itself.

Shit.

"Uh…" She blinked at André, then at Johnny. Purposely, she closed her mouth and shuffled back the way she'd come.

Was she running away?

Fuck yeah.

She just needed a minute to get her head together and find some more freaking Advil and *then* she'd deal with…whatever this was.

Except that neither man was about to let her go that easily.

She reached her office with Johnny right behind her, and André right behind him. Which wasn't a surprise considering she was moving at the speed of a peg leg pirate in deep mud.

The door closed behind all three of them and Nikki started rifling through her desk drawers.

"So, just to get the ball rolling," Johnny started. "Remember when I used to work for Ortega Construction?"

"Sure. Mr. O. The guy who taught you how to build a house."

"Right. Well, I called him a couple months ago to see if he had room for what we needed."

So far this made sense.

"But he's too busy right now and it would be a twelve-month wait."

She made a face and kept digging. There had to be an aspirin or a Midol in here somewhere.

"He referred me to André Debois. Said he did freelance carpentry in the summer, and he might be available. I interviewed him last night, found out he's Sabine's brother, and I was going to ask you how you felt about him working here after he'd hit you, but then you started yelling at me."

Nikki gagged.

"What's going on, Nikki?" Johnny asked in that "dad" tone he used on his younger brother, Shawn.

"I'm just trying to find some Advil, boss. Because *someone* hit me with their car last night and wow does it hurt."

She shut the desk drawer with more force than she intended and her gaze tangled with Johnny's.

So not just the dad tone but the dad frown too.

Awesome.

"Start talking," Johnny said calmly. Not mad, not upset. Just Johnny being Johnny.

"I get it, okay," she started. "Nikki Talks Too Much has a secret? What? How could that be?" She scratched her cheek and forced a closed-mouth smile. "It was embarrassing, okay?" She waved a hand at André but didn't look at him. "We dated, we were engaged, he dumped me." She twitched at the lack of truth in her words. "I mean, he ghosted me without an explanation, but getting dumped is getting dumped." She huffed. "It was more than two years ago and I haven't seen him since."

She looked at André then.

"Until he hit me with his car."

Johnny ran his tongue over his lower lip and pumped his eyebrows. "'Kay." He turned to André. "Now you."

André rubbed the back of his neck. "She said it all."

But Johnny wasn't satisfied with that answer and frankly neither was Nikki.

"Did you know she worked here?" Johnny asked.

André grimaced. "Yeah."

"Did you hit her on purpose?" Johnny asked.

André's eyes snapped up and his frown turned severe. "No!"

Nikki almost laughed.

Johnny held up his hands but he didn't look apologetic at all. "I had to ask."

"I hadn't seen her in so long I wasn't sure how to bring all that up." André's eyes flicked to Nikki. "It didn't seem relevant anymore."

Those words hit like a bullet to her heart.

Of course.

He'd ended the relationship without looking back.

Of course, he'd moved past it and wouldn't think to bring it up in a job interview nearly three years later.

How sad was she?

Hadn't she just told Asa last night that she was fine? If that were true, she wouldn't have had such a huge reaction to André doing some construction work down the hall. It wasn't like he was her new gynecologist or something.

And in throwing her fit, she'd inadvertently revealed her true feelings on the matter. To everyone. Including herself.

Ugh.

She didn't want to be that person.

Relationships ended all the time. André was right. It had been over two and a half years. It shouldn't matter.

Johnny took a breath and turned back to Nikki.

"Should I fire him?" He didn't wait for a response. "He's fired. It's done."

Nikki did laugh then. "No, that's not…" She shook her head and sighed. "I was just surprised is all. I shouldn't have yelled at you for not knowing what you didn't know."

Johnny grunted in agreement.

Her neck spasmed again and she hissed in pain. "Fuck!" She reached for her neck, squeezed her eyes shut, and breathed through the pain.

They'd thoroughly checked her out at the hospital. Done all kinds of X-rays and examined her in ways that felt invasive but probably weren't. The ER doc had warned her that the pain the next few days might be severe. Which was why they'd given her a prescription painkiller.

And she understood that, she did.

But she was never going to fill that script.

She'd experience firsthand what prescription pain pills could do to an individual. What it could do to a family. She was never going to risk the people she loved like that.

André made a frustrated sound, opened the door, and left the office.

She couldn't say she blamed him.

After all, she'd just run away from this awkward conversation a few minutes prior.

Johnny came closer, his expression more earnest.

"He was just here to take some measurements. I was literally on my way to ask you if you'd be uncomfortable with this. I had no idea you two had a history."

She exhaled and sat down in her chair. "I know. Little Miss Overshare left out some key moments in her life."

He smiled softly at her. "It's okay to have secrets, kiddo. But maybe don't yell at me for not knowing them."

She let her gaze drift to the floor and smiled sadly. "We hadn't been engaged very long. Just a few days. We hadn't made it official yet. We wanted to tell our families first. I was going to tell you after that. And then it ended and it didn't matter anymore."

Johnny's frown flickered between confused and angry and her heart warmed.

They'd known each other for over a decade. He wasn't mad at her; he was mad on her behalf.

"It's okay, Johnny," she said with a small smile. "It hurt initially, but I really have moved past it."

"Has he?"

She snorted and swiveled her chair to face her desk. "I think hitting me was definitely an accident. And as much as I hate to admit it, he's right. It was a long time ago. It wouldn't make sense for him to tell you."

André returned then and strode to her desk with purpose. He handed her two pills. "Advil," he said. He plopped them in her palm and then screwed off the lid to the water bottle he carried. He set the bottle on the desk.

"Thank you," Nikki muttered, taking the pills.

He'd gone and found her exactly what she needed.

Which just reminded her of how great he used to be.

Until he wasn't.

Wasn't there a Lizzo song about that exact issue with men?

Whatever.

"Nicole—"

She held up a hand to stop him. "My name is Nikki."

He flinched.

Sure, Nicole was her full name. And once upon a freaking time, she'd loved that he called her Nicole. It had felt special and elegant.

But that story was over.

"If my being here makes you uncomfortable, then I'll go—"

"No," Nikki stopped him. "It's fine." She nearly gagged on the words.

"Yeah, you sound fine," Johnny said flatly.

Nikki rolled her eyes. She knew she was being uncharacteristically mean. It wasn't in her nature. She was both the shiny and the happy that drove everyone around her into the arms of optimism whether they wanted to be there or not.

"I'll be fine." She glared at Johnny who smirked. "I'm sore and hungry. Those are my main issues at the moment."

"Can I get you lunch?" André offered.

She wanted to throw her hands in the air in exasperation. But her shoulders and neck were telling her that that would be a bad idea.

So she sighed and narrowed her eyes to the tiniest slits she could muster.

He arched an eyebrow and a corner of his mouth twitched ever so slightly.

"I'll have it brought in. You don't have to move." André glanced at Johnny. "I'll get lunch for everyone. Just as a way to say thank you and sorry."

Johnny pursed his lips and looked to Nikki to give the answer.

She relaxed her jaw but her eyes remained narrow.

"Tacos from La Morena?" André asked.

She didn't reply vocally but her stomach rumbled with an embarrassing growl.

André lifted his chin and took a step backward.

Fine.

He wanted to buy her lunch so bad, then she wasn't going to stop him. But she was going to push it for all it was worth.

"A lot of tacos," she said. "I'm *very* hungry."

The corner of his mouth tugged into the softest of smirks and she had to look away. It had been those micro expressions that had won her over years ago. Those tiny little promises of more below the surface.

But he'd wanted to keep his secrets and maybe she'd pushed too hard.

It didn't matter now.

Anything he held below the surface was his. She had no rights to it, and she wasn't going to turn herself inside out to reach it.

She busied herself with her phone again.

"I'll return shortly," he murmured, and she sensed him leave.

Good.

"I'll make him work extra hard. I promise," Johnny broke into her thoughts.

She smiled. "Please do that."

"I'm going to ask again," Johnny said.

"It's fine," she replied with a sigh. "It's probably a good idea for me anyway."

"How do you mean?"

She shrugged. "I don't know. Usually if I embrace horrible things, I learn a valuable lesson somewhere."

Johnny studied her for a beat, his lips tipped up on the side. "You're a great person, Nikki. One of the best. I have always admired your ability to not only find the silver lining, but somehow dig diamonds out of it." He chewed on his bottom lip. "But you don't have to force yourself to do something that hurts you. Ever."

Her nose tingled and she inhaled to keep from tearing up. "I promise I'll let you know if I change my mind."

Johnny left her alone then and she adjusted her chair until she was mostly comfortable.

Justin started carrying amps into her office and stacking them in various places. He sent out a text to Chase since she'd been struggling to text with her left hand.

After a bit André reappeared with Johnny and a huge bag of food.

Johnny started clearing a place for her to eat at her desk and she immediately felt like a burden.

She made a face.

"Knock it off," Johnny chastised her, reading her expression. "It's not that bad."

"This whole office is horrible. I actually meant to clean most of it out this week." She gestured to her sling. "I guess it'll have to wait."

"I can help you." André propped his hands on his hips and gave the room a once-over. Then he looked to her for what? Permission?

Johnny coughed around a laugh. "Did you just growl?" he asked her.

Had she growled?

"Probably," she replied, her eyes narrowed at André. "I don't need your help."

He was unfazed by her frosty tone. He shrugged. "I'm working here anyway." He lifted his chin, indicating her sling. "I owe it to you."

"I'm positive your insurance company will get me what I'm owed." She blinked at him and smiled sweetly.

His gaze dropped to her mouth and bounced back to her eyes. A ghost of a smile graced his lips.

There was something there, in his eyes. Something complicated and confusing and she didn't have time for it!

"Thank you for getting us lunch. You may go now." She waved him away with her uninjured hand.

Johnny coughed again and this time Justin joined him.

She almost felt bad. Being snippy wasn't natural to her. But then she glanced up and saw his stupid handsome face and his stupid muscles and his stupid small smile and she decided that being a little snippy wasn't so bad when he deserved worse.

André held her gaze and then he nodded slowly.

He didn't say goodbye, he just left.

She should have felt relieved. Or satisfied at least. She'd gotten exactly what she'd wanted.

Right?

But all she felt was sad.

Apparently, she still had some healing to do.

Johnny handed her her food and she didn't like that André had gotten her favorite. Or that he included utensils so she could eat it easier.

Nope.

It didn't feel good to know that he'd remembered.

It felt awful.

Like breaking up all over again.

But she couldn't say that because no one would understand. So she ate her food and acted like the avocado salsa was the reason her eyes kept watering.

But it wasn't.

CHAPTER FOUR

OH WELL

ANDRÉ

Okay, new plan.

Don't be a twat.

CHAPTER FIVE

INCINERATE

NIKKI

She wasn't sure what she'd expected.

Of course, Ryan would take her to a baseball game since she'd missed the last one.

She hadn't gone home to change her clothes and stayed in what she'd worn all day—gray, wide-leg linen pants, a boxy cropped pink tee with Janis Joplin on it, and Chucks with no laces so she could just slip them on and off. Her hair was down, and she'd only applied mascara. And even that had been annoying.

Her wrist wasn't feeling too bad, so she'd ditched the sling and just wore one of those braces.

Her body wasn't as sore that day. Plus, she'd found a bottle of ibuprofen on her desk when she'd gotten to work that morning. Probably from Johnny.

Ryan had picked her up from work, and when they made it to the stadium, she wasn't even a little bit surprised.

"I can't believe you've lived in Chicago your entire life and never been to a baseball game." Ryan had placed a hat on her head very carefully. "Our seats are in the sun for a little while," he'd said by way of explanation.

Once he'd gotten them to their seats, he'd taken off to get beer.

So there she sat, in the bleachers at a game she knew nothing about, waiting for her date to return.

She took out her phone and read the texts from Al but didn't respond because she still wasn't happy about having to text with her left hand.

She was probably making a bigger deal out of it than she needed to.

The voice of her dad echoed in her head, telling her to stop pouting and try to enjoy herself.

She smiled to herself.

She needed to go up north and see him before the end of summer. Sure, she'd just been up there a month ago, but when your parents were as cool as hers, missing them was a byproduct of the relationship.

Maybe Dad would have some words of wisdom for how to deal with André working just down the hall from her.

Ryan shuffled back to his seat with three beers in his hands. He held them out and waited for her to take one.

"Beer at a baseball game is the most American thing in America," Ryan said, sitting down and watching the field as the players warmed up.

Nikki smiled as she watched his enamored expression.

There was something incredibly wholesome about Ryan. She could see why Al had set them up.

He hadn't been rude or creepy. He'd always been on time, paid for her food and drinks, opened all the doors. Fundamentally, there was nothing *wrong* with Ryan.

Not really.

Except that baseball appeared to be his entire personality.

But you know who he wasn't?

He wasn't André.

And that gave him, like, a thousand more points in the personality department as far as Nikki was concerned.

Ugh.

She needed to stop thinking about André.

She had successfully avoided him all day.

Mostly.

He'd already been working on the lounge when she'd arrived and so she knew what areas to stay away from.

Though she'd taken a peek in the afternoon when he'd left to get something at the hardware store.

What? She was only avoiding having to *see* him. She couldn't do much about *hearing* him.

He'd cleaned out the rest of the equipment in there and cleaned it up in half the time it would've taken her.

Probably because of those glorious muscles he had all over his body.

Which she'd gotten a good look at after he'd returned from the hardware store.

He'd walked into the lounge and had taken off his shirt without realizing she was in there. Or at least, she assumed he hadn't known she was in there.

So many muscles.

And tan too.

Like he spent time with his shirt off doing muscly things outside.

Stop it! No! she chastised herself.

Picturing André all sweaty and shirtless was…

Sigh...

Who had triceps like that? Was it genetic? It didn't make any sense. No one else had triceps that looked like that.

Where was she again?

She shook her head and took a deep breath. She needed to clear the images from her brain. They were too distracting.

Someone took the seat next to her. Ryan leaned across her to hand off one of his beers.

Nikki tracked the movement of the beer as it passed before her from one male hand to another. Her gaze traveled up the arm of the newcomer, and when her eyes landed on André's handsome face, she wasn't even surprised.

He'd obviously gone home after work and showered, unlike her. His hair was still wet and he was wearing charcoal shorts and a lavender t-shirt that made the green in his hazel eyes pop.

He waited for her to react, his gaze bouncing all around her face, to the hat on her head, and landing on her eyes.

And then he had the nerve to smile.

Not a huge smile.

Nothing so garish.

Just a small, barely there, whisper of a smile on his perfectly symmetrical lips.

"And I ask the universe one more time," she said low and with a slow blink. "What the fuck?"

His smile grew a fraction and something that looked a little like remorse flickered in his gaze. "Hello, Nikki."

She sighed with her whole body.

And not in the tingly, sexy way she had a few moments prior when she'd been thinking about the shape of André's triceps.

No. This was the sigh of a woman who was nearing the end of her reserves of polite behavior.

That's right.

She was one more surprise reveal away from needing to be handcuffed.

Again, not in a sexy way.

"André," she said tightly. "What are you doing here?"

He inhaled and his eyes flicked over her shoulder. His mouth opened, but before words came out, Ryan answered.

"I invited him."

Slowly, deliberately, Nikki swiveled in her seat to stare at her date.

His bright smile was in no way dimmed by her glare.

"You invited my ex on our date?" she asked.

Ryan nodded. "Do you want peanuts? I meant to ask earlier but forgot. I mean, they can be messy and make you thirsty. But there is something magical about the whole peanuts-and-crackerjacks thing at the ballpark."

She stared at him, slack-jawed and a little impressed that he was this devoted.

"You know what?" Ryan continued when she hadn't spoken in at least a minute. "Hold my beer. I'll get both and you can try them and see what you think."

She watched the beer pass in front of her as he handed it to André. Then he stepped over his bleacher chair going up, made a sharp left, and bounded up the stairs.

"He's very attentive."

Her mouth grew small and her jaw clenched as she swiveled back the way she'd come.

André didn't look at her though. His eyes were on the field as he drank his own beer.

"Seriously, man. What are you doing here?" She leaned toward him and hissed, "I am on a *date*."

He nodded, still watching the field. "Yes, you are."

"And not with you," she pointed out.

He pressed his lips together but she caught the little tremble that said he wanted to smile.

"I am well aware." He glanced her way briefly. "For the record, I didn't know. Ryan invited me and I accepted."

She reared back. "Since when do you know Ryan?"

André hummed in the back of his throat. "We met that night at your house."

"Wait." She shook her head as if that would help. "What are you saying?"

André swallowed and turned to face her. "After Asa kicked us out that night, Ryan offered me your ticket to the ballgame. I'd never been to a professional baseball game and I thought it sounded fun."

She squinted one eye at him, trying to make sense of what he was saying. "You went on my *date?"*

He thought for a moment and nodded. "I suppose that's accurate."

"And now you two are besties?" she asked.

André lifted one shoulder. "He's a nice guy. A little obsessed with baseball, but not a bad person to spend an evening with."

Her left eye twitched.

This wasn't happening.

Why was this happening?

Was this actually happening?

Maybe she should go back to the hospital and have them reevaluate her for a concussion.

Maybe she'd been injured very badly in the car accident and she was in a coma and this was a nightmare.

Yes. That one made the most sense. None of this was real and she was just stuck in a nightmare loop somewhere in a hospital room. Hopefully someone would call her mom and let her know where she was.

André was speaking again and she had to blink to focus on his mouth and the words that were coming out of it.

"I'm really not trying to drive you crazy—"

She held up a hand and stopped him.

"Please stop talking. I've had to see and hear you a lot over the past few days and I'm tired." The moment she said the words she felt it in her body and face. The burn in her eyes, the ache in her joints, the tension in her shoulders. "I'm so damn tired I could cry. I have this date and one more with Ryan before I end it. I just want to get through it in a respectable way." She waved her splinted arm in a circle indicating André's presence. "I need less from you.

Which should be easy, seeing as you haven't spoken to me in two and a half years."

André frowned and then nodded once.

She glugged back her beer. When it was empty, André handed her his and took her empty cup. She faced the field and waited for her date to return.

So, André was there.

Fine.

It didn't matter.

Her phone buzzed in her pocket, and she growled.

André took her beer from her so she could get her phone out of her pocket. She knew who it was. She glanced at the screen and shook her head.

AL: how's the date?

Nikki closed her eyes and dropped her head back.

"What's wrong?" André asked.

"Nothing except that I can't reply to any of my texts." She waved her splint.

"What about voice to text?"

She frowned his direction. What about voice to text? "How do you do that?"

He put both cups in the holders on either side of him and gestured at her phone. "May I?"

She handed him her phone and he was very careful not to touch her as he took it. He cued up the text and showed her the tiny microphone icon on the bottom of the keyboard.

She'd seen it many times but had never even thought about it.

"You just tap the microphone and speak into the phone." He demonstrated. "Date is going well. Period. André is a twat. Period. And send."

She smiled despite herself.

He chanced a smile of his own as he handed the phone back to her.

He'd said twat.

Why did that amuse her so much?

It always had though.

André had been born in America—Texas, maybe—but his parents split up when he was ten. His dad took him to England, his mom kept his sister and stayed in the States. André moved to Chicago just after he'd finished school.

He'd only lived in London for twelve years and most of the time you'd never know it. But sometimes he'd say something so British that there was no mistaking where he'd spent his formative years.

For instance, when he said twat.

"Thank you. I didn't know how to do that," she admitted.

He adjusted in his seat, glancing over his shoulder. "I remember you preferring to use your hands for things."

She eyed him. "Yeah," she replied slowly. "I'm tactile."

He nodded and crossed his arms over his chest. "Where are those crackerjacks? I'm feeling peckish. What *is* a crackerjack?"

"Um," she swallowed and looked away from him. "I don't think I know. Caramel corn, maybe?"

He twisted around again and his arm brushed against hers. The heat tickled the hairs on her arm and she took a deep breath.

Chill out, Harry. It's been almost three years. You shouldn't have any kind of reaction to him at all.

Indifference. That's what she should be feeling.

Her phone buzzed and she glanced down at the screen.

AL: André IS a twat.

She smiled and set the phone in her lap.

"How is Allison these days?" André asked.

She glanced over at him. He made no apology for reading her text.

"She's good." Nikki stretched her legs out and braced her feet on the back of the seat in front of her.

Small talk was probably a good idea. Maybe it would help diffuse the swirling thoughts and emotions inside her. Help her see him as a regular person and not the guy that broke her heart and left her devastated.

Too dramatic?

Fine.

The guy who lost the best thing he'd ever had.

Better?

"She and Steiny just got back from touring. We haven't had a chance to talk. She's still resetting her clock."

"New band? Old band?" he asked.

Nikki chuckled and made a face. "New-*ish*. Al, Steinhoff, and Des. And they found some guy named Carter something or other to sing." She scrunched her nose. "I don't think he plays anything though." She shrugged. "I haven't met him."

"Are you still playing?" he asked, and she could barely detect the hesitancy in his voice.

Other people were a safe subject. Asking about her? That tested the boundaries.

She sent him a flat smile. "No bands for me. I don't need that kind of drama in my life. I'm happy where I'm at."

He nodded and they sat in silence for a few minutes.

She imagined he was remembering the last time he'd been to one of their shows. It had been the last one, but no one had known that at the time.

Old shame welled inside her chest and she took a deep breath to dilute it.

The things Shelby had said about her on stage, and even more backstage, in front of her friends, strangers, and André…

She shivered, trying to shake off the old memories.

"What about you? Still professing?" She was so proud of herself for how cool and chill she sounded she almost fist-pumped and ruined the entire thing.

Small talk for the win.

"Mm-hm," he confirmed. "And I just spent a month in the Badlands overseeing a dig."

"Shut up!" She smacked his bicep and twisted toward him. "You're kidding!"

Oh God. That was too big a reaction, wasn't it?

But that was Nikki; too excitable to be contained. Even when she knew she should be reserved. Like a haphazard roman candle of happiness.

Her gaze tangled with his and his hazel eyes were lit from within making them glow. He smiled wide and let out a small laugh.

"It was pretty cool." He ducked his head and red crept into his cheeks.

"What the hell, André?" she asked excitedly, blazing past polite and going straight for familiar. "That's amazing!"

He scrubbed a hand over his face, but it didn't clear the happy smile.

"What was it like? Everything you ever wanted?" she asked.

He sucked in a breath to answer and something passed through his eyes. Just a shadow—there and gone—but it dimmed his smile. "Almost. Yeah."

She wanted to ask more but knew it wasn't her business.

Thankfully, Ryan returned with snacks.

So, baseball was okay.

She wasn't going to have a favorite team after this or anything, but Ryan had been right. There was something super magical about watching baseball, drinking beer, and watching the sunset.

The heat from the day had started to dissipate and the colors of sunset drifted across the sky. Reds, yellows, purples, pinks, and oranges.

Nikki took a deep breath and let it out.

"Sometimes I forget about sunsets," she said.

André's head swiveled her direction. "Forget they exist or just forget what they look like?"

"Maybe both," she answered honestly. "I don't spend time looking for them and so they catch me by surprise."

She glanced to her right where Ryan was supposed to be, but he'd left to get more beer.

He'd done a great job of explaining the game without being a jerk about it. But there was still such a disconnect with him. As if he were only listening to half of what she said.

She eyed the empty stack of plastic cups in Ryan's cup holder.

How many beers had he had?

She'd only had two. André hadn't finished his first one.

Yeah, she'd be getting an Uber home.

"You know he thinks you're an auto mechanic, right?" André asked, having leaned into her space.

She chuckled deeply. "I know. I have told him what I do countless times."

André snickered and she joined him. He laughed harder because she was laughing, and it just fueled her to keep going.

God, it felt good to laugh. Laughing had to be in her top five favorite things to do. The release of energy was like an explosion of joy. A common way to celebrate just being alive.

Because being alive was always cause for celebration.

And there was something about laughing with André that felt…simple. Like untying a shoelace or turning on a light when you entered a room.

It was normal and familiar and *regular.*

Her phone buzzed and she checked it, still hoping to hear from Chase.

It was just a social media notification. She opened it and smiled at the picture of her dad holding up a fish he'd caught. She left a heart emoji and put her phone down again.

"How is your dad?" André asked.

She gave him a narrowed side-eye. "You just read people's messages all the time? You know that's rude, right?"

His smile was unrepentant.

"You know Dad," she said taking off the hat Ryan had given her and smoothing her hair down. "Finding ways to stay busy despite all the orders to relax."

She put the hat on André's head. He didn't react.

"For my birthday this year he got me a bandolier—that I'm fairly certain he had custom made—for my tools and stuff. He still can't accept that I prefer to shove everything in my pockets and leave it where it doesn't belong." Nikki rolled her eyes at herself. She knew her methods were a pain in the ass to those around her.

"Have you used it?" André asked, lips twitching because he knew the answer.

She growled. "I can't find it."

He chuckled low and deep.

"How are the renovations at the homestead?"

Oh boy. This was a tricky subject.

They had used to discuss carpentry work back in the day. He was always going to teach her what he knew and together they were going to fix up her old house. Her dad had taught her the basics, but she wanted to know how to do it all. She wanted to be able to build a house from the ground up.

It was just a weird hobby she'd gotten into in high school. Someone had said that girls couldn't take shop class and she thought that was idiotic.

She found out she really liked it.

Not enough to make it a career.

But she liked to drywall the same way some people liked to knit or play video games.

She shook her head and heaved a sigh. "Slow. I'm doing what I can, but it takes me so long to learn how to do something correctly. Learning how to use a bandsaw took way longer than it should have."

"Yeah, but once you've learned it, it's locked in there," he encouraged.

She licked her lips. "Yeah. Still. I'm better with electricity."

He shuddered. "That's scary to me. I still doubt myself every time I have to do electrical work."

"You don't really want to make mistakes in that area," she said, her lips pulled into a teasing smile.

"Not more than once anyway," he agreed.

She barked a laugh. He folded his arms over his chest, a pleased smile on his mouth.

"André…" she said, not quite sure where she was going but feeling like something should be said.

He glanced her way, hope in the arch of his eyebrows.

"This has been nice," she admitted. "Thank you."

He started to smile but his gaze drifted past her and he frowned.

She twisted back around as Ryan returned with more beer.

He offered her and André a cup but they both declined and then watched in silence as he chugged all three beers, one after the other.

André hummed and Nikki pressed her lips together.

The home team (the one Ryan was rooting for) hit a home run and the stadium exploded in cheers as the sky lit up with fireworks.

"How long are baseball games again?" Nikki asked André.

He looked around at the people around them, checked his watch, looked at Ryan. His jaw firmed and he frowned at Nikki. "His team is up by five. Ryan," he called.

Ryan was still standing and cheering. He swung around and almost lost his balance.

André stood and grabbed Ryan by the shoulder and spoke into his ear. Nikki could tell the shoulder grab was one part being friendly, but also to keep Ryan from falling into the stands.

Before she knew what was happening, André was hustling Ryan toward the steps. He jerked his chin, indicating that Nikki should come along.

She checked the seats and made sure she hadn't left anything behind, saw André's phone on the ground, grabbed it, and hurried after them.

André kept one strong arm around Ryan as they made it from the stadium to the parking lot.

"I love baseball!" Ryan yelled. "Wooooo!"

Oh boy.

"I know you do, buddy. And baseball loves you," André said, keeping Ryan on his feet.

He made it look effortless—carrying a full-grown man upright—even though Ryan was doing hell all to make it any easier.

They made it to Ryan's car and somehow André already had the keys. He clicked the unlock.

"Back seat, Nik," he instructed with a grunt.

Nikki opened the door to the back seat and André carefully laid Ryan inside.

André backed out of the car and stretched his arms over his head and then arched his back.

"I think he may have changed the shape of my spine."

Nikki chuckled and shook her head. "He owes you a professional massage for that. Thank you for getting him out here. I would not have been able to do that by myself." She frowned, realizing that if André hadn't crashed her date, she'd have been in a bad way.

The stadium cheered again and André closed the door of the back seat. He opened the front passenger door and rounded the hood to the other side. "Get in. If we hurry, we can get out of here before the worst of the traffic."

"I—what?"

He lifted his chin at the open door. "Get in. I'll drop you off and then take him home."

"You don't have to do that…" She said even though she had no idea how she was going to get Ryan *out* of the car.

"Get in, Nik." This time he said it in his bossy teacher voice that she liked more than she wanted to admit.

She got in the car.

"Ryan, buddy," André called when they exited the parking lot.

"Yup," came from the back seat.

"Where do you live?" André asked.

"We should get tacos. Do you guys want tacos? Who's driving my car?"

"I'm driving. We can get tacos," André said.

Nikki shot him a surprised look and he shook his head. "We're not getting tacos."

She snorted.

"Please don't crash my car," Ryan pleaded from the back.

"You don't want me to crash your car?"

"Nooo," came the mournful reply.

"What if I just crash it a little bit?"

"I'll be so sad," Ryan replied.

"Okay, I won't crash it," André said.

"Thank you. André's the best."

Nikki faced the window and tried not to laugh.

What had this night become?

"Check the glovebox for his registration," André said quietly. "Maybe his address is on there."

She rifled through Ryan's papers and found the address. Then she plugged it into André's phone.

But André didn't go that direction. Instead, he headed towards Avondale.

"You don't have to take me home first," she told him.

The look he gave her said she was an idiot.

"You're going to need help getting him home," she pointed out.

André glanced in the rearview mirror. "Nah. We'll manage. Won't we, Ryan?"

"André, you'd make a great shortstop. And, Nikki, you could sing the national anthem," Ryan slurred from the back. Then he rolled the window down and hung his head out like a dog.

Nikki lifted her eyebrows at André, feeling like her point had been made.

And what did he do?

He fucking grinned like it was just the most hilarious night of his life.

You know what he didn't do?

He didn't change the direction he was driving.

When they pulled up outside her house, she wasn't going to argue anymore. She got out of the car and André got out as well.

She stopped before moving to the walkway, and stood in front of him on the sidewalk.

He slid his hands into his pockets and waited.

"Thank you," she said. She wanted to say more but had no idea what.

Mostly, she just didn't want to be done with the night, as weird as it sounded.

"You two are a beautiful couple, you know that?" Ryan said from the back window.

Nikki snorted. "You sure you got him?" she asked.

"He's not the first party boy I've carried home," André reassured her. "I'll see you tomorrow."

"I'll see you," she said and went inside.

It wasn't until she was in bed and almost asleep that she realized she hadn't had to take any ibuprofen that night.

CHAPTER SIX

SWIMMING POOL

ANDRÉ

When he rolled out of bed the next day, it was in a very literal sense.

His muscles ached and groaned as he reached for his alarm.

Two days of cleaning out equipment in the studio lounge had left him sore in a way he hadn't been in years. Though, he probably didn't have to go as hard as he had.

It was just that Nikki was there, and the work was extensive and…

Okay, fine.

He'd wanted to impress her.

Stretching his arms over his head, he both heard and felt his back pop in three different places. Maybe carrying Ryan all over last night had had an effect as well. The man was deceptively heavy.

He liked Ryan, he did. Sweet guy.

But it killed him to think that's who Nikki was dating these days.

She deserved someone who…

Well, it didn't matter, did it?

She'd already mentioned Ryan wasn't getting more than one more date. He'd wanted to ask more about that setup, but didn't think she'd be too keen to discuss her dating habits with him.

He made his way to the bathroom where he brushed his teeth and shaved. He'd showered when he gotten home last night because he'd smelled like sweaty baseball fan and beer.

He couldn't remember the last time he'd been this tired.

Probably not since grad school.

Except he wasn't in his twenties anymore. It took longer for his body to recover from the combination of physical labor *and* lack of sleep.

His phone buzzed and he picked it up off the nightstand.

Text from his sister.

SABINE: Um, Dad called?? I was sleeping and he didn't leave a message. That's a misdial, right?

André let out a noise that was half gag, half snarl. It wasn't attractive.

He typed out a reply telling her to ignore it and tossed the phone on the bed so he could get dressed.

One of the reasons he had to keep reminding himself to not be a twat was because that's what their father was.

A selfish, ambitious prick. André had spent far too much of his life trying to win his respect and approval.

He'd never gotten it.

It didn't matter that he'd sacrificed any kind of a social life as a child, teen, and adult in order to excel at school. Which he had. He'd graduated early, with honors. Then he'd gotten dual degrees in geology and archeology. No time to breathe, he got his master's in paleontology.

He'd decided to go to graduate school in America though.

And that's really where the cracks in their relationship began to show through.

He was tired of living half a world away from his sister. Who was the only family member he liked.

So as soon as he could, he'd moved to Chicago, where he'd earned his master's.

Having spent twelve years in London, the transition back wasn't as difficult as his father warned it would be. Maybe that was because he embraced being an American as aggressively as his father had rejected it.

He'd never regretted it.

And for the most part, Dad left them both alone.

The only reason he'd be calling Sabine would be to get something out of it for himself.

She'd married a rock star a couple months ago. The media storm had probably breached René's thick cloud of football and football-related interests.

It was best if Sabine didn't take his call.

André made a mental note to call his dad and distract him from bothering Sabine. She didn't need to deal with him. André had had years of practice; he could do it.

He went to a drive-through and got a coffee and a breakfast sandwich, then headed toward Avondale for another day of trying inconspicuously to impress a certain producer.

The song "The World's a Mess, It's in My Kiss" by X came on his playlist and he froze.

Every other time this had happened he'd automatically skipped it.

He hadn't willingly listened to this song in, well, more than two and a half years. Instead of reaching for his phone to skip the track as he usually did, he turned the volume up.

He turned off the AC and rolled the windows down.

The hot July wind whipped through his BMW, and he breathed deeply.

His body relaxed in his seat, and he rested an arm along the open window, propping his opposite wrist on top of his steering wheel.

The fatigue he'd been feeling from his lack of sleep the night before swept away with the wind and the driving beat of one of his favorite bands of all time.

His previous thoughts about his father faded, and he went back to thinking about how last night had ended.

How lucky he felt being able to make sure Nikki got home safe. He didn't even care that he'd had to deal with drunk Ryan for that to happen.

He'd gotten Ryan home without issue last night and helped him get to bed. But not before Ryan made him a grilled cheese for his trouble. Then André had had to Uber back to the stadium for his car before he could go home himself.

It had been a weird night.

Weird but awesome.

His brain was still buzzing from having spent hours seated beside Nikki at the ballgame.

She was just so…great.

Funny.

Clever.

Ridiculous.

It was something he'd tried to forget. He'd even looked for it in others, but it wasn't there. He'd only found that kind of easy connection with one other human.

When he was with her, he felt amazing.

She felt like home.

Which was saying something, because he'd never had a safe home. Not emotionally anyway.

And yeah, when he'd shown up at XY Records a few days ago, he'd been hoping to "win her back" or whatever that meant.

But at that moment, he knew he'd be content to just have her in his life in any capacity.

Was he still impossibly in love with her?

Yes.

And he would be forever.

But he could love her from whatever distance she would allow, and he'd still be better for it than when he was away from her.

The clarity that came with that realization rushed through him and he smiled.

He pulled into the back parking lot of the studio.

It was empty, which was to be expected since it was just after dawn.

He got his tools from the truck and went to the back door where he plugged in the security code Johnny had given him the day before.

The lounge was mostly cleaned out. He would start pulling up the carpet today and seeing what the floors looked like. They might not be anything they could use. But Johnny had mentioned installing hardwood if that was the case.

André agreed.

The carpet had to go.

From what he could tell, it was old bowling alley carpet. Hilarious. But it was so worn down it wasn't functional anymore.

He flipped the lights on in the lounge and grimaced. He could replace those too. They weren't adequate for the direction the studio was headed.

Johnny had given him a tour the day before so André might get a feel for how the place was growing and in what ways.

He glanced around, making a mental list of what he'd do, and in what order. Then he headed down the hall to Nikki's office.

She deserved something functional and gorgeous.

This was not that.

What a mess.

How did she get anything done in this disaster?

He clicked his tongue as he surveyed the office.

Where to begin?

He knew exactly why her workspace looked this way. It was because the rest of the studio was exquisite. Organized and clean and beautiful.

It seemed Nikki was still putting herself last on every list in her life.

His chest compressed with regret and shame. He'd taken advantage of that in the past.

It had been easy to do. She had made it seem like she preferred taking care of everyone else's needs. He'd had no idea hers weren't being met until he'd overheard the fight she'd had with Shelby the night the band broke up.

As usual, his ability to make everything about him was truly remarkable.

It hadn't been special behavior for him. It was just who Nikki was.

She enjoyed caring for those around her.

It didn't mean she shouldn't be cared for in return.

He took out his tape measure and small field journal and began measuring everything: the floors, the walls, the ceiling, her desk, the amplifiers in the corner.

The room was actually bigger than it appeared. It was just so stuffed with equipment that it looked tiny.

And the carpet had to go.

If it could even be classified as carpet anymore.

He put his tape measure back and took out his knife. He crouched down, cut a two-inch slit in the fabric and pulled it back slightly.

Same hardwood as in the lounge.

Johnny had explained the front of the building had once been a general store. The owner had lived in the rooms upstairs. But then it had gotten sold and reshaped a few times over the years until being turned into a recording studio. Most of the structure was newer, from the last twenty years or so, and Johnny had every intention of redoing all of it a little at a time. But the front rooms had been saved for last.

He explored the rest of the studio, taking inventory of any under- or unutilized space and making notes in his journal.

Back in the lounge, he connected his phone to the large speakers Justin had lent him and cued up a playlist he hadn't listened to in a very long time.

NIKKI

Ugh.

She made a face at the wasps swarming the front door of the studio.

The sun made the door hot in the mornings and apparently some paper wasps had decided to build a home right there.

They were waking up for the day and flying all over the place.

No, thank you.

She wasn't going to mess with that.

Thankfully she didn't have to walk all the way around the block to get to the back door. She could use the small footpath between the walk-up apartments and the brick building. It wasn't meant for thru traffic on most days, but it would do.

Her phone alerted her to a text message and she hadn't even opened it before the phone started ringing.

The screen displayed the name "Z" and Nikki shook her head.

"Hello?" she asked, trying not to laugh and failing.

"Did you listen to it yet?"

"Listen to what?" Nikki asked, playing stupid. She picked her way through the overgrowth that crowded the stone pathway.

"I sent you a thing!" came the excited reply.

"I'm just getting to work now. Where did you send it? My email?" As Nikki turned the corner, branches reached out and brushed along her bare thighs.

She'd had an easier time getting dressed that morning and had opted for shorts that were probably too short for the workplace but oh well. It was a thousand degrees outside, and Johnny had never set a dress code.

Her shorts were hot-pink dolphin-cut running shorts with white piping on the trim. She'd paired them with a white t-shirt with Blondie on it and her lace-less Chucks. Because tying shoes was still difficult.

Her hair…

Well, her hair looked a lot like it did when she'd been a child running wild at the lake house all summer long—free and messy and probably tangled. But she'd done her best.

A huff came through the other side of the phone.

"No. I texted it to you."

Nikki chuckled. "The text you sent four point one milliseconds before you called me?"

No reply.

Nikki grinned and ducked, pushing some overgrowth out of her face. She needed to tell their maintenance service to get over to this side of the building before the vegetation swallowed the building. How was this better than braving the wasps at the front door? She was going to have to check herself for ticks after her small trek through the jungle. "I haven't listened to it yet, Z."

"Call me back when you do."

The line went dead.

Nikki looked down at the screen to verify the pop star had hung up on her and she snorted.

On one hand, her spontaneous and secret friendship with Zara Lorna, award-winning recording artist, was one of her favorite things about her life. On the other hand, it often gave her indigestion.

Today was an example of the former.

She slid the phone into her side pocket and finally emerged from the wilderness.

And stopped short.

"Ohhh no," she said to no one. Well, she said it to herself. But herself wasn't listening.

Because there, at the back door to the studio, the very door she was going to need to walk through to get to her job, the one that paid her bills and gave her joy, was André.

No, wait.

Not *just* André.

It was André without a shirt.

Wait again.

It was André, sans shirt, in jeans that were slung waaaaay too low to be legal, those stupid suspenders the only thing keeping his pants from showing the world what the good Lord had made with love.

And that was not all.

He was carrying a roll of carpet over one shoulder out to the dumpster which had been moved to the back door from its usual place in the alley.

She inhaled slowly, trying not to think about how André had probably been the one to move the dumpster. He'd probably done it by himself with no help, his back muscles straining and his glutes and thighs testing the seams of his jeans.

Were those Wranglers?

André owned Wranglers?

In one fluid motion he heaved the roll of carpet into the open bin. He placed his hands on his hips and took a step back, his chest rising and falling with his exertion.

Nikki's mind and heart became a tumble of competing things.

Once upon a time, that body had been hers to explore and touch and hold. That man had made her laugh and smile and *feel* more than she knew she could.

And all that was over now.

He didn't love her, and she'd accepted that.

But there he stood. The most perfect heartbreak of her life wrapped in golden muscles.

He spotted her and she wanted to bolt but her feet were anchored to the concrete.

She wiggled her fingers in a wave and he smiled.

Really smiled.

Not an almost smile, but a wide-open, happy, genuine smile.

Then he turned and went back inside the studio.

Her left thigh buzzed and she jumped, realizing too late it was her phone and not the wasps chasing her down.

She slipped the phone out of her pocket, relieved she had a distraction.

"I haven't listened to it yet," she said as greeting.

"I'm just going to stay on the phone with you until you do," Zara replied.

Nikki smiled. The turbulent storm of emotions swirling in her chest dissipated to a gentle breeze that she could ignore for a minute.

She entered the studio and went straight to her office, not looking for André and kind of hoping she wouldn't see him again.

Yes, last night had been...unexpected.

And if pressed she would even admit to having fun with him and being thankful that he'd been there to help with Ryan.

Oh yeah. She should check on Ryan and see how he'd fared after last night.

On her way down the hall, she passed the open door to the lounge and closed her eyes to the activity inside.

She tried to close the door to her office but the couch from the lounge was in the hall blocking it. She growled under her breath and gave up.

"What's going on there today?" Zara asked.

"Um, renovations?" Nikki answered with the simplest explanation. She opened the sound file on her phone. "I don't know if it'll play while I'm on the phone, so be quiet."

She pressed the volume button up to as loud as it would go and hit play.

The voice memo Zara sent started to play.

Nikki's eyebrows lifted. She paced across the room and replayed it.

It was a beat she'd made up a few months ago. Zara had walked in on her messing with it and asked if she could play with it.

Zara was singing a spunky verse over the top of the music Nikki had written. The combination made it something new.

Something important.

She played it again.

Her heart fluttered and her fingertips tingled.

She played it again.

"What do you think?" Zara asked.

Nikki, having forgotten Zara was on the phone and also that she'd turned the volume to max, yelped and dropped the phone.

"Sorry," she called, picking the phone up. "Hold on." She adjusted the volume and turned the speaker off.

"What do you think? Do you love it?" Zara asked excitedly.

Nikki snickered. "I do love it. It's…it's incredible." And she wasn't just saying that.

"Yay!" Zara squealed. "I have to go but I'll text you later, 'kay?"

"Okay, bye." Nikki ended the call and stared at her phone.

Of all the dreams she'd dared to dream, this one had seemed the furthest from reality.

"Hey."

Speaking of far-flung hopes and dreams.

André stood in the doorway, all sweaty and hardworking.

But instead of the heart-twisting reaction from earlier, she was still buzzing from her call with Zara and so she smiled like a dope.

He smiled too and she realized what she was doing and tried to look serious. Or at least less dopey.

"Was that an important call?" he asked, nodding at the phone she was clutching to her chest like it was precious.

The song Zara had sent rang through her mind and she smiled again.

"I'll take that as a yes," André said with a grin.

"What?" She moved her phone away from her chest. "No. It's— Can I help you with something?"

He rolled his lips inward and swallowed his smile. "I need to ask you what you want for the walls in here." He jerked a thumb over his well-sculpted shoulder.

He had been pretty athletic when they'd dated, but she wouldn't have described him as jacked.

Now?

Definitely jacked.

Though you wouldn't know it when he wore his professor clothes. His pressed shirts and silly bowties successfully hid *allll of that.*

His suspenders curved over his shoulders and lay flat against his pectoral muscles but didn't touch the six perfectly proportioned rectangles making up his abs. Or were there eight? It was hard to tell without inspecting them more closely. Something about the straight lines of the suspender straps drew attention to the deep lines of the V at his hips that disappeared into the waistband of the denim.

On anyone else, the shirtless suspenders look would appear kind of trashy and try-hard. But not on André. It looked like he lived in those things. Which he kind of did.

She rolled her eyes, more so she could look away. But the image was burned into her brain forever.

Thank God.

He led the way back to the lounge and she stared at his back wondering when and why he'd decided to get totally ripped.

A small tattoo on his right shoulder caught her eye. *That* was new as well.

She squinted, trying to see it clearly.

Was that a…?

Yep.

It was a T. rex skeleton on a leash being led by a human skeleton.

He stopped moving and she wasn't ready. She placed her hands on his hips to keep from smashing her face against his back. Her hands burned on his hot bare skin and she immediately removed them.

If he'd noticed, he didn't say. He turned to the side and waved an arm towards the far wall.

"I want to paint that back wall matte black. But Johnny said I needed to check with you first."

Nikki's attention bounced from the wall he'd indicated to the bare floor and the rest of the room.

Music came from the speakers nearby and she stared at them for a moment, trying to figure out if what she was hearing and seeing was real.

"What?" she started, taking a step into what used to be an overcrowded and disorganized lounge. "How long have you been here? Are you listening to Slant 6?"

"I've been here a minute." His feet shuffled on the hardwood, and she glanced down. That carpet he'd been throwing into the dumpster a minute ago? That had come from the lounge.

The room had been completely gutted. Not just in terms of the storage that had been in there, but everything was gone. The carpet, the built-ins, the lights.

Objectively, she knew this had been the plan. The space was in desperate need of renovation and she and Johnny had discussed for years what their "dream studio" would look like.

Those kinds of changes took time and, more importantly, money. Both of which had been difficult to come by.

Well, until Sunshine Capone had begun operating out of it like it was his second home.

And if this thing with Zara became a real thing and not a dream thing—

All of her thoughts screeched to a stop like a careless needle on a vinyl record.

André had his hands braced above the door and was leaning his upper body into the room like he was stretching out his arms and chest.

Her mouth filled with saliva and she reached up to make sure it was closed and that no drool was leaking out.

He didn't look real. He looked like he'd walked out of an Avengers film and stopped by to be the handyman in a very Nikki-specific fantasy.

It was normal to still find your ex attractive, right? That wasn't some sort of self-betrayal, was it?

No.

It was fine.

Of course she still found him attractive.

She was human. He was human. They were both humans.

Really? Is that what she was going with? That they were both humans? And that's why she was imagining running her hands over his chest and shoulders and grabbing hold of those suspender straps—

Oh geez, she needed to stop. She was officially disappointed with herself.

"I like the wood better, myself. I guess I knew the floor had always been there but I never realized what great shape it was in," Johnny said.

When had Johnny joined them? Had she really been that far gone in her André-inspired fantasy that she missed an entire person?

She needed to get a grip.

And not on André's suspender straps.

Nikki glanced down at the floor.

Well, look at that. It *was* in great shape. Better than the one in her house anyway.

It was enough of a distraction to get her eyes off André's gorgeous body and refocus on why she was in there in the first place.

She crossed one arm over her chest and gripped her opposite elbow as she turned back to the wall André wanted to paint.

It would look cool black. Especially if they kept the floor this bright color. One of the three remaining walls was mostly windows and exposed brick. It faced the street. And yeah, it had bars on the windows, but it was Chicago. What didn't have bars these days? At least the bars looked cool.

The wall with the door could be black too, she supposed. The remaining wall used to have the built-ins and she was glad they were gone. They had never been anything but a place to hide junk.

There was a reason the more major clients used the lounge upstairs.

But if they revamped it (finally), they'd have a nicer space for *all* their clients.

They'd have a space that could continue to grow.

What if Zara was just the beginning? What if they made this album and then suddenly Nikki was an actual producer? A recognized one.

With a client list!

She whirled back around and opened her mouth to spill all of her secret hopes to Johnny, but she stopped when both men looked at her. Her gaze bounced back and forth between them, and she realized she wasn't ready to tell yet.

Not until it was real.

A voice memo on her phone wasn't real.

And anyway, she didn't want André to know. Not because she thought he'd blab, but because he didn't get those things from her anymore. Important, from-her-heart things.

"Something to share, Nikki?" Johnny asked, eyeing her carefully.

"I think black is a good idea." She smiled and it felt tight. She wanted to confess all of everything right there. It was in her nature to overshare.

She bit her lip to keep the words inside.

André's lips tipped up on one side like he knew it was killing her not to say more.

"Cool," André said. "I can get the walls stripped and prepped. There might be some repair work, but it doesn't look like much." He canted his head to the side. "Depending on when I can get the floor done, this room could be complete in a couple weeks." He dipped his chin at Nikki and then Johnny. "If that works for the two of you."

"I didn't know you knew how to do floors, Bob Vila." It just popped out. She hadn't meant to tease him; teasing implied a cozier relationship than she was ready to have with him despite how much fun he'd been the night before.

Also teasing was very close to flirting and she was *not* flirting with him.

André glanced at Johnny, confused. "Who's Bob Vila?"

"Her celebrity crush," Johnny answered, completely serious.

André nodded like that explanation made sense and *it did not.*

Nikki's mouth fell open. Both men moved on.

"I have a friend who refinishes wood floors." André pulled his phone out of his pocket. "I'll see if he's busy this weekend."

Nikki swallowed. André had a hookup who could do wood floors?

She'd been on a waiting list with a company for six months. Six months and she still didn't have an appointment for an estimate.

Of all the things she could do on her own, refinishing wood floors was not one of them. There was a talent to it that had apparently been left out of her box of weird and unnecessary biological gifts she'd inherited from her father. Though he couldn't do floors either, so maybe that gift was in a separate box entirely.

Johnny had the gift. He'd done his own townhome and the floors upstairs. But that was back before he was in a serious relationship with the legendary Ashton James and before he was producing award-winning albums for Sunshine Capone. His calendar was so booked at this point, every day was a pink highlighter day.

She would know.

She was the keeper of the calendar.

Which was exactly why Johnny didn't know she needed her own floors done because he would already be there doing them. And the studio could not function without him.

But if André knew someone who could get to her floors sooner…

She should *not* be looking for more reasons to talk to or be around André.

Also, getting her floors done was starting to sound like a euphemism.

Her head swung around when Naked Raygun came from the speakers.

What was happening?

"Ty," André greeted. "Hey, I have a floor that needs your expertise. What's your weekend look like?" André's light eyes flitted up to Nikki and back to the floor in question. "That's right. The fundraiser." He listened for a beat and then took his call out into the hall.

Well, it was probably too good to be true.

"I mean, I could do it, like I did the ones upstairs," Johnny said.

Nikki made a face. "You don't have time."

See?

Johnny's cheek twitched. "I could move some things around—"

"Johnny," Nikki stopped him. "You don't have time," she repeated slowly.

He shrugged one shoulder.

André returned, no longer on the phone and a highly suspicious look on his face. "My friend is going to stop by after work and look at the room."

Nikki narrowed her eyes at him.

André scratched his forehead and cleared his throat. "From the photos I sent him, he thinks he can get it done in a couple days."

"Whoa," Johnny said. "That's great. How much will it cost?"

André's eyes bounced to Nikki and back to Johnny. He took a deep breath. "His firm bought a table at this benefit cocktail thing at the Field Museum. It's to raise money for children and art, or artistic children. I don't know. He's been asking me for a while to fill one of the spots. So that's the payment."

Johnny arched his eyebrows. "Oh yeah. The studio was invited but we couldn't afford an entire table." He chuckled. "Wouldn't have been able to fill it. So, you have to go to a fancy dinner and we get refinished floors?"

That was a logical question.

Because Johnny didn't know how much André hated social events like that.

But she did.

"Events like that aren't very fun for me. I try to avoid them," André said, downplaying his dislike. "But Tyrone seems to think an academic as his guest will go over well with his boss." His hazel eyes jumped to hers as he added, "I won't be able to leave this one early."

Her heart did a tiny hop at the memory it sparked.

The night they'd met, both of them had been running for it over the same hedge at a fancy gala in Winnetka.

If Al caught her, she'd never hear the end of it.

Nikki slid ever closer to the three stone steps that led off the veranda and into the dark. She pretended to gaze at the moon.

"Ooh, look at the moon! I'm so elegant and artsy! I'm just so lost in the moment." She threw back the last swallow of champagne and carefully set the glass on the stone railing.

While her chin was pointed towards the moon, her eyes checked her surroundings.

The party was still buzzing inside. A few people were near the open door, but their backs were turned to her.

This was it.

She gathered her swishy ballgown in both hands, hiked it above her ankles and bolted for the dark. Her short legs pumped and propelled her toward the back hedge and she was kind of surprised her high heels stayed stuck to her feet instead of being thrown asunder. To be fair, her feet had been sweating in them for the better part of two hours, so they were probably just a part of her anatomy at that point.

The hedge came up fast and she decided to just tuck and roll.

Maybe there was more lawn on the other side, maybe a pond, maybe an electric fence.

She didn't care.

She was going full throttle and she wasn't slowing down.

Movement out of the corner of her eye caught her attention, but not enough to change her actions.

Maybe it was security come to stop her.

They could fucking try.

She let go of her skirt and hurled her well-dressed tiny body over the immaculately manicured shrubbery.

For a moment she was airborne.

The night in her lungs and freedom within reach.

And then she landed and all that glorious night air in her lungs came rushing out.

She flopped onto her back, sucking in and blinking against the spots in her vision.

Vaguely, she realized she wasn't alone.

Swiveling her head to the side, she saw a man lying in the same position she was. Also gasping for air. But he was in a tux and not an evening gown.

"Hey," she said, flopping a hand his direction in greeting, still not breathing normally yet.

"Hello," he replied in much the same way.

The moon was bright enough that she could make out most of his features but not in great detail.

"Do you think anyone saw us?" she asked.

"I hope not," he replied. And then he chuckled.

And she joined him.

They lay on their backs laughing quietly for a few minutes.

What a ridiculous situation.

She knew she was going to hear it from Al. And probably Asa too. But she'd stayed as long as she physically could.

What kind of a person bolts from a fancy party and dives headfirst over a hedge into the unknown?

Her for sure. And obviously this guy.

"I'm Nikki," she introduced herself, giving a finger wiggle his direction.

"André," he replied.

"Nice to meet you, André," she said, her heart rate finally returning to a normal pace. "I need a drink. How about you?"

"Love to. Just give me a minute to find my wallet. I think it went into the hedge."

She laughed again but didn't move to get up. Instead, she took a deep breath and rested her hands on her stomach and gazed up at the moon.

"Nikki?"

She looked back to André.

He was frowning at her, curiously amused. "You appear to have shrimp cocktail in your décolletage."

She looked at her cleavage, and sure enough, the handful of shrimp she'd stolen before she'd bolted were falling out of the extra room in her bustier.

"Huh. So I do."

He laughed.

André cleared his throat, and she was back in the present. Not tucked away in a corner booth of a dive bar with a handsome stranger making him laugh until beer came out his nose.

She used to really make him laugh.

"I'm happy to do it," André said, holding her gaze.

She took a breath to say something, like "thank you" but that's not what came out.

"I can go with you to the fundraiser." Nikki's chin jerked back. "What I mean to say is, um, I could go with you."

She'd said it again!

Johnny's eyes grew round and he covered his mouth with a hand and she just knew he was smiling back there.

André sucked in his bottom lip and bit down. He blinked those dark eyelashes at her and she wanted to fall through the floor.

"For the studio, I mean," she said quickly. "If the floor is for us, then one of us should go. Right?" she asked Johnny who just nodded slowly. "You could go, Johnny," she offered. His slow nod changed direction as he declined her idea.

The music playing out of the speakers caught her focus again and she threw her hands in the air. "Richard Hell and the Voidoids? *Nobody* listens to them. Who *are* you?" she asked André.

His answering lopsided smile had her even more confused.

He walked past her to the far wall. "I can get all this sanded and taped today. Do you want that one painted too?" He pointed to the wall with the door as if he'd read her mind a few minutes ago.

But that had been a thing once too, hadn't it? Their similar style and the art they were drawn to.

Johnny and André discussed the details and she just stood there, trying to figure out where she was in time and space.

It was as if those couple of hours they'd spent at the ballgame last night had reset her nervous system. Her mind was a mixture of all the fun they'd had in the past, the fun they'd had last night, interspersed with flashes of the confusion and heartbreak that had followed his startling absence.

This was the guy who had broken her heart without saying a word. And he was also the guy who made her laugh and feel seen.

Which one was real?

It couldn't be both, right?

The song switched, and again, she was caught off guard.

Was this The Damned?

At least his music kicked ass.

She glanced at André.

Who would finish the lounge if he just didn't show up one day? If he just disappeared and wouldn't return anyone's calls?

He'd done it before.

She could ask but knew it would sound accusatory. And hadn't they all agreed that it had been a long time ago?

Okay, time to take stock of the facts.

Fact one. André was superhot. Let's get that one out of the way.

Fact two. He had been hired to do a job.

Fact three. She would be fine.

It was that last fact that had her releasing the tension and confusion that had been building in her body. She let out a deep breath and reminded herself that she had been fine the first time. If he disappeared again, she would be okay.

She knew how to do all the renovations herself. It might take her a while, but she could do it. She had the tools and the skill.

Having André do the renovations was *convenient*. Not necessary.

She turned in a circle again, looking at the open space with new eyes and ideas. She could bring in the old leather chair her grandmother had given her. And she had some vintage band posters from her travels in Europe that would look fucking awesome on the walls. Ooh! That lamp that she'd found at the yard sale down the street!

Yes. She could make this work.

And it would be a beautiful space for artists to chill and create and she could do it. On her own. Without André.

"Are you okay?"

She came back to André who had put a shirt on, it was blue. He was watching her carefully. Johnny had gone.

She nodded.

"You sure?" he asked, eyeing her skeptically.

Was she okay? Of course.

Nikki had long been a roll-with-the-punches kind of gal.

"I mean, everything about this is weird, but I'll be fine," she told him honestly and shrugged. What else was there to say?

"So, the benefit…" he said after a beat.

She braced. This was where he would tell her thanks but no, thanks, or that he was taking someone else.

And honestly, she should take the out. It had been absolutely ridiculous to offer to go. Even though it made sense to show up on behalf of the studio. She'd offered because she'd been mesmerized by his muscles. But now he was covered again and she was back in her right mind.

"Thursday. It starts at six. Black tie—"

"I can meet you there," she said before he offered to pick her up.

And again with the volunteering!

She had no one to blame but herself that time.

André's eyes narrowed slightly as he zeroed in on her. He took two steps closer. "Are you sure you want to go to this? It has all the things you hate, including me."

"I don't hate you, André," she said before she could stop herself.

His eyebrow twitched in surprise.

Is that what he thought? That she hated him?

Why did that make her sad?

She cleared her throat. "And it will be good for the studio to have some positive exposure. People adore me. I'm very lovable." She posed, tilting her head, and resting her cheek against the back of her left hand as she flashed a demure smile.

He smirked but the suspicion didn't leave his gaze.

"I'm not worried about you being lovable. That's a given." He licked his lips and planted his hands on his hips.

Her heart dipped.

His phone rang and he answered it, still staring at her like he had more to say.

"Javi," he said into the phone. "Yeah. I'll be right there." He hung up and slid the phone into his back pocket. "What do you want for lunch today?"

She blinked a few times. "What?"

"Lunch. Thai okay?" he asked, his expression too serious and too unreadable.

"I like Thai," she replied.

He nodded once and then turned around and left.

The music shut off and she heard the back door open and close.

Nothing had happened.

So why was her heart galloping in her chest?

She shook it off and returned to her office.

Nothing. Had. Happened.

Except for some intense eye contact and plans to meet each other in formal-wear in a few days.

But that was nothing!

She planted her elbows on her desk, closed her eyes, and caught her forehead with her hands.

"Get it together, Harry," she whispered to herself.

She opened her eyes and saw an envelope on her desk that said, "A Special Gift to Restore and Replenish." The logo looked familiar.

She opened it and found a gift certificate to a luxury spa for a full-body massage.

Damn. This had to be from Hannah. Johnny must've told her about the car accident.

Perfect timing though. She could use this before the benefit. That way she'd be all relaxed and zen and would *not* run for the hedges.

She would need a dress.

CHAPTER SEVEN

DEATH BY A THOUSAND CUTS

ANDRÉ

First, he met Javier at the hardware store. They picked out the paint—they decided on a dark charcoal that was almost black but not quite—had it mixed, and got what he needed to clean and repair the walls.

Then he went to get lunch.

While he waited for his order, he tried to think about anything other than what he wanted to think about. Which was Nikki.

Nikki in those short shorts.

Nikki's rose tattoo on the back of her right thigh.

Nikki being excited about that phone call he'd walked in on.

Nikki asking to go to the benefit.

And one repeating thought on loop: he had been an absolute idiot. Which, yeah, he knew that. But being around her in close proximity just really drove that point home.

He was so wrapped up in his thoughts, he missed his order number being called. The woman at the counter poked his shoulder with the eraser side of a pencil. He straightened from where he'd been leaning and took the bag from her.

When he returned to the studio, he went straight to her office.

"What's that?" he asked, referring to the music coming from her computer that she'd turned off when he'd walked in.

"Um. Nothing," she hedged and then chuckled. She fiddled with the mouse on her desk and then shoved it away.

"It sounded cool." He shrugged and set the bag of food on the desk. "I got you spring rolls and pad thai." He handed the food out. "I hope that's right."

"Thank you." She took the food.

He turned to the door, planning on going back to the lounge to eat his meal.

"You can eat in here."

He twisted his neck to look at her.

"If you want," she added, shrugging. Her attention wasn't on him but on the screen of her computer.

He glanced around the crowded office and took a seat on a box amp that had clearly been used as a seat by someone before. She cleared room for him on the desk.

They ate in companionable silence for several minutes. Both focused on their food and scrolling on the phones.

His sister had texted him asking if he wanted to try to get together before she left to go on tour with her superstar husband. He needed to talk to her anyway. About what he'd gotten himself into with Nik.

He also sent a text to Tyrone letting him know he was bringing a plus-one. Actually, he said he was bringing one of the studio's producers. After it sent, he realized he didn't know if that part was true.

"Are you producing yet?" he asked. His voice sounded loud in the quiet of the office.

"Hmm." She hummed and pointed at her full cheeks. She grabbed a napkin and her water bottle and took a few sips before speaking. "Not officially."

The way her eyes skated over her phone and her computer made him think she was withholding some key piece of information.

"Maybe what I should have asked is if you still *want* to produce." He kept his gaze on his food so as not to pressure her for an answer.

Delicate was the ground on which they walked.

"I do," she replied softly.

He darted a glance up, but she was gazing off into the distance, a gentle expression taking over her features.

"But it's scary." She shrugged and blinked, and she was back in the present. "I see how hard it is and I worry I don't have the skills I need." She took a bite, chewed, swallowed. "Johnny handles artists so well. Managers, assistants, entourages, all march through the studio and he somehow navigates those relationships while keeping the project focused."

"You're not Johnny," he pointed out and immediately rolled his eyes at his own unhelpfulness.

"Duh." She snorted.

"What I mean is, your methods might be different, but you handle difficult people very well. And you know that's only a small part of the process. Your ear is unmatched. You hear more than others. You listen to the soul of the artist that gets lost in the technical. You help them get their true voice across."

He took a bite, and when he looked up again, she was staring at him.

"What?"

"Nothing." She shook her head. "You just don't usually say things like that."

"Like what?" But he knew what she meant.

It wasn't as if he was the stoic, silent type. He talked, he did. But he never said things that *mattered.*

Not really.

He could go on for hours and hours about history and artifacts and process. And he had. He was paid to do exactly that on most days.

But saying things that left him vulnerable and transparent? Saying things that revealed how much he'd been paying attention?

Not really his style.

Nikki snickered, propped her right elbow on the desk and rested her chin on her fist. He tried not to let his gaze linger on the brace still on her wrist. Every time he saw it, he heard the sound of her hitting the hood of his car and his stomach filled with lead.

"It's weird, right?" she asked. "It's weird for me anyway. Tell me it's weird for you."

He wasn't positive he knew what she was talking about, though he had a pretty good idea, so he stayed silent.

"Like," she went on, unbothered by his hesitation. "We know each other. We remember these useless facts about one another that normal people don't know about us. And yet we're essentially strangers. It's weird, right?"

He dropped his gaze to his food to collect his thoughts on the matter.

She wasn't wrong.

He knew her in ways he'd never known another woman.

The way she looked early in the morning with messy hair and a sleepy smile.

That she couldn't cook eggs worth a damn. That she cried more at the part in the movie where the hero gets it right than when he gets it wrong. That she liked shrimp in an above-average way but was too afraid to cook it herself because cooking seafood "freaked her out."

He wondered what things she remembered about him.

Though it was probably best if he didn't find that out.

While he had been pining for two and a half years, she'd been trying to move on with her life.

"It's weird," he conceded. "Do you really see us as strangers?"

She shrugged. "I can't think of a word for it."

Her phone buzzed and she picked it up, leaving him to his spinning thoughts.

"Fuck," she muttered. Her phone clattered onto the desk. She moved the mouse of her computer to wake it up.

"What happened?" he asked.

"I heard from a friend that Chase is working at this studio across town. Just as I'd suspected. You know, would it have killed him to give notice? What's with the cut and run? Am I that terrifying that people can't just be straight with me?"

He rubbed the back of his neck. Sure, she was speaking about someone else's actions, but those words could have been said about him too.

"And I *knew* it too." Nikki clicked furiously on the computer and sometimes punched a few keys with angry fingers. "My gut doesn't lie. They'd been trying to woo him since Thanksgiving. And I don't have proof, but I am fairly certain he oversold his abilities in order to leverage a better position."

André's lips pulled up on one side as he listened to her rant.

He'd missed the rants.

More than he realized.

She was so damn cute when she went off. So much passion and hilarity in a tiny punk rock package.

"Yes. Having Sunshine Capone release an album with *our* name on it has gotten some attention. As it should. Also yes, Ashton fucking James's surprise drop came from our humble hole… Why did I say humble hole? That's so gross," she chastised herself. "That's not what I meant. Whatever. You can take the girl out of the scene, but you can't take the scene out of the girl."

She closed her eyes and growled. When she opened her eyes, they were on André. "I'm not—that wasn't about porn. I've never done porn."

He rolled his lips inward and nodded once.

She went back to the computer.

"But Chase had nothing to do with either record. Though I'm sure they don't know that." She snorted. "They will soon enough. They want him? They can have him. We don't need Chase to make this place run. I will find a replacement." She leaned forward, examining something on her computer screen. "Sure, a year ago I would have taken over his duties, no problem. But we're busier now. Which is awesome because who doesn't like to be able to pay their bills, right? And I want to do—" Her gaze snapped to André. "The thing."

The thing she kept thinking about but not saying out loud?

He was starting to put it together. And if it was what he thought it was, he wanted her to do the thing too.

"What did Chase do here?" André asked.

"Mostly tracking and some light mixing for commercials. Like TV spots."

"Doesn't Asa know how to do that?" he asked. He had no idea what Asa was doing these days. He might be just as busy as Nikki. "Or maybe he knows someone who does that."

Nikki stared at him without really seeing him.

She touched her lips with her fingertips which she did when she was having a memory or thinking really hard—one of those useless facts he remembered.

"Nikki."

They both jerked their heads around to find Johnny leaning casually in the doorway.

"Remember when we talked about you giving away too much information?"

André's gaze darted to Nikki in time to see her cheeks glow pink.

"Yeah," she said softly. "Sorry, boss."

"I signed that NDA," André reminded Johnny. "Technically she wasn't spilling house secrets."

Johnny's lips pressed into a firm line. He sent a meaningful glare in Nikki's direction and left.

Nikki sagged back into her chair.

"I'm not going to say anything to anyone," André tried to reassure her.

"It's not just that," she said. "He's looking out for someone."

"Who?"

Her mouth relaxed and she smiled in a dreamy sort of way. Her eyes shone with unexpected emotion. "Oh, just his one true love. That's all."

See? When the hero makes the right choice.

She sucked in a breath, blinked a few times, and forced a smile. "I know I talk too much. I'm pretending to work on it. Anyway. Yes. That's a very good idea. I'm going to call Asa. He owes me so many favors anyway."

She picked up her phone and he stood.

"I need to get back to it." He gathered their respective garbage and headed out.

And while he'd had the beginning of an idea for what to do with the lounge, it solidified in his mind.

He knew exactly what the lounge needed.

And her office was going to match.

She just didn't know it yet.

CHAPTER EIGHT

PULL APART HEART

ANDRÉ

Renovating was a lot like archeology.

It was a lot of uncovering, discovering, and judging the hell out of choices made by the people who'd been there before you.

"What are you doing here?"

André was at the top of the ladder and glanced over his shoulder to find Asa standing in the doorway. He looked around the room and tugged on the wallpaper he'd spent the last hour trying to remove. He thought it was pretty obvious what he was doing but he answered anyway.

"Stripping." André demonstrated by carefully pulling the large piece he'd managed to keep intact further down the wall while scraping the wall behind it with his putty knife.

He hated wallpaper.

He hated putting it up and he hated stripping it even more.

What an enormous time waster.

He took careful steps down the ladder, keeping the same applied pressure on the strip of paper until he reached the bottom.

Though, to be fair, this wasn't as hard to remove as he'd thought it would be.

Someone had started to remove it years ago, given up halfway, and painted over it.

Could have been the reason it wasn't so hard to remove given that they'd painted over it with forty-five layers of acrylic paint.

Yes, he was exaggerating.

A little.

He looked back at Asa with his eyebrows lifted.

Asa blinked.

"No, dipshit. What are you doing *here?*" He moved his hand in a circle to indicate the building.

André knew what he was asking of course but he hadn't given Asa shit in way too long a time.

"What are *you* doing here?" André countered.

"Nikki asked me to stop by for a… I actually don't know." Asa frowned and shook his head.

André smiled at the wall and resumed working. "Ah, so she took my advice."

Now he was just pushing buttons for the fun of it.

"What? Are you back now?" Asa asked, clearly unhappy about the idea.

"Maybe." André went to grin over his shoulder, but Nikki was there and caught him.

She crossed her arms over her chest and huffed.

André sobered instantly.

Shit. He had not meant for her to hear that.

"No. He's not back," she said. "But he is working here this summer."

André saluted with his putty knife.

A glob of wallpaper paste dripped onto the drop cloth below him.

And yeah, she was trying to be serious with her arms crossed and a frown on her face, but those lips could never lie to him.

"C'mon, Asa." She tugged her friend out of the doorway, but before she was gone, she cast a glance at André. "Are you okay?"

"Hunky-dory," he replied. He climbed back up the ladder, unhooked his little spray bottle from his tool belt, and soaked the next strip.

She didn't leave right away, and he glanced over his shoulder at her.

"I keep forgetting to ask. Have you heard from Ryan today?" she asked.

"Not since I left his house last night. By the way, the guy makes a killer grilled cheese in case you ever have the opportunity to have him cook for you."

He re-hooked the spray bottle to his tool belt. "I think he used Havarti and muenster. I highly recommend."

"So he was okay when you left him?"

"For sure." He pried the paper away from the crease of the ceiling with the sharp edge of his putty knife.

"It reeks like vinegar in here. Make sure you get some fresh air," she said. And then she left.

André smiled to himself as he slowly peeled the paper down.

That was just Nikki. She cared for people. Even the ones who had been complete asses to her.

And he'd really missed that.

He needed more of that type of energy in his life.

NIKKI

"What's going on with André?" Asa asked, slouching on the amp in front of her desk. The same one André had used for lunch.

Because they'd had lunch together.

And it had been really nice.

Nikki didn't have any answers. She was just happy André had been wearing a shirt when she'd gone in there a minute ago, so Asa didn't have to see her forget how to act like a respectable human being.

She blew raspberries and rolled her eyes. "Yeah, so much we need to go over. He's doing some renovations in the studio. He was also on my date with Ryan last night—"

"What?" Asa sputtered.

"Yeah." Nikki bugged her eyes out. "And he brought me lunch today and he's been super chill and then I did what I always do and blurted out exactly what I was thinking and—"

She side-eyed her closed office door. Closed because she'd hurled her body at the side of the couch repeatedly until Justin took pity on her and moved it out of the way. Actually, Justin and André had carried it out to the dumpster. She'd pretended not to notice all the heavy lifting.

Pretended, being the operative word there. She'd definitely noticed.

Oh no.

Had André's sweaty hardworking body unlocked a physical labor kink?

She'd have to think about that later.

"I don't want to talk about it here," she finished what she'd been saying.

Asa narrowed his eyes suspiciously. "Is he stalking you?"

Nikki barked a surprised laugh. "No. I mean, I don't think so…" Asa arched an eyebrow. She blinked rapidly and shook her head. "No. Absolutely not. No." She took a deep breath and sighed. She needed to start over.

"The reason I asked you here is because I—we—have a job opportunity for you."

Asa snorted. "As what? A runner? That's all I'm qualified to do."

His response was expected. He'd been avoiding getting back into a studio for years. She'd probably enabled his avoidance a little more than necessary. Mostly because she understood.

When the band broke up, it had hurt in a way that none of them saw coming. Especially Asa.

Nikki had always known the studio was her endgame. The band had been a short-term project to do with her friends for fun. For Asa, the band had been his dream.

But when André had mentioned Asa as a replacement for Chase, it had made so much sense. Asa was better than Chase in all the ways that counted. All she had to do was convince him of that.

"Asa," Nikki said patiently. "You are a talented and gifted musician and engineer."

Asa's eyes narrowed even further. "Why do you sound like Al right now?"

"I do not!" Nikki argued with a laugh. "Now stop it. I'm trying to be serious right now."

"Okay." Asa's smile softened, and she was reminded of how much they'd been through together.

"Okay," she decided to try again. "Chase, one of the audio engineers, quit. Well—" She made a face. "He won't return our calls and he hasn't come in—"

"What if he died?" Asa asked.

Nikki rolled her eyes. "I already thought of that. He's been seen around."

Maybe that seemed like a dark question, but it was expected. Asa and Nikki usually thought the worst-case scenario. Asa because his dad was a homicide detective. And Nikki because she spent a lot of time with Asa.

Also, all the true crime shows they watched didn't help.

"Anyway," she went on. "We'd like you to do it."

Asa didn't move. He sat perfectly still like a statue. He didn't even blink.

"Obviously," Nikki said. "You are overqualified for what I'm suggesting. But we have room in the budget to pay you what you're worth."

Thank God for Sunshine Capone.

And Ashton James.

And Zara Lorna. Probably.

Maybe.

Gah!

"My duties may be changing around here and I would really like the basic engineering to be done by someone I trust. And not…" She sighed and swallowed.

"A stealth idiot."

"Right." Nikki folded her hands together on the desk, realized how stupid that looked with the brace and then put them in her lap.

Please say yes, please say yes.

She knew what she was asking. But in another sense, she didn't know what she was asking because Asa didn't like to talk about it. He'd just made it very clear that he wasn't going to be making or recording music of any kind anymore for as long as he decided to hang it up.

He'd never said never.

So she was asking.

Al had pushed him to get back out there. In much the same way she'd pushed Nikki to keep giving dating a chance. She pushed because she cared.

Asa had been more stubborn than Nikki.

And now Nikki was on the side of pushing.

This could go very badly.

Not "ruin the friendship" bad, but it might make things frosty between them. She was willing to risk it. They'd gotten through worse.

He leaned forward and messed with the cup of pens on her desk. Most of them didn't even work anymore. She just didn't know what to do with them.

"Is André back?" he asked, his brown eyes darting up to hers.

Nikki sucked in a breath and frowned. "No. I said that."

Asa's brow furrowed and he kept messing with the pens.

He was sorting them by color.

"What are you not telling me, Asa?" she asked, sitting back in her chair.

He flicked his gaze up but only briefly.

"You know when you get wrapped in your head, and the only voice you're listening to is telling you that you suck no matter what, and you know it's not true, but because you don't want to actually ask anyone else to back you up on that, you start to believe that it's true?"

"Of course," she replied obviously. Because, duh.

His lips twitched. He finished with the pens. Not only were they sorted by color, but the colors went in the correct order. And if you didn't know colors had an order, now you do.

He took a deep breath and finally looked at her. *Really* looked at her. In a present sort of way.

"What if I suck?" he asked. "Like, ruin the whole studio, mega-size sucking."

She squashed the laugh that wanted to bubble out of her. Asa could never suck. But she understood exactly what he was asking.

"I'll tell you."

"Promise?" he asked, eyebrows raised.

"A thousand pinky swears."

He pressed his lips into a hard line, and she held her breath.

She really needed this. She needed him and his skills. What they had booked for the coming weeks…he could do in his sleep! It would be the easiest paycheck he'd ever made.

"Can I think about it?"

Her stomach dropped and she rolled her lips inward.

"Nikki, it's not you," he argued when he saw her reaction. "I'm just not ready to get back into all that."

"So let's talk about it. What's bothering you? Is it the Shelby stuff still?"

He clamped his mouth shut and looked away. Shutting her out.

She pressed her palm to her forehead and closed her eyes.

"I am surrounded by emotional men who don't want to discuss their feelings." She sighed and dropped her hand back to her lap.

Maybe if he actually *talked* about it, but *nooo.*

She knew it wasn't personal.

But for fuck's sake! It was starting to feel pretty personal!

"Okay," she said, resigned. "Fine. I'll have to make some calls."

And put off her secret session with Zara. But if she did that, she could track the next few clients and let Justin handle mixing.

She knew that none of this was Asa's fault. He was obviously dealing with something. He wasn't the only one keeping secrets. She hadn't said anything about Zara. Though, now she felt like she couldn't because that would be manipulative.

No, this was fine.

Or it would be.

The secret session had been a long shot anyway.

A knock at her door saved her from having to respond to Asa.

Well, "saved" was subjective.

It was Justin. And he didn't look happy.

"Chase is over at Chi-Town Hits."

Nikki licked her lips and nodded slowly. "Yeah. I heard from Cassandra." It made sense. They had tried poaching her once upon a time.

But they didn't have the kind of operation that she and Johnny had built from the ground up for years and years. They had some fancy funding and a nice address, but other than that, they may as well have been a radio station recording booth.

Not to disparage radio stations.

Behind the scenes, Nikki and Johnny usually referred to them as Chi-Town Shits.

Her phone lit up on her desk and she glanced at the screen.

It was Zara.

Her heart ached in a special place. The place she used when she made music and when she was on tour with Winking Pete.

Zara wasn't the kind of artist that would wait for her.

And she shouldn't.

She should get her art out into the world as soon as possible because the world needed it.

"When do I start?"

Nikki turned her head to look at Asa who was waiting with arched eyebrows.

She swallowed and tried to figure out what to say.

"I've thought about it and you're right. You guys need me." Asa pressed his palms onto the top of his thighs and stood. He approached Justin with a hand extended. "Asa, audio engineer wizard, at your service."

Justin cracked a slight smile, his eyes bouncing back and forth between

Nikki's slightly dumbfounded expression and Asa. He took Asa's hand and shook it. "Justin."

"Wait." Nikki shot to her feet. "Asa, are you sure about this?"

Asa nodded and his expression *seemed* okay with it. He shook her shoulder with a hand. "Don't worry. I won't fuck it up."

"I never—" She huffed. She hadn't said that. Or even thought it. *She* had come to *him.* What was happening?

"Show me around?" Asa asked Justin.

"Yup," Justin replied with a pop.

He turned and Asa followed him out of Nikki's office. But not before he pointed at Nikki and said, "We're talking about André tonight. And if you don't tell Al, I will. And whatever other secret you're keeping."

"Oh. Okay," she said. Even though she wasn't great at keeping secrets anyway. And the André thing wasn't a secret. Not deliberately anyway.

Though from Asa's perspective she could see why he had questions and concerns.

If only she knew what to say about all of it.

Speaking of André… Nikki went the opposite direction to where Justin and Asa had gone and returned to the lounge in progress like she was drawn there.

André had the music going again.

It was Rites of Spring's "For Want Of."

This playlist was fire. She was going to have to steal it from him.

She leaned against the doorframe and crossed one ankle over the other.

She'd always been a joyful person. Joy, optimism, and excitability, those were the cornerstones of her personality.

But if she was being honest with herself, those traits had been a little less present since he'd quit returning her phone calls.

She'd worked through it, she understood as much of it as she could, and she knew it hadn't been her fault.

But it also felt like her optimism had betrayed her.

Her tendency to look for the good in everyone had backfired with André.

Hadn't it?

She watched his back as he reached over his head and pushed the ceiling tiles aside. His shirt was covered in wallpaper paste and something about that hit a soft spot in her heart.

They'd talked at length of buying a home and then completely remodeling the inside for the fun of it.

Together.

He knew so many of her secrets. And she knew almost none of his.

It wasn't until much, much later that she had seen the imbalance of their relationship.

She was a blabbermouth, constantly spilling her heart all over the place as if to trick someone into slipping and falling in love with her.

And André kept his heart locked inside a vault surrounded by puzzles and mazes and miles of jungle overgrowth like a treasure hunter's one last quest.

But she wasn't going back into that wilderness.

On one hand she wished he'd just stayed gone.

But on the other hand, she wasn't sure she'd ever be able to describe the relief she had felt when she saw him again.

As if her heart had needed to verify that he was alive and beautiful and thriving.

He spotted her and grinned while pointing up. "The ceiling is hollow."

She dragged her eyes away from his uncharacteristically bright smile and looked up at the ceiling.

"What do you want to do with the ceiling?" she asked.

Was this what it would have been like to redo their first house together? Just making it up as they went?

A thrill rolled through her that ended in sadness.

How could it be so great and so painful at the same time?

He, of course, had no idea her insides were a confetti cannon of broken hearts and wishing stars. He came down the ladder and took a step towards the middle of the room where he pointed up.

"I think we could remove these ceiling tiles. The ductwork looks a little worse for wear, but I can change that out. I took a peek and there's copper pipe throughout. And I thought we could polish that up and paint the rest." He shrugged. "Unless the wood matches the floor. And then maybe we should just stain it." He turned those swirling green and amber irises on her. "What do you think?"

I think I need to lie down.

She tucked a strand of hair behind her ear and looked up like she could see beyond the ceiling tiles. "I like that idea. Kind of reminds me of that place in…" She trailed off and scratched her ear while swallowing.

If he noticed her discomfort, he hid it well by going back up the ladder.

"That hotel in Paris," he said, finishing what she hadn't been able to.

“Hm, yeah. That place.”

The hotel he’d taken her to for the best week of her life. They’d lived a lifetime in seven days—drinking wine, eating good food, exploring the city. No one expecting them, no schedules to keep, no fears to ruin it.

She watched him work for several minutes. Finally, she straightened and prepared to leave. She needed to get back to work.

“Do you need anything?” she asked before she left for good. She didn’t need to give him an explanation of any kind. And yet she still felt the urge to let him know she was leaving.

He glanced over his shoulder and shook his head. “No.”

“Okay, cool.” She cleared her throat and tucked her fingertips into her front pockets. “I have some projects I need to focus on, so… I probably won’t see you for…” She backed into the hallway as she let her sentence fade away.

“Go be incredible,” he called as he continued working.

“Right,” she whispered to herself as she turned in the hall and headed back to her office.

CHAPTER NINE

OH!

NIKKI

"Nikki!" Asa yelled from the two floors above her. His voice rang through the ductwork to where she stood in the basement, and she flinched.

"Sorry!" she called back and flicked the circuit breaker back on.

She jotted "upstairs bathroom" in pencil on the label.

She thought that particular switch was to the kitchen.

Nope.

One of these days Asa was going to have enough of her "home improvements" and either move out or hide her toolbox.

Nah.

He didn't have anywhere to go. He was stuck with her. And as far as hiding her tools? He wouldn't dare. Her little hobby was what kept her mind from flying apart when she was trying to work through her feelings.

Okay, so that was the bathroom. What about this one? She flicked the switch and held her breath.

She checked to be sure the voltmeter was still in her back pocket and turned to leave the utility room. The door to the room was still open, and for the one thousandth time since she'd moved in, she thought about just removing the door completely.

The people who owned the house before her had used this tiny room as a place to store old paint and the cat litter box. They had kept the door closed all the time whether by choice or by chance, she didn't know. The door handle had broken off long ago, and when she'd moved in, she'd found a screwdriver along the top of the unfinished doorframe that happened to fit perfectly in the empty hole where the knob belonged.

Had the handle been removed deliberately because the lady had small children and she didn't want them wandering into that room? Perhaps. They had installed a cat-flap so there wasn't a huge need to leave the door open.

But Nikki didn't have children. Or a cat.

So, she could just remove the old door, which was original to the house, and use it upstairs somewhere.

"Later," she promised the door, patting it on the way by. One thing at a time.

She ran up the narrow stairs and straight into the kitchen where she'd already started to take apart the light fixture above the sink.

She climbed onto the counter, her focus on the light that had only ever worked intermittently.

She'd gotten home from work the night before and gone straight to bed. But since her body was used to a very different sleep schedule, she'd woken up around five in the morning and just stayed up.

It was Saturday.

She didn't have anywhere she needed to be and she usually tried to catch up on her house projects on the weekends.

Which meant she'd been tinkering for hours.

The frustrating part was that the more she worked on her own tasks, the more she thought about André. She wondered if he was working on the lounge over the weekend or if he took the weekends off.

She could go look. It wouldn't be anything for her to walk up the street and down the block to see if his car was in the parking lot.

But as soon as she arrived at that idea, she doubled back and asked herself *why* she wanted to do that.

And herself didn't answer.

Asa had been right yesterday, she needed to talk to Al. If only to have someone tell her she was being stupid so she could immediately stop being stupid. That's how things worked, right?

"What are you doing?"

"Fixing this light," she answered, but didn't glance in Asa's direction.

"Did you climb onto the counter all by yourself?"

"No. The woodland elves helped me."

She was still wearing the wrist brace. It hadn't been a week yet and the doctor said to give it two weeks with the brace. But she'd decided on her own that she would give it one unless it was hurting. And it wasn't hurting at all.

It was basically her newest fashion accessory.

She flashed him a sassy smile and tugged the screwdriver out of her pocket and began removing the screws in the fixture.

"You're stubborn, you know that."

She hummed in agreement and slipped the screws into the front pocket of her jeans one at a time as she removed them.

She detached the cover and handed it to Asa who stood beside her waiting. After living with each other for as many years as they had, they had a comfortable routine by that point. She tinkered with the electricity, and he stood nearby "assisting" and ready to dial 911.

Which, for the record, he'd never had to do.

She slid the screwdriver back into her back pocket and pulled out the voltmeter.

After a few minutes of checking various areas in and around the electric box, she was satisfied that she'd turned off the correct breaker.

She put the voltmeter back and exchanged it for the slim pocketknife she carried with her everywhere.

If her father could see her right now, he'd be so disappointed.

How many tool belts had he bought her over the years? Too many to count. And they were all beautiful and practical and exactly the kind of thing she should be using.

But she was a bad planner and always in a hurry.

And that's why she usually stuffed whatever she needed in whatever article of clothing she was wearing and moved on with her life.

It was also why her tools were never where she thought she'd left them and more often than not wound up in terrible places.

Remind Asa to tell the story about when he found a socket wrench where his toothbrush should have been.

After a bit of fidgeting and only a handful of curse words, she installed the new light.

"Where did you get that one?" Asa asked.

"Home Depot. This morning."

He hissed. "How long have you been awake?"

"A while." She hopped off the counter, skirted Asa, and jogged back to the basement. She flipped the breaker and ran back upstairs. When she flipped the switch and the light not only turned on but did not flicker and in fact made the entire sink area look brand new, she hummed, satisfied.

Being able to fix something had the settling effect she'd been looking for.

Maybe it was just a light fixture, but it felt like stability in her otherwise topsy-turvy week.

She planted her hands on her hips and admired her work. Asa helped himself to a cup of coffee.

"I also changed the furnace filter and cleaned up the front rooms. Des is going to have to take her shit. It can't live here anymore."

Asa nodded. "I'll let her know." He took a sip of his coffee. "Should we go wake up Al?"

Nikki glanced at the clock above the stove. It was just after ten. Not exactly early. "Is she still claiming jet lag?"

Asa nodded, hiding his smile behind his cup.

"I guess it's time." Nikki sighed like it was a hardship when it totally wasn't. "She brings this upon herself."

Asa followed her out of the kitchen and down the short hall, up the stairs to Al's room.

Allison "Al" King, rock star in training and general badass, did not like to keep normal hours. Probably one of the reasons she gravitated to the rock star life in the first place. She liked to stay up all night and sleep all day.

Which wasn't a problem except that they missed her.

And the only way to spend time with Al was to either adopt her hours or annoy her into waking up to hang out with them.

At Al's door, Nikki pulled out her phone and cued up the song so she could have it ready.

She gripped the doorknob and turned it slowly. The old wooden door popped as it cleared the frame and Nikki made a face and waited.

Asa just grinned. He took too much delight in this particular torture method even though Nikki was the one who had come up with it.

The blackout curtains created a cozy cave devoid of light. Nikki closed her eyes because it was easier to remember where to go when she wasn't also trying to see when that was impossible. She crept along the edges of the room until she reached the huge speakers on Al's bookshelf.

Feeling carefully around the top of the shelf, she found the audio cable and plugged it into her phone.

What kind of music would be annoying enough to get a punk rocker out of bed without also making them violent?

There's literally only one answer.

Weird Al Yankovic.

She hit play on her phone and Asa, who had crept in silently behind her on the opposite side of the room, yanked open the curtains.

As Weird Al sang out "Waffle King," Nikki toed off her shoes and jumped onto the bed.

A mournful wail came from the pile of blankets beneath her.

Asa stomped one foot on the floor to the beat of the music and Nikki bounced as they both sang along at the top of their lungs.

Al flung the blankets off herself, and Nikki tackled her.

The long-limbed, dark-skinned beauty wrapped her arms around Nikki's tiny frame and hugged her tight.

"I missed you, goof."

"I missed you, goof." Al kissed the top of her head and then pushed her away.

Asa and Nikki had been besties since childhood, but Al fit with them in a way that felt like she'd always been there. Even though they hadn't met her until high school. It had been automatic and simple. Her easy laugh and strong personality had been exactly what Asa and Nikki's duo needed to become a trio.

They'd been together ever since.

When Winking Pete had dissolved, Al didn't even blink. She started a new band with their drummer, Des. She'd wanted Nikki and Asa to come with her, but they couldn't. And they didn't ask Al to wait.

So even though Al was out there living the life that they had all talked about, there was no love lost. They were happy she'd kept going.

It had made the most sense. She hadn't been as close to Shelby as they had been.

"Why don't you ever wake up Steiny like that?" Al asked with a pout. Her hair was mostly in her face, but she didn't seem to notice or care.

"Because Steinhoff is a cranky old man and we don't want to give him a heart attack." Nikki snuggled up next to her best friend, wrapped an arm around her middle and closed her eyes. "I missed you."

Al picked up the arm across her belly and looked at the wrist brace. "What the hell happened to you?"

Nikki growled and snuggled closer. "Nothing."

"André is back," Asa supplied, oh so helpfully.

Al gasped and sat up. Nikki rolled onto her back and glared at Asa.

"He is not back."

Al pushed her hair out of her face and waved her hands in front of her.

"Start at the beginning."

Nikki rolled her eyes but she told Al everything.

Mostly everything.

She talked about André hitting her with his car, that he was working at the studio, that he showed up on her date with Ryan… She left out the parts about Zara Lorna and some of the "you had to be there" moments.

Like the eye contact and the jokes.

"And I offered to go to this benefit with him on Thursday, so I will need a dress from you. Again." Nikki avoided the open-mouth stares from both her besties.

"What do you mean offered?" Asa asked.

"You know how I am," Nikki said with a shrug that she hoped looked blasé. "I say things. My mouth opens and words fall out."

Al didn't say anything for several minutes and then she tucked her long, black hair behind both ears and smiled at Asa. "Would you mind getting me a cup of coffee?"

Asa opened his mouth to object but the expression on Al's face had him rethinking that. Once he was gone, Al turned worried eyes on Nikki.

"Don't look at me like that." Nikki got out of the bed and went to Al's closet. "Is there a dress in here that might work for me on short notice?"

Al scooted to the end of the bed.

"Babe. This isn't just some rando. This is André. I know what he meant to you."

Nikki swallowed the tightness in her throat and started flipping through the dresses on the hangers. "It's been a long time." That's what André had said, right? And she'd agreed. "It's not even a thing. I feel nothing."

"Really."

Nikki glanced over at Al who clearly didn't believe her.

"Yes, really." Nikki pulled out a red dress. Too short. She put it back.

"So you've talked about how things ended and he's apologized for being a dick?" Al asked.

Nikki snorted. "No. Because it doesn't matter. If I still had feelings for him, that might matter. But I don't." She found a light blue dress and pulled it out of the closet.

"That would work for you. It's too small in the chest for me," Al said.

Nikki brought the floor-length ballgown over to the mirror and held it up in front of herself. It had a plunging neckline with matching back and shimmery straps. The skirt was tulle and had a dreamy, romantic quality that appealed to her.

It reminded her of something, but she couldn't place it.

"The back is open, so your tattoo will be visible," Al warned. "How fancy is this thing? Are tattoos acceptable?"

"Hmm." She could wear a shawl or something. Even though it was July.

"Though if I recall, André really liked your tattoo."

Nikki shot a glare to Al who remained unfazed.

Maybe it didn't matter if her tattoo was visible. It was the 21st century, people had tattoos.

"What's the benefit for?" Al got up and went inside the closet.

"It's to raise money for kids in the arts or something."

Al came out and handed her a pair of nude heels. "These. And those aquamarine earrings your parents gave you. I'll pin your hair up." She moved behind Nikki and pulled her hair back, pulling little tendrils out. "Like that."

Nikki nodded and her gaze connected with Al's in the mirror. "I'm so glad you're good at this stuff."

Al was still messing with her hair. "I like to be able to reach into any world I want and feel at home." She let go of Nikki's hair and sat back down on the bed.

"I know you're worried about André," Nikki said gathering the dress and shoes in her arms. "But all that's over. We happen to be working near each other for a couple weeks and then I suspect I'll never see him again."

Al crossed her arms. "How does that make you feel?"

"Fine." Nikki took a deep breath and really tried to exude honesty with her next statement. "I have no feelings for André."

"Okay," Al said, though her tone said "whatever."

Asa re-entered the room and handed Al a steaming cup of coffee.

"Hey," Al said, after she'd taken a sip. "Let's hang out tonight."

"I have a gig at the Iggy," Asa said.

"That's perfect! We'll come support you!" Al looked to Nikki. "You want to?"

The Iggy was a piano bar downtown actually called The Blue Iguana. They called it the Iggy for short. It was small, sometimes crowded, sometimes not.

Tonight was not a crowded night.

For a Saturday it was actually pretty calm which worked for them because that way they got to visit Asa in between songs.

Asa worked there off and on, playing the piano for tips. He took requests and usually people asked for the classics. Though Asa's catalogue was probably deeper than the other players. If someone had an obscure request, he almost always knew it.

"Go save us a table." Nikki pointed to a high-top table near the middle where they'd be able to see Asa easily. "I'll get us drinks."

"Got it." Al started that way and spotted someone she knew. She swerved to give hugs and hellos.

She'd been gone for a few months, so the first part of the night would be her running into everyone who hadn't seen her. Which felt like half the city. Al knew everyone. But Nikki was used to the routine.

She pushed her way to the bar. She didn't recognize either of the bartenders, though it had been a while since she'd been to the Iggy. She scanned the barback as she waited for them to be free to take her order.

Would she stick with tradition, or would she try something new tonight?

"What can I get you?" the bartender asked.

"A rum and Coke and an old-fashioned," she rattled off.

The bartender nodded and started getting the drinks together.

"I always loved that you drank old-fashioneds," came an all too familiar voice at her shoulder.

She huffed a laugh. At this point she wasn't even surprised.

She hadn't seen André in two and a half years and now he was everywhere.

"Really." She pursed her lips and bobbed her head. She didn't want to look. Didn't need to look. But after a beat she glanced up and found his eyes already on her.

"I do have to ask," he said before she could say anything. "Are you following me?"

"Ha!" Her mouth tried to form words, but his audacity had taken them.

He grinned down at her, and she knew she was smiling. She knew it and she couldn't stop it. Didn't want to stop it.

"Put it on my tab," he said to the bartender as he slid a tip across the bar.

That was a cool move.

She'd have to remember it for later in case she needed to be cool. He handed her the old-fashioned, he took the rum and Coke and picked up his own drink. She scanned him up and down.

If he'd worked that day, he'd showered and changed afterward. He was wearing dark jeans, a white button-up with the sleeves rolled up to his elbows, and gray suspenders. It was a decidedly delicious look. His dark hair was combed back but it looked like he'd run his fingers through it a few times.

"What do you have?" she asked, eyeing the highball glass he carried.

"Gin and tonic," he replied and gestured with it to the far end of the seating area. "I see Allison."

Yep. She'd managed to commandeer a high-top table with three stools. How convenient.

She started that way and took a breath and stopped. "Are you here with people?"

André's eyes skated over her face but didn't stay. "I was. They just left. I was just going to finish my drink. I'll say hello to Allison and I'll go."

She hadn't meant it like that, but she nodded.

She waved to Asa on her way past him. André nudged her elbow.

"I already bought Asa a drink. He didn't seem quite as hostile this evening as he did yesterday."

Nikki chuckled. "Well, I explained things to him, so…"

Shit fuck. That was the kind of statement that usually begot follow-up questions which she did not want.

"Oh good. I was afraid you were going to leave that to me."

He shot a lopsided smile her direction and she nearly stumbled. What the hell was that supposed to mean? What would André have said by way of explanation?

The same thing, right?

Of course the same thing.

They were working in the same vicinity and no feelings were being had by anyone, either negative or positive. They were a neutral zone of nothing.

"André!" Al greeted with an enthusiastic hug that had Nikki making a what-the-fuck face. "It's been so long! How the heck are ya?"

"Allison," André said, he handed the rum and Coke to her.

"Wow!" Al took a drink and slid onto a stool. "*Every*one is here tonight." She rattled off names that were somewhat familiar but Nikki wouldn't have had a clue who they were. "And even André's here. That's crazy. What have you been up to, Professor?"

Nikki tried to communicate to Al that these questions weren't necessary because André was just leaving. But she wasn't using her words, she was using her eyes and Al refused to look at her.

"Nothing exciting," André replied.

Nikki frowned at him. What about the dino dig? That had been pretty exciting.

He shook his head once at her as if reading her mind.

Oh. He'd told her but he wasn't telling other people?

That should not have felt as good as it did.

Fucking hell.

"What was that?" Al pointed between Nikki and André.

"Huh?" Nikki played stupid, setting her drink on the table. She pulled the stool out and tried to launch an ass cheek onto it. She was too short for these stools. And normally she just stood at the table because it was more comfortable but Al had made her nervous.

She was an idiot now, obviously.

Her ass cheek didn't get anywhere close to where it needed to be.

"That thing. You looked like you were sharing a secret," Al pressed.

"Nope." Nikki attempted another ass-cheek launch. This time she lost her balance.

She wobbled on one foot and fully anticipated eating shit right there in the piano bar. But then she was on the stool.

Ass firmly on the center of the seat.

She sucked in a startled breath and stared into André's eyes.

They hadn't been this close in…

She smelled gin and soap and his aftershave.

She licked her lips and swallowed.

The skin around his eyes crinkled as he smiled but she dared not look at his mouth.

That's when she felt the heat at her hips where his hands rested. Her hands gripped his forearms and she let go.

"You alright?" he asked.

She nodded and he backed away immediately.

Nikki reached for her drink on the table and focused on breathing.

"Another round?" André asked the two of them and then walked away.

Al leaned over the table.

"He *snatched* you right out of the air!" she hissed, quoting one of their favorite movies, *The Emperor's New Groove.*

"That he did," Nikki replied as flat as she could muster. She finally chanced a glance at her friend.

Al was looking at her, perplexed. "Nothing, huh? No feelings whatsoever."

"I feel nothing," Nikki replied, still flat.

Al backed away and waved her face with a hand. "You are a stronger woman than me because I felt things and I wasn't even involved."

Nikki chuckled and looked to Asa who was singing and playing some Elton John medley. He was so stupid talented it was ridiculous.

André returned and Nikki didn't acknowledge him.

Because she needed to prove a point to herself. Right now, their lives intersected. But as soon as the lounge was finished, he'd be gone, and she was not going to spend another two years hoping he'd come back.

André eased onto a stool and regaled Al with all the same information that Nikki had told her that morning about the renovation and the baseball game and the car accident. Which just made Nikki that much more relieved that she'd told her friend what was happening. Otherwise, this night could have been hella awkward.

She took a sip of her drink and glanced through the people around her.

Who was she kidding?

It was still hella awkward.

"I just want to thank everyone for always being so gracious with their tips and compliments," Asa said from the piano bench. "Right now, I want to invite a friend of mine up here to sing with me. Nikki?"

Nikki bugged her eyes out at Asa and shook her head. The small bar crowd easily found her and began making noise for her to get up there.

"C'mon, Nik," Asa said, his fingers tickling the keys. "I can't do this one without you."

"Bullshit," she said loud enough that the people closest to them laughed.

"Are you going up there?" André asked.

"What?" Nikki shook her head. "I don't sing."

André slow blinked. "I don't remember it that way."

Gah!

Her heart dipped and she darted her eyes to Al who was watching their interaction with amused suspicion.

Dammit!

Which meant her choices were to go up there and embarrass herself, or stay where she was and risk more heavy eye contact.

She slid off the stool and finished her second drink in one smooth swallow.

Asa made room for her on the piano bench and she happened to look out into the crowd and immediately found André.

Son of a motherfucker.

"You're joking, right?" she asked Asa.

Asa shook his head. "Please. I love it when you sing."

"I don't think this is a good idea," she said.

"C'mon. What was it you said to me yesterday? You're a talented and gifted musician. I think we've both been stuck in the worst breakup of our lives."

Her shoulders slumped as she realized he was right.

The band breaking up had shaped them in sad ways. And they had both sort of sat in the moment for years, waiting to feel better.

Singing poorly at the piano bar used to be just another night. And now she was so afraid of failing, that she was avoiding the stupid things that had once brought her joy.

She looked out and her eyes connected with André's again. Something about his presence soothed her anxiety.

It shouldn't have, and she knew that.

But sometimes the truth just existed and all anyone could do was live with it.

"Okay, bud. What do you have in mind?"

Asa moved the microphone so it was in front of her, and then he started playing a song she knew quite well. She was thankful he'd picked one she could sing without thinking about.

"Vienna" by Billy Joel.

Had Asa chosen this one because he was trying to tell her something? Probably.

Her voice started out soft and timid but grew with confidence as Asa carried her with his talent.

Love him or hate him, Billy Joel had a certain magic about his music. By the end of the song the entire bar was singing along. They did the chorus one more time just because the moment called for it.

Nikki smiled wide, bathed in the sound of strangers singing about how she had all the time she needed.

She rested her head on Asa's shoulder.

Yeah.

He'd made a good call.

"One more?" Asa asked after the song had ended.

"Okay. One more."

ANDRÉ

He should have left.

The moment he saw Nikki walk in he should have closed his tab and gone home.

That would have been the smart thing.

That's what the old André would have done.

But he was trying this new thing where he went after what he wanted.

And when he'd swerved to catch her at the bar, he knew he was flying too close to the sun.

And he didn't care.

She was wearing ripped-up jeans and a white scoop-neck tee a couple sizes too large. It hung open in the front exposing a black lacy bralette. And several necklaces of differing lengths and material on top of that. Her hair was loose and wavy, heavy eyeliner that made her blue eyes look crystalline.

She could burn him to the ground and he'd kiss her feet and thank her for it.

But it wasn't until he'd grabbed her hips and set her down on the stool that he realized how much danger he was really in.

She'd looked up at him, those blue eyes big and round, her lips forming a stunned "o."

He almost hadn't let her go.

"Are you dating anyone these days, André?" Allison asked.

"No," he replied, never taking his eyes from where Nikki sat beside Asa.

Was it his imagination, or was she looking right at him?

She sang "Vienna" much the same way she used to sing it in the shower which also happened to be the way she used to kiss him. Slow, deep, and sweet.

He should've left when the song was over.

But he stayed because his head and his heart were trying to tell him something. They'd been trying to tell him something for years where Nikki was concerned. And he was pretty sure he finally heard what they were saying.

Listen.

Asa began to play again, and it was familiar but he didn't identify it in time.

Nikki brought the microphone to her mouth and began to sing "Long Road to Ruin" by the Foo Fighters.

Chills raced over his arms, and he leaned forward.

The entire bar fell into a quiet repose.

Nikki didn't have the kind of powerhouse vocals of the big singers. Hers were more of a sweet, gentle rain. A refreshing sound to refill a weary soul and bring it back to life.

He'd never heard her sing this song before and maybe that was why it all felt so new.

Or maybe he was new, and he was just now realizing it.

She held his gaze as she sang about sealed fate and not turning back. Her every word seemed to strip him bare and demand he confess.

Confess that no matter how much time had passed, he was still hers.

And he always would be.

CHAPTER TEN

CRUEL SUMMER

NIKKI

After the intensity that had been her Saturday night, Nikki decided she needed a break from all of the meaningful yet confusing exchanges she'd been sharing with André.

Mostly it was the eye contact.

She thought she kept seeing something that wasn't there and it was starting to drive her crazy.

On Sunday she only left the house to get that massage with her gift certificate. It had helped to relax her but only until Monday when she'd gotten to work and saw his car already there.

She went to her office and closed the door.

She could do this.

A couple days of not seeing him or talking to him and this little crush she'd developed would clear right up. Because it wasn't like she was *really* crushing on him. It was probably just pheromones and her body remembering his body.

But it would fade, and she'd be fine.

She spotted a small, black, round tin on her desk. It was tattoo balm. From a company she'd used for years. But this wasn't hers. She opened the lid; it was brand new.

Huh.

She'd have to ask…someone about that later.

Music and male laughter trickled down the hall and she envisioned the lounge being walled off. That helped.

Kind of.

When lunch rolled around, she grabbed Asa and made him eat with her outside. No one else was invited. If Asa thought she was being weird, he didn't say.

Tuesday and Wednesday were filled to the brim with her favorite kinds of distraction. She helped get Asa acquainted with their process and equipment. She sat in on a few commercial clients before leaving Asa to work his magic.

He really was an audio wizard.

And having him in the studio had alleviated a lot of the stress that had been back-building for God knew how long. It was just one of those instances when she hadn't realized how heavy something had gotten until she was no longer carrying it.

And she hadn't seen André.

Or talked to him or talked about him or thought about him at all.

Okay, that last part was a lie. She'd thought about him. But only when she was trying not to. You know? Like, she'd have the thought, "I'm so glad I'm not thinking about André and all his muscles. Crap!"

She and Asa had finally discussed all the things that they needed to.

Mostly.

She still got the impression that he wasn't being totally forthcoming with her about his more complicated feelings. Especially when it came to his sister. And that was okay.

He was back to making music again and that was his happy place. The rest they could work on later.

By the time Thursday began, she was feeling very confident that whatever had been happening between her and André had been a fluke. Leftover chemistry that just needed to burn itself out.

The lounge would be finished, and he would be gone again. And her heart would not be rebroken. It would stay intact from the last time she'd superglued it back together.

It was her overconfidence that kept her from bracing when someone knocked on her open door.

She glanced up, completely unprepared.

"Hey," André said with a smile. He braced his hands on the top of the doorframe and leaned into her office. "Are you still coming to the benefit tonight?"

"Mm-hm," she confirmed, her eyes darting all around him and trying very hard not to notice the tanned sliver of skin showing between the hem of his shirt and his jeans. But his biceps were extra muscly today and his t-shirt sleeves were bunched up near his armpits. As if his biceps had had enough of their nonsense and exiled them to the tops of his shoulders.

Good God damn.

"Do you need a ride?" he asked.

"Asa is dropping me off."

"Cool." André dropped his arms and tucked his hands in his pockets. "I'm really looking forward to you meeting my friends tonight." And then he left.

But Nikki sat there for at least ten minutes going over their small interaction. He didn't seem fazed the slightest bit that she'd been avoiding him all week. That was good, right?

And also, his friends?

She'd met some of his friends when they were together. None of them had been introduced as close friends. They were more like colleagues or acquaintances. And the one time she'd met his dad, he hadn't wanted to introduce them.

Therefore, the fact that he was *excited* about sharing any part of his life with her was...confusing.

She checked the time.

Gah.

She had to get home so she would be ready in time.

For a benefit she had invited herself to and a date that wasn't a date at all.

Yeah, André was the confusing one.

ANDRÉ

He got to the end of the stone steps and spun around, pacing the other way.

She wasn't late.

He was just very early.

He hadn't wanted to be late and had overcompensated, so now he was dressed in a tux and pacing the stone steps of the Field Museum in the hot July sun.

And hoping she didn't give him everything he deserved.

He'd suspected that she'd been avoiding him all week. His mind had ping-ponged back and forth between two competing ideas. Sometimes they would collide with one another and turn into a super reason for why she was avoiding him.

First, she had changed her mind about coming to the benefit with him and wasn't going to tell him.

Or, he'd imagined the intense looks they'd shared at the Blue Iguana and he'd made her uncomfortable.

And then the combination of, she was uncomfortable with him around and she wasn't going to show up.

Though being stood up for a benefit was not the same thing as the night he'd ruined both of their lives.

He released his seat belt and paused.

The most beautiful woman in the world stopped outside the door as an older man with wispy blond hair held the door open. She laughed at something he said and then did an overexaggerated waltz through the door. The black dress she wore was super short and he could see where her rose tattoo ended on the back of her thigh. She wore her hair down and the blue and pink tips looked freshly updated. But it was her shoes that made the outfit.

Huge platform boots with black spikes all over them.

They looked like two heavy metal puffer fish attached to her slender legs and made her at least five inches taller.

The man, who was no doubt her dad, tossed his head back and held a hand to his chest as he laughed at his daughter's antics.

Laughed.

Not berated.

Not scolded.

He didn't shake his head in shame and make her go home to change.

Nope. He followed his punk rock princess into the fancy restaurant with a smile on his face.

André's stomach soured and he swallowed.

The ring he'd gotten for her sat hot in his pocket.

Tonight was supposed to be the beginning of the rest of their lives. He'd alluded to the proposal. They'd discussed getting married. She had made a joke just that morning when they talked and called him her fiancé.

He had planned on proposing tonight with her parents and his father there. Properly.

But his dad wasn't coming.

Not only was he not coming but he'd reminded André that he had no idea what he was getting into.

And he was right.

What did he really have to offer? At some point she'd figure out that he wasn't the man she thought he was and she'd be gone. He'd fooled her. But she was smart and eventually she'd see it and then what?

And then he'd lose even more.

He'd sat in his car outside the restaurant for over an hour.

She probably didn't know that. And it honestly didn't matter. He hadn't shown up for her and then he'd cut off all contact because she'd want to know why.

And he couldn't tell her at the time.

"I'm here! I'm here!"

He turned to see Nikki running towards him in a light blue ballgown. She held the skirt up with both hands as she sprinted in high heels.

Her blonde hair was pinned back and her cheeks were flushed.

She bounded up the stairs, the dress floating around her in a way that looked like she was bouncing and not running.

"Asa decided to drop me off where the school buses park. A tour must've just ended or something. I was surrounded by children and most of them were larger than me. Which is terrifying, by the way. When did children get so large?" She smoothed her skirt and fanned her face with both hands.

The wrist brace was gone.

"I had to run around the building. I'm a sweaty mess, and I may or may not have rolled my ankle, but I'm here now." She exhaled on a smile and beamed up at him.

The relief that flooded through him when she came running towards him was unexpected. He sought the correct reply, but no words would come out.

She came closer until they shared the same stair.

"André?" she asked with a soft frown tugging at her smile.

"You look beautiful," he finally mustered.

She looked down and back up. "I do rock a ballgown, don't I?" she agreed. "Are you okay?" she asked, inspecting him carefully.

He took a deep breath and let it out. "I am now."

"Were you worried I wasn't going to show?" she asked.

He knew she was teasing. It was obvious in her voice and the sparkle in her eyes.

But he said it anyway.

"It's what I deserve."

It was the closest they had come to talking about The Ghosting.

Her lips parted and a shadow passed across her bright blue eyes.

They hadn't talked about it for a reason, right? Now it was up to him to get them to the next moment.

He offered his elbow. "Milady."

She took the offered arm but didn't respond.

They walked silently into the museum.

He'd just made the entire night weird, hadn't he?

But it was always there for him. In the back of his mind. How things had ended, the decision he'd made that night because he *thought* it would hurt less in the long run.

The "what if" that never disappeared.

Was he crazy to assume she had similar thoughts?

Would she be here if she didn't want to be?

They reached their table and André introduced her to Tyrone and his wife, Tara, and Charles and his wife, Heidi.

He pulled her chair out for her and when she went to sit down is when he caught the first glimpse of her exposed back.

The rose vine started high on her right shoulder and curved across her back in an "S" shape where it disappeared into the dress. But he knew it wrapped around her right hip and then her right thigh. A thin line ran from the nape of her neck to the center of her back where it connected to the vine.

On first glance it looked like a smaller vine without roses.

But it was words inked vertically that said "*L'amour c'est être stupide ensemble.*"

She'd gotten it in Paris.

It meant "love is being stupid together." A quote from the French poet Paul Valéry.

He tucked in her chair while his eyes remained on the tattoo. His hands flexed at his sides before he took his own seat.

He wanted to touch it.

To run his fingers down her spine and press his lips to each rose.

How could he be so close to everything he had ever wanted and still be so far away?

She leaned closer to him and he reciprocated as she spoke in hushed tones.

"Do you think they have a shrimp platter around here?" she asked.

He chuckled and reached for his water. "Do you have room in your dress for it?" he asked behind his glass.

The look she gave him had him arching his eyebrows.

She glanced around at their table companions, but no one was paying attention to them.

"Sir, you have no idea what's under this dress."

He choked on his water.

Knowing Nikki and how she always did things the way she wanted, regardless of what was expected or proper, he should have been worried.

But instead, he was amused, curious, and just a little bit aroused.

Which was to say, how he felt around Nikki all the time anyway.

Did she have to-go containers hidden under her skirt? Or plastic bags ready to be filled?

Maybe.

Or maybe it was just bare legs and temptation.

Cocktails were served and Nikki was very happy when they brought out the shrimp. André got her an old-fashioned at the bar which she sipped carefully as she conversed with the people around her.

By the time dinner was served, she was making everyone at their table laugh.

How she did that, he had no idea.

She just put people around her at ease.

It was probably because she accepted people for who they were. She didn't put them in a box because to her, boxes didn't exist. People were people and it was that simple to her.

A few people got up and gave some moving speeches about why everyone should donate money.

They had a live band that started after that while they wheeled out dessert. But no one got up to dance.

The band had a female singer with a voice like velvet.

"She's fabulous," Nikki whispered to him and he had to agree.

"Why isn't anyone dancing?" Nikki asked, looking around.

He put his arm along the back of her chair. "Maybe they don't like dancing."

She rolled her eyes at him. "That's stupid."

His eyes dropped to her mouth as she smiled. It held.

God, that smile.

The things it did to him.

He sucked in a breath and darted his gaze back to her eyes, hoping she hadn't noticed his lingering stare.

She blinked at him.

"C'mon." She stood, shoving her chair back and his arm dropped away. She held out her hand toward him.

He stared at it.

"What?" he asked, suddenly not sure what was happening.

"We're dancing." She said it so confidently that he didn't think he had a choice in the matter. He took her hand, and she tugged him towards the dance floor.

The band switched to a different song as they approached, and the singer pointed at the two of them like they had planned it this way.

"Twirl me, Professor," Nikki said.

She swung their connected hands to her left, his right and he took over. He twirled her under his arm and her skirt flared out around her like she was floating across the floor. Then he pulled her in and caught her waist with his other hand. They eased into a slow waltz.

"I love Billie Holiday," she said, her eyes never leaving his.

"Is there anything you don't know about music?" he asked, not hiding how fascinated he found her endless fount of facts and trivia.

She gave a slight shrug. "Probably. But if there is something I don't know, I'll find it. And then that'll be mine too."

He chuckled because he knew that's exactly how she'd handle it. Like a huntress.

But she also shared what she knew with anyone willing to listen. She wasn't stingy with her information.

The first time they'd met, she'd intimidated him with her wide breadth of music knowledge. He'd been afraid to let her know he secretly listed to punk rock. He knew it didn't fit with his perceived persona. But she wasn't a gatekeeper and she hated it when people were.

"Music should be enjoyed. That's the point," she'd said. "No one gets to decide what art moves you. Just be moved."

He was pretty sure that was the moment he'd fallen in love with her.

And he'd never stopped falling.

A few more people joined them on the dance floor and Nikki waggled her eyebrows.

"See? People love dancing. They just get scared sometimes."

"But not you," he pointed out and then spun her out and back.

They made a few more turns on the floor before she spoke again.

"I just know how it feels to be up there." She nodded her head at the band. "And if I was up there, I'd want people to dance."

She eyed his chest and shoulders. He was about to ask what she was looking at when she told him.

"Not everyone can pull off suspenders, but you manage to make it look good." She flashed him a smile. "I don't think I told you when I got here but you look beautiful tonight as well."

They both chuckled and he realized what it was he'd been feeling deep in his gut.

Joy.

She had helped him find joy again.

"Did I tell you what happened in the Badlands?" he asked, a pressing need for her to know taking hold in his chest.

She shook her head. "Did you dig up a dinosaur?"

He smiled, wishing that would have even been possible. "Unfortunately, there aren't any dinosaur bones in the Badlands."

Her delicate frown warmed a spot inside his chest. She was disappointed on his behalf and that was so Nikki. And so not anything he deserved.

"The entire month was hot and dry and difficult," he went on, ignoring how her reaction had made him want to fold her into his arms and never let go. "We found nothing most days. On the days we did find something, it was usually just pieces of an oreodont."

"What's an oreodont?" she asked.

"It's like a camel-sheep-pig. Most of the fossils found in the Badlands are those. But one day, we found something kind of huge. At first, we thought it was just another oreodont, but the more we uncovered, the more excited we got."

He twirled her out and back, they settled back into their rhythm. Distantly he recognized the new song but didn't know the name.

"What's this song?" he asked Nikki.

"'They Can't Take That Away From Me.' Written by the Gershwins and made popular by Ella Fitzgerald. Now stop changing the subject and tell me about the super-sized camel-sheep-pig you found," she answered in a hurry.

He grinned and was struck with the sudden urge to kiss her.

Nope. Don't do that. That would be bad.

He cleared his throat and pretended like he was trying to remember where he'd been in his story.

"The more we uncovered, the more I began to suspect—to hope, rather—that we'd found something quite massive." He glanced down at her. Her attention was fixed on him. She wasn't bored with his story or trying to change the subject.

That concentration, the pure kind that came from her, was dangerous.

The kind of danger that a man would die to have.

"Long story short," he said and then smirked when she frowned in response. She really did like to hear his stories. And he would tell her all the boring details eventually, but he wanted to get to the part that mattered.

"It was part of a mosasaur. It was actually several intact vertebrae—"

"André!" she said excitedly. "That's amazing!"

"You know what a mosasaur is?"

"Uh, duh." She made a face. "Giant lizard that ate sharks."

He laughed and pulled her in for a hug. When he pulled back, her eyes were shining.

"That's so cool," she said. "Did you find more?"

He wagged his head back and forth. "I won't be there for the rest of it, but I still get credit for the first part."

Her happiness on his behalf made his heart pound. How could he feel both happy and sad at the same time?

Because this was what he'd wanted, and now that he was getting it, it felt too good to be true.

"André," she said softly, her eyebrows dipping in concern.

"Yes?" he asked, knowing he wasn't hiding his complicated feelings the way he wished he could.

"What's going on?"

"It was the most exciting day of my life, Nik. And I had no one to tell." He swallowed and his heart thundered in his chest. He could do this. He could be vulnerable without expectation. He could confess to her and let it exist for what it was.

"The only one I wanted to share it with was you."

Her eyes scanned his face, probably looking for the lie.

But she wouldn't find it because it just wasn't there.

She didn't say anything, which only made him want to take back what he'd just said. Claim it was a joke or that he'd had too much wine despite him not having any wine at all.

But he had promised himself that he wasn't going to run away anymore.

And if he couldn't keep this promise to himself, then there would never be a reason for anyone to believe anything he ever said.

It had to start with him.

And it had to start now.

She placed her hands on his shoulders and then ran them up to the back of his neck. She pressed her cheek to his chest, and he wrapped his arms around her. They continued to sway to the music until the song ended.

He took her hand and led her back to their table, but he didn't take a seat with her.

He needed a minute.

She caught his hand before he walked away.

"Are you leaving?" she asked. Panic washed through her features, and he hated himself in that moment. That's what he'd taught her to expect from him, wasn't it?

"No," he replied solidly. "Unless you have a strange impulse to hurdle a few hedges. In which case, please count me in."

The panic disappeared and she smiled. She nodded and let go of his hand.

He went to the restroom and took a few extra minutes to collect his thoughts. When he'd gathered himself sufficiently, he went to the bar to refresh their drinks.

"Two old-fashioneds," he requested.

"You helped get the dancing started," a woman said at his side.

He turned slightly to face her. She was in a long, black, glittery gown, but it was her gorgeous red hair that stole the show. He nodded in answer to her statement, trying to figure out if he knew her from somewhere.

"You make a lovely couple," she observed with a knowing smile.

"Not a couple," he replied tightly as he flipped a few dollars into the bartender's tip glass.

"Are you sure about that?" she asked, she signaled the bartender for her own drink.

André turned. He spotted Nikki immediately. She was laughing at something Tyrone was saying, her face the picture of joy and freedom and everything he wanted in his life.

She didn't need him coming into her stable life and making a mess of it.

"I already ruined any hope of that," he said sadly.

Why was he confessing things to a stranger? He hadn't even said these things to his sister yet.

"Why do you think that is?" she asked.

He took a breath, already knowing the answer.

"Because I have daddy issues," he said.

Wow, just spill all your deepest, most embarrassing secrets to the Bond Girl, André. Very smart.

"Who doesn't?" the redhead quipped.

He snorted and looked at her again. He still couldn't figure out where he knew her from.

"Here." She handed him a business card. "Tell him Sandra sent you and you'll get a discount on your first two sessions."

"A therapist, huh?" he asked, staring at the information on the card. He knew he sounded skeptical but internally he was thinking what a good idea it was.

"Daddy issues aren't a death sentence." She patted his shoulder, took her drink, and walked away.

André tucked the card in his pocket, gathered his drinks, and returned to Nikki.

He hadn't been able to figure out his issues on his own. Maybe it was time to call in professional reinforcements.

Because at the very least, he couldn't risk his baggage damaging Nikki again.

NIKKI

. . .

She tried not to make it obvious that she was keeping an eye out for André.

After his unexpected confession on the dance floor, she worried he'd bolt.

And if he left her at this benefit on her own at a table full of his friends, she was going to kill him. After she made sure he was okay.

A fresh drink was placed on the table in front of her. She followed the arm up to André's reserved smile and breathed a tiny sigh of relief.

But he was decidedly less open than before he'd brought her back to the table.

He took his seat beside her and remained quiet.

On impulse, she reached over and grabbed his hand under the table. She had no idea what was going on in his head and it wasn't like she could just ask him in front of all his friends. They were cool people, that wasn't the issue.

But the last thing she wanted to do was draw attention to his discomfort.

She squeezed his hand for a solid three seconds and then relaxed her hold, but didn't let go.

He took a deep breath and flipped his palm over, lacing their fingers together.

She smiled at Tara's story while her heart settled into a gentle rhythm, glad she was the one at André's side.

If there was one thing Nikki was good at, it was talking. She told stories about being on tour, making music, her home improvement projects—those ones had Tyrone wiping tears—and what it was like to live in a crash house.

"Wait. What did you call it?" Tara asked, eyes bright with humor.

"The Lil Snugs House," Nikki repeated, trying not to giggle. "It was because the first year I bought it, I couldn't afford heat. So, we had to wrap all the pipes in blankets to keep them from freezing. We only ran the heat when absolutely necessary. Bands passing through would crash in the living room and it was just a massive pile of sleeping bags and pillows. Everyone snuggling together like littermates. Thus, it became known as the Lil Snugs House."

She sighed and sat back in her chair. "I have since been able to afford heat. But the name still stands."

Everyone laughed and she took a drink of her old-fashioned while glancing at André. He had relaxed considerably since returning from the bathroom. But they were still holding hands under the table.

His lips twitched and he squeezed her hand.

She wondered what was going through his mind.

Did he regret letting her come along tonight? Was he second-guessing what he'd said to her on the dance floor?

It was probably the latter.

Their whole situation was confusing, and it reassured her that maybe she wasn't the only one a little mixed up in what was going on.

The more time she spent with him, the easier it was to forget that she needed to keep her heart detached.

But even without their hearts involved, she'd always enjoyed André as a person. He was sweet and funny and curious. It was his curiosity that really appealed to her. He asked questions and wasn't afraid to learn something new.

He never treated her like she was weird or embarrassing. Even tonight when she'd gone on and on in front of his friends about her obsession with analog recording.

If anything, she loved him.

Like a friend!

Like a friend. Geez.

She wasn't looking for a repeat of the greatest heartbreak of her life.

But she could always use another friend.

Who couldn't?

"You don't have to walk me."

André tucked his hands in his pockets and didn't say anything. But he didn't leave her either.

Which was actually kind of nice.

She really didn't want to be walking around Near South Side alone, in a ball-gown, in the middle of the night.

They walked around the building toward the south entrance, where Asa was supposed to pick her up. Or at least, that's where she'd told him to pick her up.

The night had been really fun. The dancing, the band, the company.

She cast another sideways glance at André.

He hadn't said much but that was typical for him.

They arrived at the bottom of the stone steps and she turned to face him, intending to thank him for the night but he got there first.

"Thank you," he said. "For coming with me tonight. I'm not sure I would have had as fine a time had you not been there."

"Oh." *That was nice.* She smiled. "I had a lot of fun." And then, because she could never resist teasing him a little, "Do you think all events are as fun as this one and we've just been missing out because we ditch early?"

He laughed lightly, looked around the stone entrance, brought his eyes back to her. "No."

"No?"

"No. I think tonight was incredible because of you."

Her heart stumbled and she flashed a smile. "I am pretty cool."

She meant to sound cocky and make him laugh, but it came out entirely too soft.

He studied her in the yellow glow of the lights of the museum front.

"Nik," he started, voice low, serious. "I'm really glad you were here with me tonight."

"You said that." She licked her lips and tried to look away from him but found her eyes only wanted to be on his.

His smile was small and tender. "It bears repeating." He stepped forward and caught under her chin with a crooked finger. His gaze drifted to her mouth.

He bent toward her and her eyes closed, her heart thudding in her chest.

Did she want him to kiss her?

Was it just the formalwear and familiarity?

She should really decide what she wanted out of this moment before something happened that they couldn't come back from.

His lips brushed her forehead and her eyes fluttered open. Both thankful and disappointed.

At least one of them knew what they were doing. Because it certainly wasn't her.

He inhaled and his hand fell away. "Besides, I was able to practice my dancing. I had been getting rusty."

He took her hand, a step back, and then twirled her.

She laughed as he spun her back into his arms.

"You were a little stiff at first," she agreed, falling into an easy waltz.

He danced her around the base of the stone steps, and even though there was no music, she could hear the tune anyway.

Something special and sweet, just for them. It broke the tension of the previous moment, and she was grateful. Too many more seconds of staring into his eyes in the moonlight and she was going to start confessing things of her own.

This was better.

Having fun was safe and what friends did.

Headlights bounced around them and he brought them to a stop.

He bowed and she curtsied before laughing.

"Goodnight, André," she said, backing toward the curb where Asa had flung open the passenger door to his Mazda.

André just smiled and lifted his chin at Asa.

"How did it go?" Asa asked as he pulled away from the curb.

"It went fine," she replied.

She watched André in the side mirror until she couldn't see him.

CHAPTER ELEVEN

GET A HOLD OF YOU

NIKKI

"How was the benefit?"

Nikki looked up from her phone. Johnny stood in the doorway of the control room for Studio X which was where she was due to be working the following day.

Asa sat beside her, headphones on. But she knew nothing was playing through those headphones.

"It was nice." She shrugged.

It *was* nice. But it had left her with little flutters in her belly that she didn't know what to do with. Hence why she was hiding in the control room with Asa.

If anyone could suck the sexual tension out of a room, it was him.

Just don't tell him she said that.

Johnny nodded once. "Are we on schedule for the cat food jingle?"

"Actually, we're ahead," she replied, going back to her phone. "Sending them an email right now to let them know."

Johnny's shoulders relaxed just enough that she noticed. But she wasn't going to point it out. They didn't need the commercial jingles anymore to make sure the bills got paid. But he still treated every client like they were the last client he might ever have.

"Let me know if you need anything. I'll be in Y with Shawn all day."

She lifted her eyes to Johnny in interest.

"Messing around or…?"

Shawn was Johnny's younger brother. Johnny had raised him when their mom had gone back to Honduras when Shawn was five. Shawn, now almost twenty, had his sights on being a rock star, much to Johnny's dismay.

"He's determined to do this thing and I'm not going to let it sound like crap so…" He shrugged.

Nikki bit her lower lip to keep from smiling and failed. "Let me know if I can help."

He nodded his thanks, turned to leave, and doubled back. "Are you still out of here this weekend?"

She frowned at him, her mind blanking. Why would she be gone this weekend?

"For that board install in Malibu?" Johnny reminded, concern entering his expression. "Did they reschedule?"

She sucked in a breath as it all came racing back to her. "Right! The install in Malibu this weekend!"

That was this weekend?

She nodded, her movements jerky. "Yes. I will be gone this weekend."

Johnny narrowed his gaze but didn't push. "Okay." He slowly left the control room.

When she thought he had been gone a long enough time for it to be safe, she dropped her head back and slapped a palm to her forehead.

"Fuck," she hissed.

"You forgot about Malibu?" Asa guessed.

She straightened in her chair and checked her phone for her flight information.

"It can't possibly be tomorrow." She clicked through her calendar. "It's tomorrow. My flight is at eight in the morning. Ugh." She dropped her phone in her lap and held her face with both hands. "How did this happen?"

She knew exactly how it had happened. She'd been so distracted by the hunky carpenter working down the hall that she'd lost track of things.

If Johnny hadn't said anything, she'd have missed it.

And then where would she be?

Probably fired.

Okay, probably not. Johnny wouldn't fire her for one mistake. But she'd disappoint him. And somehow, that was worse.

"I have to go home and pack. Like right now."

"You don't have to be in here with me. I think I can do this without supervision," Asa said.

"I know." She chewed on her bottom lip, thinking. It was a simple board install. She could do it drunk and with one hand tied behind her back—not that she would do that.

"It's a three-day trip," she said more to herself than to Asa. "I won't be back until late Monday."

"Do you need a ride?" Asa offered.

She glanced over at him. "Yeah."

Why did her stomach feel like it was falling through space?

"Are you okay?" Asa asked, peering at her, concern lining his brow.

She nodded but knew her frown relayed something else.

"I just feel…" She shook her head because she didn't know how she felt. Everything inside was a jumbled mess without clear definition.

"Did something happen last night? With André? Because when I picked you up, you seemed fine. Happy even."

Did something happen?

That was the question on Nikki's mind as well.

Because no, nothing had *happened.*

But everything felt very big.

And precarious.

On the outside she was calm, cool, collected.

Inside was another matter. She felt like her head and heart were pulling her in different directions. And then for one spontaneous and ill-prepared moment, they'd both wanted the same thing.

"Hey," Asa got her attention. "Go home, pack. I can finish this no problem. And then let's go see a movie." He turned back to the board. "Get chill before you have to leave. They're playing *Phantom Menace* at the Logan tonight."

That sounded amazing actually.

"I'm supposed to go on a date with Ryan tonight," she said.

She sensed rather than saw Asa spin around in his chair and stare at her. She glanced up, trying not to smile. "What?"

"That's still happening?"

"Four dates. That's the deal. He gets one more."

"Wow. You're truly magnanimous," Asa deadpanned.

Nikki chuckled. "Listen, he's nice and who I date is none of your business anyway."

"Is it André's business?"

Nikki made a face and Asa chuckled as he spun back around.

No. It was none of André's business either.

And yet she felt queasy about it.

Even though she shouldn't!

"Have you talked to him about…you know."

She stared at the back of Asa's head until he spun around to face her again.

"To André," Asa said. "Have you guys at least cleared the air on what happened?"

Nikki continued to stare at Asa as her mind raced with all that his question brought up.

"We talk." Nikki shrugged and knew it was too large a movement for what she was hoping to convey. "We talk a lot. Sometimes we talk so much that I'm like, 'Whoa, buddy. Leave some things a mystery.'"

"Uh-huh." Asa cleared his throat, unimpressed. After a beat he sighed and ran a hand over his short-cropped black hair. "I know I'm not exactly the poster child for dealing with difficult things. But maybe that's why you're so confused about all of this. Because you still have questions and he's the only one who has those answers."

She narrowed her eyes and growled at him.

He laughed. "Maybe I'm wrong." He put his hands up, palms facing her. "Maybe you can be in love with someone, and after a long enough time, all those pesky feelings go away."

He went back to the control board after he'd finished speaking. He didn't wait to see how Nikki reacted to his words.

And she was glad for it.

Because even though she couldn't explain it, sadness grabbed hold of her heart and squeezed.

He was right. Love didn't just go away. It lingered. Just on the edge of her awareness, it pricked at her heart. It whispered in her dreams. And it never truly left.

She hated that Asa was right.

Because that meant she was going to have to ask André why.

To "clear the air" as it were.

But she didn't want to know why. There wasn't a reason that wouldn't hurt. And she was so *tired* of hurting because of him.

Wasn't it easier to let things be as they were?

Because right now, they were getting along. Having fun even!

Right now, nothing was wrong and no promises were made.

Right now…

Well, right now she was hiding from him in the control room for Studio X.

Why was she hiding?

Why could she only think about André and his stupid hot suspenders and his stupid hot vulnerability?

Ryan had taken her to get burgers.

Not fancy burgers.

Just regular, franchise-made burgers.

He sipped from the straw of his vanilla milkshake and she realized he had a great jawline. She had never noticed.

In fact, looking at him in the light, Ryan was kind of hot.

In that all-American, Channing Tatum kind of way. Muscles and white teeth and the disposition of a golden retriever.

Again, it made sense that Al would think they'd be a match. More than once, Nikki had been told she "bounded through life like a puppy." This was the kind of guy who could match that.

So why didn't she feel anything?

It had been over two weeks between dates, and she hadn't even noticed that much time had passed.

But she'd spent hours with André last night and she couldn't stop thinking about what he might be doing at the moment. Was he having dinner alone? Or with friends?

"Listen, Nikki," Ryan said.

His serious tone had her straightening her shoulders on her side of the booth.

"I've had a lot of fun getting to know you, but I think this should be our last 'date.'" He did the air quotes and everything.

She blinked as her brain scrambled to make sense of what was happening.

He was dumping *her?*

Huh.

His brown eyes gentled and he reached across the table to take her hand. She let him of course because she wanted to see what would happen next.

"You're a really great person. Funny and gorgeous and way too smart for a guy like me."

Why did this sound like the speech that she had been planning on giving him?

"But I'm just not feeling a connection." He smiled apologetically. "I hope we can stay friends."

Nikki licked her lips. "Yeah. Of course," she agreed.

He squeezed her hand. "Thank you." He let go and sat back in the booth with one arm stretched out along the seatback. "So what else have you got going on tonight?"

She wanted to laugh but she was afraid he'd think she was losing it.

"My friend Asa is meeting some friends at a movie in a bit."

"That sounds like fun," Ryan said, interested.

"Well…" She hesitated because sometimes when people weren't used to the people she hung out with, they could get very uncomfortable. "It's *The Phantom Menace*? The *Star Wars* movie?"

Ryan shrugged and nodded. "Yeah, okay. I've seen it."

She hummed as she tried to figure out how to describe what he should expect.

"There's gonna be a lot of weirdos. Some of them will be dressed like characters. There will be people who mimic the lightsaber duels *while* they're happening on screen."

"Oh. So like *Rocky Horror* fans."

"Yeah." She chuckled, relieved. "Exactly like that. A lot of the same people actually."

"Cool." He finished his milkshake. "I could get into that." He started to crumple up his garbage.

"Seriously?" she asked.

"Yeah, text him. See if it's okay if I come."

"I'm sure it'll be fine," she said while texting Asa that her plans had changed, and she could meet him at the theater.

ANDRÉ

. . .

The next time Ryan texted him to hang out, he was going to ask if he was on a date with Nikki. Because this was the second time of the four times that he'd hung out with Ryan, that Nikki was also involved. That's fifty percent for all of you following along at home.

André wasn't complaining.

But he didn't like feeling as if he were ambushing her.

Last night's benefit had gone well for the most part. What was a little revelation of the soul between exes?

But she had successfully avoided him all day at the studio.

Not that he was looking for her, he wasn't.

But he could tell.

Did it bother him?

Fuck yes.

Was he going to do anything about it?

Fuck no.

And yet here was Ryan, doing God's work, the lovable oaf.

Asa spotted him first, followed by Ryan, then Nikki. There were other people in their group: Allison, and a handful of others who André didn't recognize.

Surprise rippled across Nikki's face, and she quickly hid it. He couldn't tell if it was a good surprise or a bad surprise.

André greeted everyone he knew, saving Nikki for last.

"Would you like me to go?" he asked, low and with total sincerity. He didn't want her to be uncomfortable. And he didn't want to draw attention to the fact that she might be.

Her shoulders relaxed at his question. "No." She looked up at him with those big blue eyes that he adored and smiled softly. "You don't have to go."

She was wearing what she'd been in at work today—jeans and a lavender t-shirt that said "Infantstructure" on it. He'd meant to ask about the shirt but didn't get an opportunity. But it also meant she hadn't gone home to change for her date with Ryan.

And he read way too much into that.

It still made him happy.

Ryan was great.

Didn't mean André wanted to see him be the one to get all of Nikki's bright smiles.

"I didn't mean to crash another date," he said. "Though it looks like I wasn't the only one this time." He eyed the large group taking up a good portion of the small lobby area.

Nikki's soft laugh brought him back to her. "You're not crashing anything. We had our final date a little earlier."

He frowned in question.

"Ryan doesn't feel that way about me. He thinks we're better as friends." She shrugged and rolled her eyes like she couldn't believe it either.

"*He* dumped *you?*"

"Right?" She waved a hand. "Thank you. Finally, someone gets it. Asa was less than sympathetic."

André was equal parts relieved and disgusted. Ryan could only be so lucky. And yes, he knew he wasn't being rational. He didn't want Nikki dating the guy, but he also hated the idea of her getting hurt.

"How are you feeling?" he asked, trying not to make this moment all about him.

Sure, she was laughing about it and being good-natured, but who really liked getting dumped?

Her lips twisted to the side, and she frowned. "I feel weird."

He nodded and took her by the elbow. "Weird is a perfectly valid response. Let me get you some sweets. Anything you want."

She cracked a smile. "Thanks."

"I'm not kidding. Let's get you all hopped up on sugar and then send you home with Asa. He'll be more sympathetic after that."

Nikki belted out a loud laugh and André wanted to pat himself on the back.

See? They had fun together. It wasn't his imagination.

"Dre!"

He spun around at the sound of his sister's voice.

She launched herself at him and he almost took a lightsaber to his nose as she flung her arms around his neck.

Sabine backed up and smacked him on the arm. "What are you doing here?"

"Uh." He coughed a light laugh. "I was invited."

Sabine was wearing a cream-colored tunic and brown robe.

And a fake beard.

"What is on your face?" he asked, shaking his head.

She tugged on her beard and grinned.

"She looks cute, right?" Dave, her rock star husband, said coming up beside her. And by rock star, André meant that literally.

Dave, aka Sunshine Capone, was dressed similarly to Sabine except his beard was gray.

"What am I looking at here?" André asked, pointing between the two of them.

"I'm young Obi-Wan and he's old Obi-Wan," Sabine explained. "But I was not expecting to see you here." She flicked her eyes to Nikki, trying to be inconspicuous, but André knew what she was asking.

"Are you sure it's okay for him to be here?" André asked, meaning Dave. Because rock star in public just seemed irresponsible.

Nikki bumped his shoulder. "These people do not care. Allison is here and no one bats an eye. And she's local-scene royalty."

Dave was nodding. "It's true. Besides, I have a bodyguard around here somewhere…" He looked around the lobby. "She's stealthy like a ninja."

Sabine nodded in agreement.

It didn't make sense to André, but he wasn't about to argue. He glanced at the people surrounding them and it did seem that no one cared. About half of the moviegoers were dressed in a costume of some kind. Perfectly content looking very out of place in the middle of the night in downtown Chicago.

He turned to say something to Nikki, but she was gone. He spotted her at the counter, buying her own candy, and disappointment twisted his gut.

Disappointment in himself.

"Brother mine," Sabine said regaining his attention. "Is this a date?"

"I wish," he said without thinking. He blew out a breath as he thought about how to answer the questions his sister had asked. They were valid questions.

He just didn't have the answers.

This was a bad idea. He shouldn't even be here.

Nikki was here with her friends, and he was being intrusive.

Again.

"Actually, I think I'm just going to—"

"I got extra butter on the popcorn," Nikki said, shoving the bag into his hands. "So, you'll have to deal. But I have a ton of napkins." She shimmied her chest at him, where at least a half a bundle of paper napkins was poking out of the collar of her shirt.

He choked on his surprised laugh.

Her pleased smile warmed him and soothed his previous anxiety.

"Also, so much candy." She held out her hands to reveal at least six packages of different candy.

"That's so much sugar," André said.

She nodded and turned to the doors of the theater. "C'mon. I like to sit in the middle."

André's eyes connected with his sister's for a moment. Sabine looked confused but happy.

So, the same as André, then.

He followed Nikki into the darkened theater and shuffled past cosplayers and other people who all seemed to know her name.

As soon as he sat down beside her, his sister sat next to him, and Asa sat on the other side of Nikki.

Asa leaned forward a bit and lifted his chin at André. André returned the gesture.

He was both self-conscious and excited. Out of place and anchored.

"I meant to ask earlier," he said, shifting in his seat more her direction. "What's your shirt about?"

She glanced down at her shirt as if to remind herself what she was wearing. Asa leaned over to look too.

"Oh." She finished the mouthful of popcorn. "It was my and Asa's first band in high school. "We were terrible."

Asa chuckled as he nodded in agreement. "We just really liked the name we'd come up with."

"You guys have been friends a long time, yeah?" André asked.

Asa's dark eyes cut to him. "Since childhood. Besties for life."

His answer sounded more like a hidden warning than a casual answer to a simple question.

André eased back in his seat and faced forward. If he was going to be friends with Nikki, he was going to have to make peace with Asa somehow.

The movie started and he allowed himself to be pulled into the story instead of worrying about what Asa thought of him.

He'd never had an experience like this at the movies; the loud banter from the audience, the lightsaber duels in front of the screen and in the aisle. It was ridiculous and amazing, and he was filled with gratitude.

Nikki had always invited him into parts of living that he never would have discovered without her. From music, to movies, to people, she opened doors to worlds that he didn't know he needed.

He spent so much of his life talking about the past. Moments forever frozen and unchanged.

Growing up had been unstable and high stress. He'd gravitated to things that didn't change on him. Like history and fossils and broken pots he hadn't broken himself.

And then he'd met Nikki and she introduced him to a living world. One where it was okay to show up and be yourself.

He could be the professor with the bowtie and also enjoy loud music and not knowing what came next.

All he had to do was open his eyes and show up for it.

She'd saved him.

And she had no idea.

The movie ended all too soon, if only because he liked being near her. He liked being around her friends that lived with such freedom.

As the crowd around them filtered out of the theater and into the night, he lingered.

They walked down the street, side by side, Asa and Allison a few meters in front of them. The hot day had cooled into a tolerable night, but the humidity still clung to the air.

As they approached Asa's car parked along the street, Nikki slowed.

She stopped and faced him.

He waited because it felt like she wanted to say something.

"I'm gonna be gone for a few days."

"Where are you going?" he asked, curious. He reached out and tucked a strand of hair behind her ear.

The action felt so natural he didn't even realize he'd done it until his eyes drifted to hers. He dropped his hand back to his side.

"Uh." She swallowed. "Malibu." She rolled her eyes. "An actor set up a studio in his house and I'm installing the soundboard. I'll be back late Monday."

"You're brilliant, you know that?" he asked with all sincerity. She was remarkable in ways that he knew she didn't see in herself. But he never tired of watching her shine.

She opened her mouth and started to say something, her brows twitched, and she sighed.

"When you get back, the floor will be done," he said.

She nodded. "Cool." She forced a smile and glanced at Asa and Allison who were waiting. "I'll see you."

She turned and walked away. She didn't look back.

André waited until they'd driven away before turning back the way he'd come to get to his own car.

He wished he knew what she'd wanted to say before she left.

Sometimes he'd look in her eyes and he could almost see what she was thinking. But then a wall would go up and she was unreadable again.

It was like they were both standing on opposite sides of a river, and he had no idea how to get them both onto the same side. There had to be a bridge or something.

But maybe she didn't want to be on the same side with him.

Saturday was spent in the studio with Tyrone as they finished the floor of the lounge.

It had turned out beautifully.

So why was he still unsettled?

He got in his car to drive home and instead pointed the BMW toward West Loop. He shot a text to his sister to warn her he was coming.

He had no idea if Sabine could help him, but he'd be foolish not to ask her.

She opened the door to the loft and narrowed her gaze.

"Brother mine," she greeted. "Are you here seeking wisdom or cookies?"

"A bit of both." He smirked and followed her into the loft.

Dave was sitting on a stool at the kitchen island.

They were an odd couple from the outside looking in. Sabine was a teacher and Dave was a rock star with face tattoos. They lived here at Sabine's loft, but Dave had a condo in the East Randolph Residence. They had every intention of keeping both places.

When you saw them together, it all made sense. Individually, they were awesome. But together they were something else. Something better.

André accepted the bottle of hard cider Sabine handed him and took a seat on the stool beside Dave.

"I love being a grownup," Dave said, clinking his bottle of cider against André's. "Cider and cookies are definitely where it's at."

"What's up with you? Do I finally get to find out what's going on with you and Nikki?" Sabine asked, getting to the point. She set a plate of cookies on the island in front of him. They looked like chocolate chip. Dave grabbed one immediately.

"You're seeing Nikki? From work?" Dave asked. "That's a trip."

André paused as he processed that Dave considered being a rock star "work" like it was any nine-to-five. He picked up a cookie as well and tried to inspect it for raisins. Sabine had fooled him before.

"Remember the night I hit her with my car?" André asked.

Dave choked on his cider.

"I seem to recall that unfortunate incident," Sabine replied.

André examined the label on his cider and blew out a large breath. Then he recounted the last two weeks to Dave and Sabine. The baseball game, having lunch in her office, the benefit.

When he was finished, he glanced up at Sabine. Her mouth was pressed into a hard line.

She shook her head at him. "What the hell are you doing?"

"Now wait," Dave broke in diplomatically. "Maybe he's trying to figure some things out."

Sabine's eyes widened and she made a little growl noise in the back of her throat. "Pretty sure the time for figuring things out has passed. When you ghost your fiancée, you don't get to have a redo."

"Wait." Dave swiveled to face André directly. "You *ghosted* her?"

André sighed and dropped his shoulders.

"Yep. Two and a half years with no communication and then boom! Hits her with his car."

André lifted his eyes to his sister. "I didn't mean to hit her with the car. And…." He sighed again. "I drunk dialed her on Christmas."

"What?" Sabine yelled.

Yes, actually *yelled.*

She shook her head and tsked.

"That's…" Dave broke off and sighed.

André studied the tattooed face of his sister's husband and saw something there he never had before.

Disappointment.

When had Dave developed so much dad energy?

"Maybe this is going to sound weird, but in my opinion, ghosting is worse than cheating." Dave's solemn declaration had both André and Sabine stunned silent.

Dave's dark blue eyes bounced between the two siblings. "Not to say cheating is ever acceptable. But for me, personally, ghosting would hurt more."

"Why do you say that?" Sabine asked quietly.

"I don't know." Dave shrugged. "Maybe there are different ways to do the same thing. I just know that I've gotten over being cheated on way easier than losing contact with someone who wouldn't at least tell me *why* it had to end." He rolled the bottle of cider between his palms. "Cheating says what they wanted: something else. Ghosting is a sentence without punctuation. I will inevitably blame myself." He dipped his head. "As is my nature. And without being able to ask what I did wrong, I'd be terrified of doing it again. I'd be caught in a loop of self-doubt and anxiety. Moving on? That would take real work."

Fucking hell.

Is that what he'd put Nikki through?

It would explain why she went back and forth from being happy to be with him, to being distant.

She'd had to put things back together without any answers from him about why and where and how.

Sabine crossed her arms over her chest and narrowed her eyes at him. "Have you told her?"

"What do you mean?' he countered, trying to buy time as his brain scrambled for an answer.

"You just heard what Dave said. She's worked hard to get over you. Have you told her why you did what you did? And what's changed since then? Why are you showing up in her life now? Because it looks bad. If a guy did this to Kara, I'd already have hidden his body in the dumpster."

André held up a finger. "Being raised in America has made you far more violent than I am comfortable with."

She rolled her eyes. Dave chuckled.

"It wasn't like I planned this, okay?" he said, a little more defensive than he needed to be. Her questions were valid. "I thought at the time that leaving her was better for the both of us. I didn't know…" He stopped and took a deep breath as his chest constricted. "But I was wrong. I just…" He shrugged because he wasn't sure if the words that wanted to come out were the right ones.

"The drunk dial was a one-off. I don't even remember the conversation. My phone said I was on it for twelve minutes. Twelve. I have no idea what I said or who I even spoke to."

"Maybe she changed her number," Dave offered helpfully.

André licked his lips. "I thought of that."

"But if you ask and her number is different, then she'd know you had called," Dave guessed.

"Right. See? You get me." He lifted his eyebrows at Sabine. "He gets me."

Dave nodded knowingly.

Sabine glared at the two of them. "But that doesn't explain why you're around *now.* You could just fade into the background of her life again and no one would even care."

André winced at her words. Which was unexpected. What she'd said was correct, of course. But it hurt like hell to hear.

After a beat he looked up and his gaze collided with his sister's. She was watching him in that way she did. With way more insight than someone her age should have.

It made him want to run away.

Both of them had kind of had to raise themselves. Separated when they were in primary school, André had been taken to England to live with his father. Sabine stayed in America with their mother.

Both of them had shit parents. He had wondered many times over the years if they had been raised together, if it would have been better than it was being apart. They had no way of knowing.

He only had a small understanding of what Sabine had gone through when their mother had decided to pursue a life of white-collar crime. Sabine had not only had to be her own parent but also had to fight for her own identity in more ways than one.

André's experience was limited to a cold and distant father with impossible expectations whose most stable relationship was with football.

As soon as André was able to move back to the States to be closer to his sister, he did.

But it had taken him a lot longer to leave emotionally.

"What happened?"

André glanced at Dave and tried to buy time by taking a long drink.

"You mean with the engagement?" he clarified, knowing exactly what Dave was asking but still not wanting to answer.

Or maybe he just didn't have an answer.

"Did you fight or something?" Dave prodded.

André's gaze darted to Sabine who was reading his soul again. "Or something," he mumbled and took another drink of his cider.

Sabine crossed her arms over her chest and cocked a hip.

"You got freaked out," she said.

André paused, held the cider in his mouth a beat, then swallowed.

"Something freaked you out and you ran away. It's your move."

André nodded once and pursed his lips. It *was* his move. He'd run away from home as soon as he'd gotten the chance.

"It was also Dad's move," she stated, unimpressed.

André paused in body and mind and stared at his sister. Small in stature and younger in age but with the self-assurance of a honey badger.

She probably got that from their mom.

But she'd chosen to use her powers for good instead of evil. Which was great for the world at large but sucked for him in that moment.

It wasn't that she was right; it was that she was right *and* unapologetic about it.

And it hurt like hell.

"You know," Dave broke in. "There *are* other moves."

André's gut twisted and his memory flashed with the image of Dave standing in the doorway on Christmas Eve night with his heart in his hands.

That moment was seared into his brain.

That moment had been the catalyst for him calling Nikki that night. It had offered him hope in a possibility that he had never dared to hope before.

"How—" His voice cracked, and he cleared his throat. "How do you learn new moves?"

Dave studied him like he was shocked by what he saw.

"Dude," Dave said softly. "You're the whole package. You have a cool job, you're smart, creative, good looking. You've got degrees I can't spell. If you want to learn something new, you can just do it." Dave shrugged.

"I don't know how to get from here to there," André confessed. "I feel like I'm within reach but it's too far away."

"You have to tell her, Dre," Sabine added gently, her frown having melted away.

He grimaced because that was not the answer he was looking for.

"You have to tell her what happened. It's the only way to get to the next step."

"What if it doesn't matter? What if I tell her all of it and she doesn't give me another chance?"

Sabine leaned her elbows onto the island and leveled her gaze at him.

"If you want to get to the other side of this, you have to do the scary thing. She might not meet you there. And that would hurt, but you'll get through it. You don't get to the life you want without taking risks."

She made it all sound so simple.

André sighed and nodded. She was right of course. Like he knew she would be. But it was not a conversation he wanted to have with Nikki.

Which was why he hadn't told her years ago because he knew it would hurt and he didn't want to have to see that.

Which wasn't fair.

Or brave.

Fine.

He'd talk to her when she got back. That gave him enough time to finish the lounge. Then, when he had something beautiful to give her, he could have the hardest conversation of his life.

CHAPTER TWELVE

FAVORITE CRIME

NIKKI

The "house call install" wasn't as glamorous as most people thought it was. Whenever she told people she had to fly to Beverly Hills or Miami or Prague, they assumed it was like a vacation.

But she never really saw the places she went to.

She showed up, did the install—which was in a windowless room in some rich dude's basement—and then flew home. It went pretty fast.

But Malibu seemed to drag.

She couldn't say why except that she was pretty sure she missed André.

Which was a stupid and irresponsible feeling to have. Irresponsible to her heart and everything that it had already been through with him.

She'd gotten back from Malibu as the sun was setting. Part of her wanted to walk over to the studio to see if André was working but she knew that would be a bad idea.

She took a shower, put on a tank top and some sleep shorts, and tried to go to bed early.

But she couldn't sleep.

She tossed and fussed until she'd thrown her pillow across the room and gotten out of bed.

The house was quiet as she crept downstairs. Asa was probably watching TV in his room. Al and Steiny would be at rehearsal for a couple more hours.

Nikki grabbed her acoustic guitar from off its stand and quietly slipped out the back door.

She set her phone to record and put it on the table in front of her and then sat cross-legged on the loveseat.

The small jungle behind her house teemed with life. Crickets', frogs', and locusts' songs hummed in the summer air.

Talking to André was obviously the right decision.

But she couldn't stress enough how much she didn't want to do that.

She pulled the guitar into her lap and breathed the night air.

It started with a few small strums and some experimental chords.

She hummed and sung with no words as she tried to find her feelings in there somewhere.

The last time she'd done this was Christmas Eve night.

André had called her, drunk and unintelligible. She couldn't understand a word he'd said and it had become obvious after a few minutes that he had pocket dialed her.

It had been an accident.

And it had hurt like fuck.

When her phone had lit up with his name, her heart had tripped all over itself trying to get to the phone before her hands did.

But it wasn't what she'd thought.

Or hoped.

Thus was born the Heartbreak Chronicles. She and Zara had confessed a dizzying amount of secrets that they hadn't told anyone else. And then they'd started writing songs about them.

That's what they'd been sending back and forth to each other for the past eight months.

Songs of love and hope and heartache.

Zara wanted her to produce the entire album. She said she didn't trust anyone else to understand what it needed to sound like.

But Nikki wasn't a producer.

Sure, she wanted to be; that was the dream.

But she was untested and inexperienced. Her first record shouldn't be for the biggest pop star in the world.

That would be like falling in love with a guy who was lightyears out of her league.

And everyone saw how that had ended.

The guitar faded back into the sounds of the night and she set it aside. She stood and picked up her phone and sent the audio file to Zara without context.

"Hey," a masculine voice broke the stillness of the night.

She jumped and screamed at the same time.

And it wasn't a glamorous May West scream. It was more of a yelp-bark, better suited for a dog getting its tail stepped on.

And her jump was more of a twirl.

She made a full one-eighty in the air and landed facing the door and the man who'd startled her.

André doubled over in laughter, putting his hands to his knees while his whole body shook.

"Oh my God, you scared me." She pressed a palm to her racing heart, too relieved that it was him to be embarrassed at her reaction.

Her body flooded with adrenaline, replacing the melancholy that had taken hold of her a moment before.

André took his time getting sober and finally righted himself.

He had to push his hair back as it had flopped onto his forehead during his merriment. And while he was fully clothed, in jeans and a clean white tee, she still felt she was seeing too much of him.

Maybe it was the smile.

Or the tired happiness in his eyes.

Or that she'd made him laugh and she hadn't even been trying.

"What are you doing here?" she asked.

He sucked in a breath and his eyes roamed over her face. "Three days felt like a long time."

She swallowed because she felt the same. And yet he'd had no problem going two and a half years without seeing her.

"I wanted to show you something. Asa said you were out back." His gaze flicked to her chest, down her legs, and back up. "If you're too tired, I can show you tomorrow."

"What do you want to show me?" she asked, crossing her arms over her chest.

"The lounge is finished." He slid his hands into his pockets and rocked back on his heels.

The floor was only being started when she'd left. He must've worked all weekend to get it done.

"Oh," she replied, interested. "Let me get my shoes."

She grabbed her guitar, and they went back inside the house. She put the guitar away and slid her feet into her lace-less Chucks by the front door.

They left the house together and she texted Asa to let him know she was going to the studio. Because again, his dad was a detective. Telling each other where they were was just habit.

She fell into step with André as they walked up her quiet street.

"How was Malibu?" he asked.

"Fine." She shrugged. "I did the thing and got paid." She flashed him a grin.

He shook his head. "You have no idea how cool you are, do you?"

They made it to the front door and she unlocked it.

"I am exactly as cool as I believe I am."

He extended an arm and ushered her to go first.

Ninety-nine percent of André's personality was perfect. At least for her. He was gracious and sweet and polite. He held the door for her like a gentleman, but he never ever asked her to comb her hair or put on more clothes before they went out in public. He laughed at her jokes, listened to her talk about music in a way that had to be annoying, but he also didn't get jealous that she had a lot of guy friends.

And then there was that one pesky detail.

That one thing that changed everything.

The Ghosting.

The door closed behind them, and André made sure to lock it. All the lights were still on. He must've been working right up until he came to get her.

Her stomach fluttered and she had to consciously keep breathing.

They arrived at the closed door of the lounge. He gave her a smile before pushing the door open.

She stepped into the room and her heart fell through the cracks of time and memory.

She'd been busy enough and disconnected from reality enough that she hadn't really been paying attention to the changes going on over the past two weeks.

And nowhere in there did she consider what he could do to her.

She was wholly unprepared.

Yes, he'd painted the walls. And the floor was finished.

But he'd also replaced the couch with a cream-colored leather one which was going to match the lounger she had at home perfectly. He'd even left a space for it near the window where he'd set up a round coffee side table that looked like a converted wine rack.

On the painted walls he'd hung art. Vintage band posters, framed albums that they'd produced, political art from the '80s. She looked up and the ceiling was what he'd described a few days before except it was so much *more*. The copper pipes gleamed. The ductwork had been replaced and was also copper now. But he'd painted the rafters to match the walls so the ceiling looked like it went on forever.

Against the wall with the built-ins, he'd created a tall worktable with stools around it.

It was a creative heart's dream come true.

And it was all so…

"I needed to do some finishing touches. I found this lamp at a flea market in…" He shook his head. "Don't worry about that part actually. It's too hard to explain." He strode across the room, his steps ringing solid on the hardwood, and wrapped his fingers around the stem of a tall floor lamp. "I thought I'd put it here." He placed it near the wine rack side table. "But this space really needs a chair too."

I have one.

She had the perfect one. They had both planned on putting it in the same place in the room and he didn't even know the damn chair even existed.

"I have a few calls out to see if I can find a chair that will work. I don't think a regular Lay-Z-Boy will do." He flashed her a grin.

She was either going to throw up or burst into tears.

"I have one," she choked out.

"I'm sorry, what was that?" he asked.

"I have one. A chair. The perfect chair actually."

"Great!" He checked his watch. "Actually, we could grab it now if you have time."

She gulped. This was…

What the hell was this?

"What do you think?" he asked, sweeping an arm around the finished room. "A good space for a creative mind?"

"Yeah," she answered honestly. "It's… I'm impressed. And I'm not just saying that."

He took a deep, pleased breath and put his hands on his hips.

Then he turned those hazel eyes on her and her heart tripped. "Doing this room first helped me decide what I wanted to do for your office."

"My office?"

"Yeah." He came within three feet, and she had to look up to see him. "Your office is terrible. I'm going to fix it for you."

"Wait. You think my office is terrible?"

He flashed perfectly white teeth at her.

"You need a workspace suitable for your creative endeavors."

She was struggling to comprehend what he was saying. "I feel like I did that time that Asa changed the audio translation on my Roku to French and it took me an entire episode of *Brooklyn Nine-Nine* before I realized something was wrong."

André chuckled.

And be still her heart, it was still one of her favorite sounds.

"Then let me translate." He was still smiling. "I am more than ready to gut that cupboard you have the audacity to call an office and build you something you will never want to leave."

She stared at him, flabbergasted.

There was a lot to address in what he'd just said.

But she didn't get a chance because he grabbed her hand and pulled her out of the room. She followed him, willingly—even though her heart was chanting *no, no, no, no, no*—down the hall to her office.

He let go and started pointing at things.

Belatedly, she realized that she should have been drunk for this.

Yes, that would have helped tremendously.

"I would like to set up a workstation for you in the lounge while construction takes place in here. I'm going to tear out all this carpet tomorrow or the day after. Tyrone will be able to do the floor next weekend." He walked further into the room, vibrating with excitement.

"Remember that restaurant we went to in Paris? The one where we danced on the couches?"

She nodded once, stunned. Overwhelmed.

And was that her heart shattering into a thousand pieces?

He continued.

"I want to do a gallery on the ceiling like they did. Paint it navy and use copper ductwork in here too. And put a couch here, along this wall. But you need a large rug to cover this space since"—he tilted his head to the side—"you wind up on the floor when you're working. The walls should be cream with gray here and here. And just pillows everywhere." He moved to the far corner of the room. "I can build a cupboard for these." He pointed to the amps. "That pulls out like ah, like a trundle…" He pinched the bridge of his nose. "Not a trundle. You know what I mean. So you can move them around easier and load and unload other large…" He clicked his fingers as he sought the correct words. He went with, "Items."

He crossed to the other side of the room.

"Your desk should be closer to the light. And bigger. This desk is small and quite damaged. I'm going to take out all the overhead lights since you prefer ambient lighting." He pointed to the one window. "I'll replace the glass in there which will brighten it up in here during the day. And then install light strips around the perimeter, top and bottom for when you're working at night. And if it's not enough light, I have a lamp guy now. He can get me cool lamps."

He put his hands on his hips and faced her, very pleased with his ideas.

She should tell him it sounded awesome. Amazing even.

That it was perfect, and she couldn't believe he'd managed to make something that spoke right to her soul in a way she hadn't felt in *years*.

But only one thing came out.

"You broke my heart," she blurted, not thinking. Or maybe not caring. Maybe both.

André's eager expression immediately went blank.

She hadn't meant to be the one to bring it up. She thought she understood what had happened enough that it didn't need to be dissected.

But watching him excitedly talk about his plans for her space and using his intimate knowledge of her to build something so perfect…it was too much.

It hurt like a sledgehammer to her sternum. The more he talked, the harder it had become for her to breathe.

"You keep doing all these great things and I can't tell if it's because you just have no idea or if you don't care. So, you should know. You broke my heart."

André's eyebrows dipped and twitched. She couldn't tell if it was confusion or concern. But now that she'd started to let it out, she couldn't stop it. Or maybe she didn't want to stop it. They had never talked about it. About how he'd disappeared and left her holding the baggage of all they'd created together. She'd never been able to express how it had felt to be left without explanation.

"I thought you didn't know me," she said, hating that her voice shook. "I thought, if you knew me, *really knew me,* you would never hurt me like this."

He didn't move. He just stood there, staring at her.

She took a step towards him and put a hand on her chest. "I was ready to spend the rest of my life with you and you just stopped speaking to me. Who does that?"

He opened his mouth, closed it.

She nodded and looked around the room. Looking for anything to anchor herself to but she was surrounded by chaos. When her eyes landed on André, they began to burn. Dammit. She didn't want to cry.

"I guess I'm not okay after all," she said. "Because listening to you just now." She swung an arm toward the doorway. "What you made in the lounge." She dropped her arm and bit the inside of her lip. "You know me very well."

She took a shaky breath.

Part of her wanted to scream at him. To yell and explode with grief and rage. But hurting people had never been her style.

"So that means that you knew exactly what you were doing back when you did it. You broke my heart, and you did it on purpose."

"Nik." He took a step toward her.

She took a step back.

"I loved you *so* much," she whispered. He flinched. She inhaled through her nose and cleared her throat. "I waited an embarrassingly long time for you that night. Long after I knew you weren't coming. I called and called and called. And you couldn't just tell me what was going on. Do you know how dehumanizing that is? How many days I tried again just to be left with no answers. None. You became a stranger overnight and I wasn't even allowed to ask why." She rolled her eyes, fresh shame pulling through her insides at how ridiculously naive she'd been.

"And now you come in here and show me that you were paying a lot more attention to me than I realized. The gallery ceiling? That's brilliant. Truly. I still can't figure out what I did that was wrong." Her thoughts were bouncing around in her head like a hot potato. She knew she was all over the map, but the entire situation was fucked up and convoluted.

"Nik," he said again, soft and careful. "It was never you. *I* was the problem."

"That's your father talking," she said, knowing it was low and saying it anyway. "I liked everything about you."

He shook his head like she didn't get it.

Maybe she didn't. But how complicated could it be?

"You were in love with a lie, Nik," he said, earnest as ever.

"I wasn't," she protested.

"You were." He took a step toward her, and she didn't retreat this time. "I withheld myself from you. I was terrified that if you saw me for who I was, you would leave. And it became too much for me. I should have talked to you. I should have told you everything. You deserved…better."

"You could tell me now." Did she want to know? No. But she needed to.

His stoic expression cracked and revealed deep lines of regret and sorrow. His hazel eyes, usually so bright, were dark with shadows.

Her heart lurched.

"That night…" He cleared the rough in his voice. "I was there. I was at the restaurant."

"What?" She studied his face, looking for the lie and not finding one. "No, you weren't."

He exhaled and rubbed the back of his neck. "I was in the lot across the street. I never got out of the car." He dropped his hand and the breath he took seemed to take more effort. "I watched you go inside with your dad. You were wearing a black dress and platform boots. The ones that I said looked like puffer fish."

Her eyes burned and she swallowed.

"Your dad laughed at something you'd said and held the door open for you and that was when I realized…"

He stopped, closed his eyes.

"What?" she whispered, not wanting the answer.

"I don't know how to be that guy."

Her breathing came heavier as she fought the urge to cry. "What guy?"

His brows dipped and he pressed his mouth into a hard line.

"André," she said, wishing her voice came out strong instead of soft. "Did I—? Did you think I expected—?"

He shook his head and stepped closer to her. "No. No, Nik. You did nothing wrong. It was never you. Not once." He licked his lips and this close she could see redness in his eyes.

"My dad got in my head. Looking at it now, I can see he was just projecting his own shit onto me, but I was too much of an idiot to understand that." He paused. "And here I am, still not taking responsibility." He dropped his gaze, lifted his eyes and took a deep breath.

"Okay, here it is. I was a coward. I hadn't been able to open up to you, not truly. And I think you know that. I held you at arm's length and used up everything you were willing to give me while I gave nothing of myself in return."

Her eyes darted to the side because she knew what he was talking about. But she'd thought that had just been her perception.

"But you…" His eyes gentled as he took her in. "You live wild open and free. It would have been horribly unfair to tie you to a man who wasn't even sure who he was."

A hot tear slipped from her eye and she quickly wiped it away.

"So, you just vanished?" she asked. "I called you so many times."

"I'm so sorry, Nik." He swallowed again and his eyes glossed over. "I was so scared," he whispered.

"Of me?"

"No." He shook his head and wiped at his eyes. "I was scared I'd hurt you." He shrugged. "It's that simple and that stupid."

She tilted her head to the side as another tear made a slow trek down her cheek. Couldn't he see that what he'd done had hurt more?

"What I did isn't okay. And I'm sorry it took me this long to say it."

She inhaled but it was shaky. "But why all this stuff now? I mean…André, these past two weeks have been…" She didn't want to say it because then it would be real but the tears in her eyes were already spilling. She sucked in a breath. "I've missed you so much. And I don't know what to do if you just disappear again. I don't know what any of this is for. Is it for you? So you can feel better about everything?"

He inhaled, his chest filled with air, and he let it out slowly. "No. I'm—fuck. I'm still doing it all wrong, aren't I?" He raked his fingers through his hair and stalked away. He paused and stared at the floor for a beat before turning around. "Fuck, I'm sorry, Nik. I'm just sorry. Admittedly, when I got the call to work here, I had hoped…" He closed his eyes and shook his head once, as if ashamed. "I thought we could start over. That I could show you how much I've grown, and I'd get a second chance."

All of her breath left her lungs.

"But it became very clear, very quickly that that was a foolish idea." He tucked his hands in his pockets and looked to the ceiling. "I'm a fuckwit. Still."

She didn't argue with him.

Her mind filtered through the past two weeks. All the times she'd noticed something off. Something different.

The honesty in his smile, the vulnerability in his quiet confessions.

They hadn't matched who she'd known him to be. Which meant everything he was saying to her now was the truth—she'd been in love with someone else.

Someone who didn't exist. He had been half a person.

It should have hurt but all she felt was relief. Like a weight had been lifted off her.

"What is it that you want now?" she asked.

His lips tilted up on the ends. "I just want to be in your life. In whatever capacity you'll have me."

"Like friends?" she asked.

He nodded.

Friends.

Friends?

She wiped at the tears that kept creeping from her eyes without her permission. Tears of hopeless understanding. So much of what he'd said made the worst kind of sense.

"I don't…" How was she supposed to say this without sounding horrible? "I don't even know you." It came out just as helpless as it felt.

He nodded and his eyes turned down.

"I want you to know me."

She sniffed a laugh. "You do?"

He came back to stand in front of her, his face earnest.

"Yes."

His answer was so firm and so simple. No excuse or over explanation. No pleading, no begging. Just "yes."

She swallowed and waved a hand between them. "I don't know how this is supposed to work. I don't know how to be friends with you. I think I'm still really mad at you."

He nodded like he understood. "You can keep yelling at me," he said, surprising her. "I deserve worse."

An unexpected laugh fell out of her. "I wasn't yelling."

"You were kind of yelling." He cracked a smile. "And if it helps, I'm fine with it."

"I don't want to yell at you." She ran her fingers under her eyes to check for more tears. She shrugged, feeling a little lost with the next steps.

"I believe you," she said. "But I'm not sure I trust you." Which was the strangest feeling because so much of her *wanted* to trust him

He nodded and took a slow breath. "That's more than fair."

Why couldn't they have had these kinds of conversations way back when? Maybe if they'd been communicating honestly, he would never have felt the need to flee, and the relationship would have taken its logical course and ended on its own. That's how most of her relationships ended.

"Do you think that if we'd have had hard talks like this, we'd have stayed friends?" she asked.

"I do." He rocked back on his heels. "You never did anything wrong. As far as I'm concerned you were absolutely perfect and still are."

She snorted.

"But I was so lost in the hope of who I could be that I dragged you along." He smiled a sad sort of smile. "And now I just want to be your friend. Authentically. Without strings or misconceptions." He paused. "If you'll have me."

Nikki closed her eyes and took stock of her emotions. There was still some confusion mingling with the relief of having said what she needed to say. Could they be friends? Maybe.

"It's so unconventional it might just work," she said, opening her eyes.

His lips tugged up on one side.

"You know I have a weakness for punk rocking the shit out of things," she said.

His smile grew a little more hopeful.

"I'm still kind of angry with you," she said.

"I'm still angry with me too," he agreed.

Part of her felt enormous relief at having been able to tell him how she felt. Or had felt. And another, softer part of her was just sad.

Because it finally felt done.

Resolved.

Final.

And no matter what you've been told, even happy endings carry their own bit of sorrow in them.

He took a step closer to her, bringing them within inches. His gaze danced over her face and her hair and settled on her eyes. A peaceful determination in his jaw. His voice dropped to a rough whisper. "I will never again not be there for you."

Despite her better judgement or what others may have done in the same situation, Nikki let her heart respond for her.

She slid her arms around his waist and hugged him. She put her head on his chest and closed her eyes. After a beat, his arms came around her and held her tight, wrapping her in warmth.

She inhaled the scent of his soap and aftershave, and it was the same as it had been two and a half years ago.

They stood there, holding one another, letting the moment fade into them.

He ran a hand up her spine and back down. Again. Again. Slow, soft, comforting.

She finally had her answers, and he was there to soothe the pain of it all.

It was more sweet than bitter, and she hoped it was a glimpse into where they were headed. Maybe now they could both find the peace and love they deserved.

Wherever that might be.

CHAPTER THIRTEEN

WHAT'D I DO WITH ALL THIS FAITH?

NIKKI

When she came into the studio the next day, all her things had been moved to the lounge.

André had set up a workstation for her just like he'd said he would.

And it was perfect.

She'd stopped by her office that morning and was surprised by the amount of work he and Javier had already done. When had he started?

Last night he'd walked her home, hugged her, and said goodnight.

And she'd slept like a rock. The moment her head had hit the pillow, she was out.

Funny how having answers, as difficult as they were to hear, gave her peace.

Though there was a brief moment that morning right before she came around the side of the building and saw his car where she worried he'd be gone again.

She wondered if she'd always have a little bit of fear first when it came to André. An apprehension. That seemed expected but she wished it wasn't.

Her phone lit up with a new text and she read it while hanging her bag on the copper coat rack in the corner of the lounge.

Z: I have the weekend off.

NIKKI: Come to Chicago

Zara replied with a *Blues Brothers* gif.

Nikki snorted.

Who was this woman?

The more time they spent together, the more Nikki was convinced that Zara Lorna was a super dork trapped in a pop star's body.

She didn't hate it.

A low whistle brought her head up. She turned the screen off on her phone and put it facedown on the high table.

Johnny stood in the doorway.

It wasn't like she didn't want to tell Johnny what she was working on with Zara. She did! She just couldn't yet.

"So is this your office for the rest of the summer?" he asked.

"Looks like it." Nikki adjusted her computer keyboard and surveyed her new "desk."

André had set it up almost exactly how she had it in the other room. Right down to the Post-its scribbled with notes she no longer needed.

"He was in here early this morning comparing photos on his phone to make sure he hadn't missed anything."

"That's…a lot," she muttered.

"Do you want me to kick him out?" Johnny asked. "I have a couple cousins who can be very menacing. And an auntie that will make him rethink all his life decisions."

"No." Nikki chuckled. "We talked last night and cleared the air." She smiled, remembering the long hug that had seemed to put them both back together. "I think we might even be friends now."

Johnny tilted his head to the side and lifted his eyebrows. "Well, you're the best kind of friend someone could have. So I hope for his sake, that's true."

The compliment hit Nikki in the heart and spread throughout her body. "Thanks, Johnny," she murmured.

He waved it off, like he would, and left her to do her job.

Which was so much easier to do for some reason.

It was mostly administrative stuff. She had to schedule a few commercial clients and show Asa how to access the scheduling app (again). And she also had to plug in a secret session with Zara that needed to be "on the books" but not really.

Every time she looked up, her eyes were met with the beauty of the lounge André had built. It kept her refreshed and inspired.

Sometime in the afternoon Sunshine Capone showed up at her door.

"There's the second-smartest woman I know."

He had the best stage name in the industry, truth be told. He was practically a walking billboard for happiness.

"I was wondering if you could do me a favor," he said, leaning in the doorway. He drummed his tattooed fingers along the doorjamb and his dark blue eyes scanned the lounge.

"Whoa. Have I never seen this room before?" he asked, stepping inside.

"André just remodeled it." She squinted at him. "It took him like two weeks. You seriously didn't notice?"

Sunshine turned in a slow circle. "André did this? My brother-in-law, André?"

"That's right," Nikki said, tugging on her earlobe. "He's your brother-in-law."

How had she forgotten that very important detail?

"You said you needed a favor?" she asked Sunshine, wondering what it would be this time. His favors ranged from needing her to listen to something to verify what he already knew, to seeing if she had an air pump.

"Yes." His eyebrows shot up and the new lounge was forgotten. "I heard a rumor that you used to play in a punk rock band."

Asa.

Her lips twitched but otherwise she didn't react. Sunshine studied her carefully.

"And that you do some light singing."

She was already shaking her head.

"C'mon, Nikki," Sunshine pleaded, taking a step her direction. "Just some background vocals. It's a very sweet song and I need a light touch."

She narrowed her eyes at him.

"I don't sing. You need a fast guitar and some mediocre tambourine? I'm your girl."

Sunshine's grin was blinding. "One take. If you hate it, we'll pull the plug."

See? This was how he'd talked Sabine into marrying him after a month. He was adorable in his persistence.

Which was how she found herself in an iso booth with headphones on and a sheet of paper in front of her.

She'd listened to the track a few times and warmed up enough to satisfy her own inner critic. Sunshine was right, it needed light backing vocals. And the song *was* very sweet. He'd probably written it for his wife, the lovable jerk.

"We can get a professional in here. I can make a few calls, schedule some—"

"Nope." Sunshine shook his head. "No schedules. This song's soul is all about being in the moment."

Nikki rolled her eyes and her shoulders back.

Fine. One take.

The track began and she did her best. She really did.

Backing vocals used to be something she enjoyed, so it wasn't a surprise when it came back so naturally.

It finished and she twirled a finger in the air. "One more time. I can do better."

No one argued and the track played again.

She did better that time, she could hear it.

When she left the iso booth, she was met by high fives.

"Good enough?" she asked Sunshine.

He flashed a happy grin and played back what they'd just recorded with the full track.

Nikki bobbed her head to the beat, listening to all the layers involved. When her vocals were added, goose bumps skated across her arms.

"It's perfect," Sunshine declared. "Why don't you do that more often? You're really good." He frowned at her.

Nikki rolled her eyes and then she noticed André in the doorway of the control room. He was leaning against the doorjamb, arms crossed, eyes on her in a way that felt oddly intimate.

She hadn't seen him all day.

Part of her had wondered if their "airing of grievances" last night would alter their connection.

And it appeared it had.

It had deepened it.

He smiled and she had the strangest urge to grab him by his suspenders and kiss the heck out of him.

"My sister ruined a lot of stuff that used to be fun," Asa said from the soundboard where he sat next to Johnny. "Like life."

"Asa," Nikki chastised with a frown. She shook her head.

Asa shrugged. Nikki took a breath and hoped no one asked follow-up questions.

She didn't want to talk about Shelby. Or Winking Pete. Unless it was good memories, and then she'd be down. But the negative stuff? Nah. She'd pass.

Nikki's phone beeped and she picked it up off the table, casually looking at the notification.

A text from Zara.

She headed for the door calling over her shoulder, "I have to get back to work now."

André joined her in the hall and walked beside her all the way back to the lounge. He stopped in the doorway while she continued inside.

"Will this work for you?" he asked, meaning the lounge as her workspace.

She nodded and slid her phone into her pocket even though she wanted to see what it said. It would have to wait until she was alone.

She really needed to tell Johnny about Zara.

When her eyes met André's, he had a sneaky smile on his face and his eyes crinkled at the corners.

"What?" she asked, feeling caught.

"What?" he mimicked followed by a chuckle. "You're damn cute when you have a secret."

"I don't have a secret," she denied even as heat spread over her cheeks.

"Of course not," he pretended to agree with her.

And then he winked.

Just one, short, blink-and-you-miss-it wink.

But it was a spark that sent electricity down her spine.

"Shut up," she said, looking away even as her pulse roared in her ears.

He chuckled again and left, not having any idea what he'd just done to her.

She didn't have a full idea either until later. When she finally remembered to check her phone.

ANDRÉ

By the time Friday rolled around, André was exhausted.

He'd hardly spent any time with Nikki but that was okay because they'd both been busy.

Not only had he had his first therapy session with Thomas, but he was hurrying to finish Nikki's office.

Therapy was not what he'd expected. For some reason he'd had it in his head that therapy was showing up to have a stranger tell him how much he sucked.

That's not what had happened.

Thomas asked some background questions, and they discussed André's goals. Thomas also gave him some homework—reading suggestions and making a list of the things that caused his anxiety as they happened.

And for the first time in a long time, André felt hopeful for his future self.

It made working on Nikki's office that much more enjoyable.

All he had left was painting the walls and ceiling and the finishing touches. But he had to wait for Tyrone to do the floor first. Which he'd be starting tomorrow.

It was late Thursday night and he was walking through the studio, making sure he hadn't left lights on in weird places, or had left tools lying about.

He came around the corner and the back door opened. He stopped and waited to see who had come in so late at night. Obviously, they had the combo to the security alarm, so he wasn't worried, just curious.

Nikki closed the door behind her, turned around, and jumped when she spotted him.

"Shit," she gasped, clutching at her chest like she had the night he'd surprised her on her deck.

He flashed a smile. "Just me."

"What are you doing here? Do you sleep anymore?" she asked, approaching him.

She was in baggy jeans and a Billy Joel shirt. Her hair was in a messy bun and her makeup was light, if she was wearing any at all.

She was stunning.

"I am making sure your office is ready for Tyrone to do the floor tomorrow. What are *you* doing here?" he countered.

She scratched the side of her neck and looked away.

"Nik," he said, narrowing his eyes. "Why do you look suspicious?"

She licked her lips, and her blue eyes—too big and bright to hide a lie—darted to his. "I have a thing?"

He eyed her, his lips twitching. "You do?"

"I do. I don't know why that came out like a question. But that's why I'm here." She pulled her shoulders back and jutted out her chin.

"Because of your thing?"

"Yep."

He watched her for a beat and then let it go. If she didn't want to tell him, he wasn't going to press.

His smile faded and he nodded. "Okay. Well. If you need help with it…"

"It's a work thing," she hurried to clarify. "Not a date thing."

His lips tipped up again on the ends. He hadn't thought it was a date. But it was adorable that she wanted to make sure he didn't think it was.

It also made him think she actually *did* want to tell him what was going on. Was this part of the secret thing she'd been hinting at for a few weeks now? Those hurried texts and phone calls? The audio recordings she kept playing when she thought no one could hear?

He waited, not asking, and not pushing. Just enjoying being in her space and feeling her energy zip all around them.

She swallowed and bounced on her toes. "The person I'm meeting tonight is a major recording artist and she wants me to produce her next album."

His smile grew with each word she said, and by the time she was finished, he was grinning with everything he had. "Nikki, that's brilliant!"

She made a face and waved her hands like she was trying to calm him down. Or maybe calm herself down. "You can't tell anyone," she said urgently.

"I won't," he promised. "I really want to hug you, though."

She threw her arms around him and squealed. When she stepped back her face was pink with excitement and he forgot how tired he'd been a few minutes ago.

"I haven't even told Johnny yet," Nikki said. "And he's just going to kill me when he finds out." She sighed. "It doesn't feel real, you know?"

He did know. It was probably very much how he felt when he'd found out that he'd gotten that gig in the Badlands. Like finally being taken seriously but not knowing if that was a good thing or not.

"Do you…" She stopped and rolled her lips inward.

"Do I what?" he asked.

"Do you want to stay and watch?"

He arched an eyebrow. "Am I allowed?"

She shrugged. "I mean, you've already signed all the paperwork. And it would be cool to have you here." She tossed a hand out. "Or it might be incredibly nerve wracking to have you here. Maybe I'll crumble under the pressure."

He chuckled and tapped the tip of her nose. "You thrive under pressure."

She made a face and looked away.

What was that about?

As usual with Nikki, he didn't have to wait long to find out. She was an open book in every sense of the word.

"I'm not a producer," she said. "Sure, I want to be, but I'm not. And it won't take long before Zara figures that out. I'm just a girl with a dream bigger than her stomach."

He chuckled. "I don't think that's how it goes."

"No?"

"No." He realized he was staring at her mouth.

That gorgeous pink mouth that smiled at him. That teased him and talked in ways so free and uninhibited that he felt like he could be free someday too.

He wanted to kiss her. To press his lips to hers and see if she tasted how she used to. To slide his fingers into her hair and hear her sigh against his mouth.

Her phone beeped and she glanced at the screen. He took a breath.

"Your thing?" he asked, his heart rate calming as he remembered where he was.

Damn, he was tired. He could hardly think clearly.

"Yeah, they're almost here. I have to let them in." She motioned to the door over her shoulder.

"I should go. I don't want you to get into trouble."

"Oh."

The disappointment was evident on her face and most of him was happy to see it.

"I'll let myself out the front, so they won't even know I was here." He took a breath and held her eyes. Did he want to stay? Yes. Absolutely.

But he was too tired, and he didn't want to be a distraction.

And with the way she was looking at him, she was already pretty distracted.

But this was too important to her. He knew it better than anyone. No way was he going to interfere with the thing she'd been working toward most of her life.

Before he knew what he was doing, he cupped the side of her face with a hand and brushed his thumb along her cheekbone.

Her soft inhale shook his convictions and he nearly changed his mind.

"Will you be safe here this late?" he asked.

She nodded, her dilated pupils skimming over his face. "She has security that will make sure I get home when we're finished."

He nodded.

"I'm so proud of you, Nik," he whispered. "You're going to be amazing."

She licked her lips and leaned toward him. The same way she had outside the museum after the benefit.

But this time it was harder for him not to give in.

He brushed a thumb over her cheek again and then pressed a soft kiss to her forehead. He lingered for a beat before stepping away.

His hand slid free, and he immediately missed the warmth of her skin.

But he needed to go. She had work to do and he wasn't rushing this.

Not this time.

CHAPTER FOURTEEN

TOO MUCH TOO FAST

NIKKI

The next few days flew by. Every night she waited until after dark before she snuck Zara and her bodyguards into the studio where they played with all the bits and pieces of music they'd been working on since December.

Zara and Nikki played that is. Her bodyguards just sat there and sometimes they checked the studio for criminals. At least that's what Nikki assumed they were doing.

Zara left Chicago early Monday morning and Nikki slipped quietly into her house for a shower before going back to work.

She froze in the entry when she spotted Asa standing in the hallway. He was facing her, one hand in his jeans pocket, the other holding a cup of coffee. His hair stuck up on one side from how he'd slept and his open flannel was so wrinkled she was positive he'd slept in that too.

But her favorite part of his ensemble had to be the bedazzled Crocs he wore as house shoes. Al had made them for him as a joke and he wore them religiously.

"Where have you been, young lady?" he asked, expression flat.

She smirked. "Hey, Dad," she teased. "Am I past curfew?"

He took a slow sip of his coffee. She kicked off her shoes and walked up to him.

"Were you with André?" he asked, concern coloring his otherwise annoyed expression.

"I was not," she replied easily. André had steered clear since Thursday and on one hand she missed him. But on the other, she was thankful because she needed to focus and he was...distracting.

Nikki went around Asa to the kitchen. He followed.

"What were you doing?" he asked, not believing her.

She grabbed one of her favorite mugs out of the cupboard—it was black and said "Hot AF" in hot pink. "Working."

"Uh-huh." He leaned his back against the counter and narrowed his eyes at her.

She poured coffee into her cup and decided to give Asa a hard time. Probably because she was exhausted. But it was a good kind of exhausted. The kind that came from depleting herself creatively and loving the results.

"Did you see what André did to the lounge?" she asked also leaning her back on the counter. She felt Asa's eyes on her.

"I saw it."

"What do you think?" she asked, trying to sound casual about it.

"What do I think about the lounge or what do I think about André?" he asked with a grumble.

Nikki chuckled. "Both."

Asa took so long to answer she finally glanced his way. He was frowning. She bit back a smile.

"The lounge looks amazing. I can say that because it's true and I'm not big on lying no matter how much I hate the guy. But I do actually hate the guy."

"I thought you might say that," she said, hiding her smile with her coffee cup.

Asa dropped his head back and looked up at the ceiling. "Jesus," he whispered under his breath. "Are you two dating again?"

"No." Nikki shook her head. "He just wants to be friends and..."

"And...?"

"And I'm considering it."

Asa shook his head, disappointment rolling off him. "You know I have to continue to hate him on principle? He made you cry."

"I know." She stepped to the side, bringing their hips together. She put her head on his shoulder. "He said he was sorry."

He rested his head on top of hers.

"You're too forgiving," he said quietly.

The heaviness of his words hit an old memory and she shrugged. He'd always said that. And maybe he was right. Maybe she gave more chances than she should.

"Though I should be grateful for that because it's benefited me a time or two," he added.

Her mind swam with old memories that she'd rather not think about. But there they were, ill-timed as always.

"Do you think Shelby was right about me?" she asked. As soon as the words had passed her lips, her heart folded in on itself and tears crawled up the back of her throat.

Asa pulled away so he could look into her eyes.

"Why would you say that?" he asked. He frowned, his dark eyes scanning her face, looking for whatever it was that had made her ask that question.

Nikki swallowed and tried to look as unconcerned as possible. "I was just thinking, what if she was a little bit right about me?"

"Shelby was wrong about everything," Asa said. The muscles in his jaw tensed and flexed under his skin. "Not some things, all the things."

She nodded. "Yeah."

"Where is this coming from?" he asked.

Valid question.

"I think I'm just tired," she admitted.

He studied her for a minute before sighing. "She does that. Gets in your head with her little rat claws and doesn't let go." He shuddered.

Nikki snickered.

"I'm glad I have you," he said seriously. "I'd still be stuck in that cycle if you hadn't been there for me."

"Same."

Asa pulled her into a hug with one arm and she wrapped her free hand around his back.

Some things were hard to talk about even after so much time had passed. Shelby and the end of Winking Pete might always be one of those raw areas that never fully healed.

Al and Des had moved on easily. But they had never been as close to Shelby as she and Asa had been. So when everything went to shit, it had hurt them deeper.

Asa the most, since it had been his sister.

He'd lost more than the band. He'd lost family.

"Ooh, are we hugging?" Al wrapped her long arms around the two of them and hummed softly. "I love hugs. They're my favorite."

After a minute, they broke apart and Al got her own coffee.

"What's going on?" she asked.

"Just reminiscing about the fork-tongued lizard witch that brought us so close together," Asa replied.

"You think she's still stuck under that house in Munchkinland?" Al asked.

Asa barked a laugh and high-fived Al.

"Why were you talking about her?" Al asked.

Asa looked to Nikki because she was the one who'd brought her up. And maybe it was time to tell her big secret.

She chewed on her bottom lip as her two closest friends waited.

"Zara Lorna was here this weekend and we worked on a track together… And she might want me to produce her next album."

The kitchen erupted in pandemonium. Asa yelled, Al yelled, coffee spilled, Nikki was hugged, shook by the shoulders, and hugged again.

She tried to settle them down.

"It's still early. She was here this weekend and we worked on a track that…" She shrugged, finding it difficult to say how much she really liked how it turned out. "Well, it's cool." She swallowed. "It doesn't mean that anything is going to happen though."

"Oh my God, are you kidding me?" Al said, excited. "When can we hear it? I bet it's badass."

"You're amazing," Asa added. "I'm so proud of you."

Nikki smiled her thanks, but she was still unsettled.

It was the biggest deal of her entire life.

So why was she so afraid of the next steps?

"But what if, you guys," she blurted. "What if Shelby was right?"

Both Al and Asa looked at her like she'd said that Sonic Youth was overrated—horrified and confused.

"Why—?" Asa cut himself off with a pained expression and a headshake, like he was physically rejecting the very idea she'd proposed.

"Yeah, I'm with Asa," Al said, her lip still curled in disgust. "Why would you give her any credibility? She's a dick."

Nikki nodded, agreeing. "But what if she was right about me and she was the only one willing to say it?"

Asa set his coffee cup down so he could wave both hands at her. "No. She was never right about anything she ever said. Not one thing. The only reason she said shitty things about you, about me, about Al, was because that's all she has—words. She has zero talent and zero skill."

Al nodded her head. "It's true. She got off on hurting people. She knew what you wanted to do with your life, and she attacked it. Just because she could."

Rationally, Nikki knew they were right.

"I get it," Asa said, voice tight. "Shelby could say the very thing you secretly feared about yourself. And that makes it hard to dismiss. But please believe the people who *love* you. Not the people who hate you."

Nikki took a deep breath and nodded.

"It's just hard," she admitted.

Al and Asa both came at her with hugs then. She held on to them and tried to push aside the fears that Shelby had put into words years ago. Words that she could never erase completely.

She was on the cusp of getting everything she'd ever dreamed of.

And those fears and doubts just kept getting louder.

She excused herself to shower so she wouldn't be late for work, promising to stop letting Shelby's wicked words have any more time in her mind.

It was probably because she was so absolutely exhausted from working all weekend. She was depleted physically and creatively.

That always led to negative self-talk and second-guessing.

The smart thing would have been to call Johnny and tell him what she'd been doing all weekend and then take a nap.

But she didn't do that.

Instead, she got dressed, drank three more cups of coffee, and went back to the studio.

By the time she reached the lounge, her heart was pounding so hard she could feel it in her teeth.

She dropped her stuff in the lounge and went to find Johnny. He was smart. Smarter than her. Maybe she'd tell him what was potentially happening and talk her out of it the way he'd talked Shawn out of a million other bad ideas.

"Hey," she said, tapping the open door of the control room for studio Y.

Johnny looked up from the board and removed his headphones. She wondered what he was working on but didn't ask.

"You look tired," he said with a worried frown.

Nikki glared but it was half-hearted. "That's not something you're supposed to say to women."

Johnny arched an eyebrow. "I'm not insulting you. You look like you haven't slept in days."

Nikki dropped onto the leather couch and sighed. "I have to tell you something."

Johnny turned his chair around and she launched into the entire thing. How she and Zara started with an idea last Christmas and everything that had happened up until the wee hours of that morning. She left out the parts about André's drunk dial because that seemed irrelevant.

When she was done, Johnny's expression was carefully neutral. He rubbed a hand along his jaw.

"What do you think?" she asked.

He took a breath and folded his hands in his lap. "I think this is a huge step."

She held her breath.

"But you're ready for it."

"She might change her mind. Or her people might change her mind," Nikki said. "I'm untested. I have no experience to speak of—"

"Let me stop you right there." Johnny held up a hand. "Your experience speaks for itself. As does your talent and dedication. How many albums have you ridden shotgun with me on?"

She sniffed a laugh.

"Nikki," he said seriously. "You can do this. And I, for one, am really fucking excited to see what you make."

Johnny didn't swear. Not unless he was trying to make a point.

Point made.

"Okay, then." She rubbed her hands on her thighs and stood.

"Let me know what you need," Johnny said. "You have all my support and access to most of my bank accounts, so have at it."

She snorted and turned to go.

"And, Nikki…"

She turned back.

"You've got this."

He sounded so convinced.

She smiled, nodded once, and left.

Everyone around her was being way too supportive. What if Zara changed her mind?

Well then, it just isn't meant to be, Nikki justified.

Maybe that's what it would take. If Zara backed out, Nikki would be fine. She'd accept it and everyone around her would console her, but she'd be fine.

Just like she always was.

Because no matter what happened, good or bad, she managed to be okay.

Some things just weren't meant to be.

She made it back to the lounge and had barely crossed the threshold when she heard someone call her name. She stepped back into the hall and there was André. And he was crooking a finger at her with a pleased smile on his gorgeous lips.

Oh, she had fantasized about those lips all weekend long.

The way they said her name, the way they smiled, the shape of his cupid's bow that was soft and subtle, but she always ended up staring at the shadow it made.

One of these days she was going to kiss him just to see if it was as amazing as she remembered.

She went down the hall to where he'd beckoned. The door to her office was pulled closed behind him.

"Do I have to close my eyes?" she asked teasingly.

He took his time looking her over. "Hello," he said, soft and careful.

"Hello," she repeated.

"Would you like to see your new office?" he asked. Again soft, his voice low and almost seductive.

"Yes," she whispered, feeling like she was saying yes to so much more.

His eyes flicked to her mouth and back to her eyes.

"Close your eyes," he commanded gently.

She did.

For a moment, nothing happened. He didn't move and neither did she and she wondered if maybe this time he just might—

He took her hand and electricity and warmth shot up her arm to her chest.

She closed her fingers around his and he tugged her forward.

After a few steps, he let go.

"Open your eyes," he said from behind her.

Her office no longer looked like her office.

"How…?" She took a step further in and her words left her.

Everything he'd said he was going to do, he had done.

But seeing it was something else.

The window had been replaced and it let in so much light that the room was bright without the help of electricity.

The floor was a bright blond and covered by a thick rug that was a rich gray with copper swirls. One wall was navy and so was the ceiling. All the fixtures and ductwork had been converted to copper and they gleamed against the dark background.

Her new desk was long and sleek and stained the same color as the floors.

A cream-colored sofa sat against the wall with the window and it was covered in pillows and a dark blue throw.

And the pillows didn't stop there. They spilled off the sofa and onto the floor.

"Where did everything go?" she asked, her voice soft because she was afraid that if she spoke too loudly, it would all disappear and she'd wakc up.

He strode to the opposite side of the room where it looked like a bare wall painted navy. But, as she looked more closely, she could see grooves like wooden planks running vertically from top to bottom and covering the wall end to end.

André slipped his fingertips into one of the grooves and slid out a section of the wall. It had three evenly spaced shelves that were full of equipment.

He pushed it closed and pulled on the next groove. That one slid out to reveal four shelves with equipment.

"Shut up." She put her hands over her mouth as she watched him pull out another one.

"All of them," he said, indicating every vertical plank. "The last two are empty."

"How did you do that? There's not enough space in here for that."

He grinned and slid his hands into his pockets. "Do you like it?"

Did she like it?

It was everything.

She turned around and stared at him. His dark, tousled hair, his jeans and dirty white shirt that still had sawdust on the front, and his suspenders, and his hesitant smile, and his hazel eyes.

"Hey," he said, stepping forward, his brows dipped. "What's wrong? Is it the navy? Not the color you wanted? I can change it—oof!"

She threw her arms around his neck, he caught her, stepping back on one foot.

"It's perfect," she said into his neck. "Better than perfect."

His arms tightened around her and she melted against his hard chest. He smelled like fresh-cut wood and paint and laundry detergent.

"She likes it," he said, sounding pleased.

It was because she was so tired.

That was why she was so emotional.

At least that's what she told herself as tears climbed up her throat.

She didn't want to let go. In André's arms she finally felt safe and warm and *understood.* Her friends, her boss, everyone was great. They were. They said and did wonderful things, but André *got* her in a way no one ever had.

Slowly, she let go and leaned back so she could see his face. She forced a watery smile. "Thank you. It's incredible."

His hand cupped her cheek, and he brushed a thumb through a tear that had spilled over. "Why the tears, love?"

She sucked in a breath, her hands flexed on his shoulders. "Sometimes you see me so clearly and it's a bit overwhelming."

He swallowed and his eyes drifted to her mouth and back to her eyes. "Most days you're all I see."

Her heart pounded and her skin zipped with electric currents as she zeroed in on his mouth. Her hands drifted down to where his suspender straps lay flat against his chest. She took hold of them, pulling him closer to her. Closer to everything she wanted.

Would he let her kiss him?

Would he push her away?

What if he kissed her back? Would it be as good as she remembered or would it be better?

She pressed her lips to the corner of his mouth, soft and unsure. His body tensed. She did it again, closer to the center of his mouth. Once more for good measure.

He didn't move.

She dropped back, her heart thundering as she attempted to save face.

"I'm sorry, that was…" She loosened her grip on his suspenders and started to pull away. "That was out of line."

She went to turn away from him, her face heated.

Oh God.

What had she done?

How was she going to go back to before? Friends didn't kiss each other. She'd never had the inclination to kiss Asa or—

His hand closed around her arm and yanked her back toward him. His mouth met hers in a crushing kiss at the same moment their bodies collided.

His tongue swept inside her mouth, an invasion of heat and electricity as his arms banded around her, keeping her body flush with his. She made a noise that was half desperation, half relief.

Yes, she thought. *This. This is everything.*

His hands were everywhere, grabbing, touching, caressing, kneading. They were in her hair, at her ass, up her back, her ribs—always searching and pulling and grasping. Like he couldn't get enough of her and didn't want to.

Her hands were much the same. In his hair, running over his shoulders, tugging at his suspenders, wherever she could reach.

He groaned into her mouth and it went straight to her center.

This was the kind of kiss that sparked addiction and need.

The kind that started something important and extraordinary.

Gradually the kiss began to slow. It grew deeper, their movements more deliberate. He rested his forehead against hers, his hands at her waist, closed his eyes, the hint of a smile on his mouth.

She ran her hands over his shoulders, down his arms, catching her breath.

A knock on the door had them stepping away from one another. She smoothed her shirt down where it had ridden up from his roaming hands.

"Come in," she called, her eyes locked on André's which were watching her with heated promise.

The door opened and Justin came in. He took one look at Nikki and then André and didn't hide his grin.

"Sorry to interrupt," Justin said.

"It's fine," Nikki said, sounding way cooler than she felt. Because she felt hot.

Her entire body felt like it was on fire and she could only imagine what she looked like. Was it obvious that she'd just had André's tongue in her mouth and his hands in her hair?

She hoped so.

That thought caused the heat pooling in her belly to coil tighter.

"What's up?" she asked.

Justin handed her her phone. "This was ringing in the lounge. I thought you might want it."

Nikki took the phone and glanced at the screen just as it started to ring again.

It was a douse of ice water on her blazing thoughts.

"Oh." She swiped quickly. "Hello."

"Oh my God, I thought you were dead," Zara said, sounding relieved.

Nikki forced a chuckle and tucked her hair behind her ear as she glanced at André.

He hadn't moved.

He was still standing in the middle of her extraordinary new office, his heated eyes on her with a promise that said they would finish what they had started.

"I landed a minute ago," Zara was saying. "I'm working on clearing my schedule and getting a place to stay in Chicago while we do this thing. What works for you and your calendar?"

"Me?" Nikki asked, not sure she understood what the pop star had just said. Her thoughts were still on André and his incredible mouth.

"Yeah. Shit. I have to take this other call. But check your timetable. What did we say? Two? Three weeks? Call me when you have dates." And then she hung up.

Wait.

What did she just say?

Did she just say what it sounded like she'd said?

They were doing this? Nikki was producing an album for her?

She stared at the phone in her hand as she tried to process what just happened.

When she looked up, Justin was gone but André was still there.

She was really glad that André was still there.

"Has something happened?" he asked carefully.

Their previous moment had passed with this new development. He must've read it on her face, because his expression had sobered.

He crossed the room to her, curiosity lining his brow.

"Yeah," Nikki said, sounding as shocked as she felt. "Zara Lorna wants to schedule studio time with me to make an album."

The words hung in the air a moment as they became real.

André scooped her into a hug and swung her around the room.

She was laughing when he set her down.

"That's the dream, right?" he asked.

"Yep." She nodded and her eyes began to burn. "That's the dream," she repeated on a hiccup.

"What's wrong?" he asked, eyes searching hers with affection.

She shook her head and tears spilled out.

"I think I'm just tired," she said after a minute. "It was a long weekend."

Because how could she tell him that even though she was getting everything she ever wanted, she was more terrified than she'd ever been in her life?

It wouldn't make any sense.

But the tears wouldn't stop, and she tried to laugh even as they poured out of her.

"I feel so stupid," she said, taking the tissue he handed her. "I'm happy." She waved her hands in front of her. "I shouldn't be crying."

"Hey." He cupped her cheek with his hand and looked tenderly in her eyes. "Crying is part of the experience. You're not stupid."

She nodded and more tears spilled out.

"I do think you're exhausted though." He pulled her into a tender embrace, and she rested her cheek on his chest. "I think—and this is just my opinion—but I think you should go home and rest."

She nodded against him.

He was right.

She hadn't slept more than a few hours in the last couple of days. All of this would look more manageable after she'd gotten some sleep.

"I'll walk you home."

ANDRÉ

"Oh, André," she said softly as she closed her eyes. "It's the God damn pressure of it all."

And then she was out.

It was her final words before she fell asleep that had him perplexed.

Of course, he understood she would feel a certain amount of pressure. It just made sense for when someone was on the path of everything she'd been striving for. Pressure was a privilege.

But he couldn't shake it.

He kept coming back to her words again and again in between reliving the hottest kiss of his life.

As far as he could tell, she hadn't told anyone else her big news before she'd gone home. Not Johnny, not Asa.

André hung around the studio for as long as he could, thinking she might come back after she'd rested a bit. He finished cleaning up his tools and any debris still floating around. By lunchtime he was looking for something to keep him busy.

By the afternoon he decided to check on her.

If she didn't want to talk about the record, then maybe she'd want to talk about that kiss they'd shared.

Or maybe they didn't need to talk about it at all. Maybe their bodies would do the talking for them.

He knocked on the front door and after a couple minutes Asa opened it. He stepped aside to let André in.

"Is she awake?" André asked.

He still wasn't sure where he stood with Asa. They weren't friends, that was clear. But were they enemies?

Time would tell.

"Awake?" Asa scoffed. "She left two hours ago."

André squinted at him because what he'd said didn't make sense.

"Where did she go?"

Asa waved a hand and let out a disgruntled sigh.

"Her dad called, and they were visiting and the next thing I know she's packing a bag. Said she couldn't let her seventy-year-old father reroof his house. She called Johnny and took the rest of the week off."

André pinched the bridge of his nose and closed his eyes. "Did she happen to mention that Zara Lorna wants to schedule studio time as soon as possible?"

"What? No." Asa gasped. "That's fucking awesome!"

André waited for it to catch up to him.

"Wait. Then what the fuck is she doing going to the lake house?"

André ran a hand through his hair and let out an exhale from deep in his chest.

It had finally clicked. Her remark about the pressure. That's why he couldn't let it go.

"We're the fucking same, Asa," André said. "Me and Nik."

He looked up at the ceiling as his mind raced with all the weird shit they'd both said and done over the years. It was almost too much information to process all at once and his ears started to ring.

"Here she is on the edge of absolutely getting her life where she wants it, and she's doubting her ability to make it happen. It's like we share the same horrible strain of imposter syndrome."

Asa's perplexed expression cleared as he registered what André had just said.

"She's sabotaging herself," he muttered.

"She's sabotaging herself," André agreed.

Where he was confident in his talents and not in his relationships, she was confident in her relationships and doubted her talents.

What a fucking pair they made.

She was him two and a half years ago sitting outside the restaurant.

But he wouldn't let her do that to herself.

"I'm going to need the address to the lake house."

Asa nodded. "Let me get it for you."

CHAPTER FIFTEEN

LONG ROAD TO RUIN

ANDRÉ

More than once on his drive north, he wondered if Asa had sent him on a wild goose chase.

But when he drove down the tree-lined drive and saw her car at the end of it, he had his answer.

He parked right behind her and slowly got out. His muscles ached from having worked all day and then sitting still for so long. He stretched his arms over his head and twisted the kinks out of his back.

The big house her car was parked by didn't seem to be having any work done to it. He listened and the unmistakable sounds of roofing shovels came from his left down a dirt path. He followed it, keeping his eyes open for signs of people.

One person specifically.

Down the path and around a bend, it opened into a clearing with a cabin that was a smaller version of the large house by where he'd parked.

And up on the roof was the love of his life.

Glaring at him.

"What are you doing here?" she asked. She was in jeans, a white tank top, and work boots. Her hair was tied back and held down with a scarf to keep the debris from flying into it. She was covered in splatters of roofing tar.

And if he wasn't mistaken, she was rather upset to see him.

"I'm here to help," he replied honestly.

She wiped her arm across her forehead. An older man, her father from the looks of it, came up and over the other side of the roof.

"Who's that, Nikki?" he asked.

She muttered something to him and he laughed.

It was a deep, rich laugh and André had to keep from smiling.

Because he knew it.

Just that small interaction he'd seen between father and daughter years ago and he'd gotten it right.

"Don't listen to her," her dad said. "There's extra gloves and shovels around the front." He held up a hand near his mouth like what he had to say next was a secret. "She's awfully touchy about her side of the roof, but you can help me on mine."

"All right," André replied with a smile.

He was still in the same clothes from working in the studio earlier. He hadn't gone home to change before heading north because he hadn't wanted to waste any time.

The tools and extra gloves were easy to find around the front of the house on a small, covered porch. It looked out over the lake and he took in the view for a minute.

He knew Nikki had grown up in the city, but she'd mentioned the lake house as a place they spent their summers.

It was easy to picture her here swimming, fishing, living flat out and happy.

He grabbed a shovel and hiked up the ladder.

"My name's Robert Harry, but you can call me Bob." Bob stuck out his hand the minute André reached the top.

André grasped it in a firm handshake. "André."

The man looked damn good for seventy. André would not have guessed his age. He was a few inches shorter than André but stood with his back and shoulders straight, effectively using every inch he'd been given.

Bob nodded and his gray eyes turned sharp. "Yeah, you're the college professor who I was supposed to meet a while back."

André braced for the scolding he deserved. Or to be told to get out and stay away from Nikki.

But that didn't happen.

"Heard you built her the perfect office recently." Bob nodded as if in approval, those eyes still sharp and calculating. "She seems to really love it."

André couldn't help the tug on his lips. "Happy to do it," he said.

Bob showed him what they had accomplished so far and what still needed to be done.

They had to finish removing the shingles and check the roof for any repairs. And then apply new stuff.

It was pretty straightforward.

And the roof wasn't that large. They could get it done in two days if all went well.

Two days and Nikki could be back in the city. That was André's goal.

Nikki came over her side of the roof and he smiled as the memory of their incredible kiss rushed through him.

Had that happened just this morning?

He hadn't allowed himself to think about it too much because her self-sabotage had taken precedence. The feel of her in his arms, the sound of her tiny gasps as her fingers twisted in his hair…

"This is stalking," she said but there was no bite in it.

He smirked and let his eyes wander over her. She was a mess, roofing tar smeared all over her arms and clothes. Her face flushed from working in the sun, sweat glistening along her hairline…

He wasn't sure if she'd ever looked sexier.

She shook her head at him when she realized what he was doing. He should probably cool it until they had time to go over all of his thoughts in detail.

Slow, deliberate, detail.

He took a breath and set aside his amorous feelings.

"Asa gave me the address," he said, surprising her. He arched an eyebrow. "We need to talk." About a lot of things. Including that kiss.

She rolled her eyes. "We'll talk later. I want to get this done." She turned around and went back to her side.

That was fine with André.

He hadn't done a roof in a while, but he knew how to get it done. He focused on the task and he and Bob had their side cleared in less than an hour. He then went over to Nikki's side and helped her finish over there.

"Show-off," she muttered on her way past him.

André grabbed her elbow and stopped her.

He was sweating profusely and breathing heavily.

"Nik," he said, making sure her dad was already down the ladder.

"I know you're worried, okay?" she said. "But you don't have to be."

"Make some time for us to talk, yeah?" he pressed. "About all of it."

She sighed but nodded once before moving away from him.

He wasn't leaving until he'd said what needed to be said. Maybe he wouldn't be able to convince her to go back. Maybe the kiss had been a one-time thing. Maybe a lot of things.

But he knew nothing would be settled until they both were able to say what they wanted.

André came down the ladder and began cleaning up the debris. He scooped old shingles and nails into his gloved hands and then deposited them in the bin nearby.

Bob brought him a bottle of water.

"You're staying for dinner, right?" Bob asked.

He hadn't made plans outside of getting to Nikki. He could probably sleep in his car if it came to that. He knew he'd passed a gas station not too far back; they might have sandwiches or something.

André glanced at Nikki.

"Mary will be disappointed if she doesn't get to meet you," the older man added.

Nikki rolled her eyes and used the motion to indicate André should join them.

André grinned. "Well, I definitely don't want to disappoint Mary."

NIKKI

She was still reeling from dinner.

Not because it had gone badly, but because it had gone so *well*.

Who knew her parents would adore André?

Well, she did.

But who knew André would adore them right back?

Since they'd all been covered with tar, Mom had set the table on the deck. They'd had spareribs and beers.

André had made her mom laugh and her dad blush.

And they'd treated him like he'd been part of the family for years.

When it had started to get late, André helped her dad cover the bare roof of the bunkhouse with tarp in case it rained.

She could hear them talking and laughing from where she still sat at the table up the hill.

Nikki drained the last of her beer and tossed it in the recycle bin with a clatter.

"Here's some extra towels." Her mom, a veritable saint, set a stack of towels on the table in front of Nikki. "Neither one of you will want to sleep without cleaning up first."

That was the other thing. It hadn't been talked about, but it was assumed that André was staying the night.

With Nikki.

In the bunkhouse.

And as sexy as that sounded, Nikki had a feeling it was about to get very *un*sexy in a minute.

André had chased her up there for a reason.

She was pretty sure she knew what it was and she wasn't looking forward to the discussion he wanted to have.

Though it was probably going to be more like a lecture.

"I like him," her mom said apropos of nothing.

Nikki huffed a small laugh. "I do too."

When she saw his car come down the drive, she'd been so shocked she said more swears in front of her dad than she usually did.

But her insides had been melted into goo.

No one had ever come after her before.

Not that she'd made a habit of running away. But usually her people let her have her space.

Not André though.

It should have bothered her.

But it didn't.

Because she could feel how much he cared by that one small action. The least she could do was listen to his lecture. He would never force her into something she was against.

And maybe, if she was very lucky, she'd get a repeat of that kiss from earlier.

Just the thought of it had her entire body blushing.

She gathered the towels in her arms and started down the path.

André and her dad met her halfway.

André eyed the towels in her arms with a quizzical look.

"Goodnight, kids. I'll be down to call you for breakfast," Dad said. He shook André's hand, pressed a kiss to Nikki's cheek, and headed on toward the house.

"C'mon, Professor," Nikki said to André's even more perplexed expression. "Do you have clothes to change into?" she asked, stopping at his car.

He retrieved a bag from the trunk.

They walked down the path side by side. The sounds of the night filling the space between them that seemed to crackle with electricity. They were alone again for the first time since their kiss that morning.

Suddenly it was all she could think about.

His mouth, his tongue, his hands, his hard body under her fingers…

She cleared her throat and tried to calm her racing heart.

She wanted him. Bad.

"You stopped to pack before racing up here to rescue me from myself?" she asked, trying to joke her way out of her lusty thoughts.

"No. I have a bag of essentials in my trunk in case of workplace emergencies." He sounded tense. Maybe he was thinking about what she was thinking about. "For instance, one day I was leaving class and I walked into a very vigorous game of ultimate frisbee that sent me into a fountain. I didn't have time to go home, I still had two classes that day."

She chuckled and he joined her. The tension broken, but only briefly.

They made it back to the bunkhouse. She flicked on the lights and crossed to the bed where she set the towels.

The bunkhouse was just a guesthouse. It was a small cabin with a queen bed, a small kitchenette, and a bathroom with a shower stall.

It was the lone bed that André was staring at.

His Adam's apple bobbed as he swallowed.

"Do you want to talk before or after showers?" she asked, ignoring the way her skin tingled with their close proximity.

He frowned and his gaze bounced between her and the bed.

"Yes, André. There's one bed. I promise I won't take advantage of you," she said with a small smile.

"Now, that sounds less fun," he countered in a low voice.

"Maybe if you ask me really nice," she teased.

The look he gave her was positively sinful and she felt her temperature start to rise as sparks shot through her limbs.

Yeah, she probably shouldn't tease him if she couldn't handle the consequences.

"I'll shower first," he announced.

He brushed her arm as he reached for a towel and she held her breath.

It was either that or something far more embarrassing.

When he was locked in the bathroom and the water was on, she called Asa.

"Hey," he greeted, unconcerned.

"Dude," she said glancing at the door to the bathroom and keeping her voice low. She didn't know what he could hear in there. "You sent him after me?"

"Uh, no. He came looking for you, and oh yeah, were you going to mention your big news at all?"

She growled. "He told you?"

"Yes, he did. But more importantly, you did not."

Nikki rolled her eyes at his tone. "So, you two are besties?"

Asa snorted. "No. But we both love you and don't want to see you do something stupid."

"Whatever. This friendship is officially on hiatus," she said haughtily.

"Bite me," came Asa's bored reply, then he hung up.

She glowered at it and then snickered because she couldn't be mad if she wanted to.

After she plugged her phone in on the bedside table, she got her sleep clothes out of her bag and froze.

When she'd packed that afternoon, she'd still been all mixed up about André and what that kiss may or may not have meant and she'd wanted to keep him near. If only symbolically.

So she'd brought one of his old shirts she'd stolen from him years ago. It was a gray t-shirt, branded with the university logo where he'd gotten his master's.

There was no way she could act as if it had come from anyone else. He'd know instantly that it had been his and why she still had it.

She dug through her bag, looking for an alternative to sleep in. She had a couple tank tops; she could just wear one of those and leave the university tee in her bag. He'd never have to know.

Though that meant she'd be in a form-fitting tank and cotton panties.

In her defense, she'd had no idea she'd be sharing a bed with the sexiest man alive. Because that's what he was. She'd fight anyone who said different.

The door to the bathroom opened and André came out in gray sweats and nothing else. He rubbed a towel over his wet hair and crossed the hardwood floor in his bare feet.

"Bathroom's yours," he said, sitting on the edge of the bed.

She grabbed the towel and her entire bag, and scurried into the bathroom.

But not before she took one last look at all his suntanned glory.

The man was a specimen.

Tight, rock-hard abs; defined chest and shoulders; long, lean arms; a sprinkle of hair on his chest and small patch visible above the waistband of his pants. And gray sweatpants? Had he done that on purpose.

She could drool.

She was drooling.

Dammit.

She closed the door to the bathroom and just focused on getting clean.

One thing at a time.

First, get clean.

Then, get lectured.

Last, try to sleep next to the most perfect body known to man and pretend you have normal, containable, non-lusty thoughts about him.

Easy.

CHAPTER SIXTEEN

PUT YOUR ARMS AROUND ME

NIKKI

She left the bathroom and stopped at the foot of the bed.

Just stopped.

In mind and body.

André lay on his back on top of the covers, his arms stretched up and folded over his eyes. The hard planes of his muscles wrapped in skin that looked like golden silk in the yellow light of the bedside lamp. The steady rise and fall of his chest suggested he was sleeping.

As well he should.

He'd worked hard for weeks to build her a workspace that wasn't just functional, but beautiful as well. And then he'd driven two hours north to start stripping shingles in the hot July sun.

When had he become this man?

The one she always suspected he'd become but had resolved she wouldn't get to see it?

When he was apart from her?

She could be sad about it if she wanted, but sadness wasn't her first emotion.

No. It was gratitude.

And happiness.

For him.

Because if anyone deserved to know what André was capable of, it was him.

Careful, trying not to disturb him, she crawled onto the bed and he sucked in a breath. She folded her legs and backed against the headboard. He stretched his arms over his head and groaned loudly, his hazel eyes tipped up to look at her.

He finished his stretch and rolled onto his side with a sleepy smile.

"I'm ready for my lecture, Professor," she said, her belly trembling with a mixture of anxiety and trepidation.

His sleepy gaze sharpened on her and he blinked slowly. "You have no idea what it does to me when you call me professor," he murmured.

"It's your proper title, right?" she said, sounding a little more breathless than she intended.

"Not when you say it." He arched an eyebrow and his gaze traveled over her chosen sleep attire.

She'd decided to wear the university tee.

It was the gray sweatpants that led her to that decision. Because if he could drive her crazy, she could do the same to him.

But the way André was looking at her, she may as well have been naked.

All at once he came up on his knees, wrapped one strong arm around her waist; lifted, turned, and placed her on her back at the other end of the bed. She clutched his shoulders and let out a surprised squeak while he was maneuvering her effortlessly through the air.

And just like that, they were lying on the bed with their feet towards the headboard, her on her back, him braced on an elbow looking down at her, one of his thighs resting gently in between hers.

Not lowering his weight, not creating friction or pressure.

Just. There.

Oh my.

Heat curled low in her belly and spread throughout her body.

He curved his palm around her rib cage, his eyes on the emblem across her chest.

He lifted his gaze to hers and she flexed her hands against his skin at what she saw. Desire and need, hope and promise. An open door to every question she had, he was answering in the way he looked at her.

"Nicole," he said, voice a heavy caress to her senses. One word. A name. Her name, on his lips and in his throat.

It was a callback to who they used to be, a reminder of what they'd been through, who they could be, who they wanted to be.

Who they wanted to be with.

No, that kiss earlier hadn't been a fluke, or an impulse.

It had been a warning.

André used his fingertips to trace her hairline, over her chin, along her jaw. His eyes followed the movement, and the gentle tease made her skin hum and buzz with awareness.

"I have some questions," he said, dragging his thumb over her lower lip.

Her eyelids dropped to half-mast and her breaths grew shallow.

His hand came back to her middle and curved around her ribs. His thumb caressed the underside of a breast and she shifted beneath him, wanting more.

His breath wafted over her cheek as he leaned close to her face.

"Nicole," he said, low, soft. "Are you running away from your dream?"

The question was asked in such an intimate tone that she was completely caught off guard.

He carefully took her arm and stretched it above her head, then he smoothed his fingers down her arm, down her side to her hip. Every movement he made was slow, deliberate, almost lazy.

"Tell me what you're afraid of," he said nuzzling the skin next to her ear as his hand made contact with skin near the waistband of her panties.

Her eyes fluttered closed as the sensations threatened to overwhelm her in the best way.

"I'm afraid of ruining it," she confessed. One of her hands trailed down the hot skin of his back. Because she needed to touch him. To feel the life humming under his skin and heating her from the outside in.

"How would you ruin it?" he asked, his lips grazing the shell of her ear. She turned her neck to give him more access.

Meanwhile, she was finding it very difficult to keep her legs still because they wanted to wrap around his thigh and hold on for dear life.

"What if I'm not as good as I think I am?" How was he getting all this out of her? *She* hadn't even had thoughts that coherent on the matter.

He was seducing the truth out of her.

And she wasn't mad about it.

"Do you think everyone around you is a liar?" he asked, moving his mouth to hover over the column of her throat.

She arched her head back, silently begging him to give her more.

"Zara, Johnny, Asa… Have they all lied to you?" he asked, the hand under her shirt slid higher, smoothed across her stomach.

"No," she dismissed that as an option. The people she surrounded herself with these days were the epitome of integrity. Her hand moved down his back and under the waistband of his sweatpants.

As she'd suspected, he wore nothing under them.

"Do you think they're foolish?" he asked into her other ear.

"No."

He lifted his head and she opened her eyes. His hazel irises were swirling with dark gold around the black of his pupil.

"You won't ruin it," he said confidently. His gaze dropped to her mouth. "And I won't ruin this."

He lowered his mouth to hers and slicked his tongue inside while he also dropped his thigh to apply pressure right where she needed it. Simultaneously, he swiped his thumb over her nipple.

A needy whimper came out of her followed by a delighted moan.

She could feel his arousal against her hip and she wanted to touch it. To taste it.

He swirled his tongue over her pulse point.

"Yess," she hissed, clutching at his hard shoulders.

"André," she said, needy and desperate.

He lifted his head and his eyes blazed in the dim light of the cabin. They were wild and possessive and there was something there she could never remember seeing before.

But she liked it.

And she wanted it.

She wanted him.

"Are you ready for me to love you proper now?" he asked, his voice rough and slow.

"Please," she whispered.

She caught a hint of a wicked smile just before he disappeared between her legs.

He lavished kisses along her inner thighs as he hooked her panties and slid them off. He drew one of her legs over his shoulder and then his mouth was right *there.*

Nikki arched into him and grasped his hair with both hands.

"André!" she whimper-gasped.

No teasing, no hinting, no prelude. Just his hot mouth on her like his existence depended on it.

He held her hips in a firm grip, keeping his mouth on her as he licked and sucked and did things to her pussy no one else in the world had ever done.

"I have missed you, darling," he rumbled against her and she didn't know if he was speaking to her or her pussy. Either way, it worked for her in a big way.

She could hear her broken cries and how desperate she sounded but she was helpless to stop. Her fingers tightened in his hair while he made appreciative sounds against her.

He speared his tongue inside and she dug her heel into his back, needing him closer. Needing to go higher.

This was what his kiss had promised in her office. All of these wicked, naughty, *exquisite* things that he could do to her.

She'd known that and yet she'd had no idea.

"That's it, darling," he coaxed. "You taste incredible." His hot mouth worked over her clit and then he plunged his tongue back inside and groaned.

"Baby! Oh my God… *yesss*." Her thighs trembled as he used his tongue to thrust in and out of her. Her hips bucked but he held fast. She grasped at him, at the sheets, at anything she could touch to keep from flying off the earth.

Her entire existence focused in on one singular sensation and she thought for a moment it might kill her.

Her back arched and her body jerked as she exploded with pleasure. André cupped her ass and held her to his mouth as she came apart.

Wave after wave of ecstasy crashed through her, making her body tremble and her voice hoarse.

As she came back down to earth, André's ministrations slowed to accommodate her new sensitively. He placed open mouth, caressing kisses along her thighs and belly.

She released a long, satisfied sigh. Amazed she'd survived and wondering if it had felt like that before. Because she didn't think so.

André moved up her body then, a smug look on his face. She touched his cheek, pushed his hair back, and shivered with aftershocks.

His hazel eyes were heated and dark with desire.

He palmed her breast under her shirt and rolled her nipple between his fingers.

"I don't want to take this off you," he said. "Seeing it on you…" He pushed the shirt up and took her nipple into his mouth with a groan.

Fuck yes, she thought. She didn't want to be done yet either.

For as incredible as her climax had been, she still felt needy.

A tortuous, unrelenting desire to feel the weight of him push inside her. To feel his pleasure combine with her own like stars born too close together, bursting into one another's existence.

She writhed and squirmed, pressing into his beautiful, talented, hot, wet mouth.

He went to move to the other breast and the shirt got in the way.

Frustrated, she pulled the t-shirt over her head and tossed it aside, leaving her naked beneath him.

He smiled knowingly. "You want my mouth here?" he asked, hovering over the straining peak.

"Yes," she hissed, trying to pull his head down to her.

"Tell me what you want, Nicole," he commanded gently.

Her clit pulsed in response to his words.

"I want you to suck my tits like you missed them," she answered honestly.

He rewarded her by doing just that. Pulling one tight nub into his hot mouth and flicking it with his tongue. He released it with an indulgent "pop" and then kissed it softly.

"World's most perfect tits," he murmured reverently as he moved back over to the other one. "I missed them every day."

The sight of her breasts being teased and tasted by him was so hot she could cry. She dropped her head back as the want built inside her again.

His hands seemed to be everywhere, kneading her hips, sliding over her ribs, gliding down her thigh to hold the bend in her knee.

She pushed at the sweatpants he still wore, wanting to feel all of his skin against her.

"I'm not done here yet," he said, lightly scraping his teeth over the swell of one breast while kneading the other with one of his very capable hands.

She made a noise that was both protest and arousal and slid her hand into the front of his pants. She wrapped her hand around his length and he hissed as she ran her thumb over the tip.

"Nicole," he warned and groaned, pressing his cock into her hand.

"I want you," she said. "I need to feel you inside me."

André kissed her, thrusting his tongue into her mouth, before moving off the bed. He took a foil square out of his pocket before dropping his pants to the floor.

His gorgeous erection stood tall and proud and she sucked her lower lip into her mouth.

Next time.

She'd taste it next time.

The knowledge that there was going to be a next time made her heart hammer and she smiled to herself.

He got back on the bed on his knees, and tore the foil open with his teeth, his eyes on her.

She held his gaze as he rolled the condom on and then kneed her legs apart. His hands came down on the bed next to her shoulders and he hovered over her.

One kiss.

Another.

Deeper this time.

She took hold of his hips and pulled them toward her.

"Say it again," he said against her jaw.

"I need you inside me," she repeated, opening her legs wider to give him easier access.

His eyes nearly crossed when his cock met her slick entrance.

"Please, André," she begged, pushing her hips up to meet him.

That's what did it.

He slid inside her and she moaned in relief.

Finally.

They were back where they were always meant to be.

He started a steady pace, filling her, reaching her.

He grabbed her hip and slid his hand all the way down to the back of her knee, the touch sending shivers throughout her body. His eyes met hers and held. He slowed his thrusts, making her feel every inch, out and back, and again.

He raised up on an arm and looked down between their bodies. He watched as he entered her over and over.

Slow.

Slow.

Slow.

His movements controlled.

Deliberate.

His dark hair flopped onto his forehead, drawing attention to his furrowed brow and earnest focus.

"Fuck," he growled, still watching their connection. "So fucking perfect."

She couldn't agree more. The feel of him moving inside her had her panting and pleading with unintelligible sighs and whimpers. He was so good at the slow build. At making her feel everything, connecting her to the moment. To him.

He slid his hand back up her thigh and in between them. He stroked her clit and her moan deepened with need. His gaze cut back to hers and he stroked her clit again.

She closed her eyes because it was too much.

"Look at me, Nicole," he said, voice jagged as her own.

She did and he rewarded her with another stroke of her clit.

Everything that existed between them—the time, the heartache, the forgiveness, the friendship—caught fire. Every thrust, every stroke, every mingled breath intensified the ecstasy building and bleeding in her veins.

She felt reborn.

A nebula in bloom.

She clung to his shoulders; raked her fingernails through the hair at the nape of his neck.

His thrusts increased in force and frequency, reaching her.

Finding her.

She cried out as pleasure fully claimed her, shattering her into a million pieces, each one a supernova. Her body convulsed and bucked as wave after wave of ecstasy washed through her.

André's rhythm grew rough and he surged into her, groaning his own release.

She felt him pulse inside her and she moaned at the sensation.

He collapsed on her, head to her chest, breathing heavy. She raked her fingers through his hair, still panting. Tingles and aftershocks coursed her body and she sighed.

Carefully, he slid free and rolled onto his back beside her.

"That was… Wow." She had no words. Just elation and satisfaction. But no words.

He chuckled and took her hand, bring it to his mouth. "I agree." He kissed her knuckles. "I'm going to take care of this and I'll be right back," he said.

He rolled out of the bed and she listened to him pad across the wooden floor to the bathroom.

She stared at the ceiling, highlights from the previous activity flashing through her mind. Her body still hummed. Content. Sated.

Everything about life was better now. She had no complaints and couldn't remember if she'd ever had any to begin with.

She got off the bed and considered wrapping the comforter around herself but decided to leave it. He opened the bathroom door and she slipped past him to go inside. On her way by, she trailed her fingers over his abs and hummed a sigh.

She caught sight of herself in the mirror and grinned.

Sex hair was the best hair. Especially when it was well-earned.

She tried to smooth it down a little but mostly didn't care.

After she was done in the bathroom she returned to André.

He'd pulled the covers back and was waiting for her.

She slid into the bed beside him and he flicked the covers over them both and immediately pulled her against his body.

He pressed slow kisses to her shoulders, neck, and face.

"Are you tired?" he asked, his voice a deep satisfied rumble.

"Mmm," she sighed, snuggling closer to him.

"Do you want me to turn the light off?" he asked.

"That would be a good idea," she conceded.

He reached behind him to the remote on the nightstand and hit a switch. The room grew dark but moonlight filtered through the skylight above them, illuminating the planes on his face and the curve of his mouth.

"I just want to hold you for a while, if that's all right," he said, slipping one of his legs between hers and pulling her even closer somehow.

She ran her hands over his shoulders, his arms, through his hair. Enjoying the feel of him under her fingertips, the warmth of his skin. She kissed his nose, his forehead, his eyebrow.

He stirred against her, shifting, adjusting. Featherlight touches all over her body.

Her eyes closed and her breathing deepened as she relaxed against him. On one hand, she didn't want to ever go to sleep again because she wanted to stay in this moment with him for as long as possible. On the other, she wanted to rest for a just a minute so they could do it all again.

"You're so beautiful," he said, brushing her cheek with his knuckles. "I hope you don't mind if I keep you forever."

She didn't answer because she was already sliding into sleep. But she thought it.

I love you.

CHAPTER SEVENTEEN

SUGAR KANE

ANDRÉ

He woke up when the light of dawn began to filter in through the blinds.

It took him a half second to remember where he was, but as soon as he did, he was reaching across the sheets to touch her one more time.

Nikki stirred in her sleep but didn't wake. Her blonde hair spread out along the pillow like strands of silk, and he brushed it aside to lay soft kisses across her shoulders and down her spine before getting up.

He slid on his sweats and went to the bathroom.

Then he figured out how to work the coffee maker.

When he had a hot cup of coffee, he went out on the covered porch and took a seat in one of the Adirondack chairs.

Last night had not gone as he'd planned.

It had been far better.

He'd had every intention of having a serious conversation about what she was running away from, but she'd walked out of that bathroom wearing his old shirt—a shirt she had kept, despite everything—and that was it.

He was deep in his peaceful ruminations when Nikki joined him. He spread his legs and patted a thigh. She had his shirt back on, and again, it did things to him to see her in it.

She slid sideways onto his lap and rested her shoulder and head against his chest while her feet went over the armrest.

He handed her his coffee and she took a sip.

"How did you sleep?" he asked, pressing his lips to the top of her head.

"Like a well-fucked woman," she murmured and then snorted.

He grinned and hugged her closer. One arm over her middle to hold her hip.

They sat in peaceful silence, listening to the lake come alive with the day.

This was it. Right there. Her, in his arms. That was all he'd ever needed.

And he had it.

"Did you know you called me on Christmas?" she asked, breaking the silence and mentioning the last thing he expected her to say.

He stiffened and she noticed. She sat up a little to see his face.

"I assumed it was a pocket dial," she said, her cheeks turning pink.

"It wasn't a pocket dial," he said.

Her eyebrows dipped and she tilted her head in question.

He watched her carefully. "I remember talking to you…"

She shook her head once. "No. It was just static and noise."

He huffed a laugh, the building tension releasing in a single breath. "To be fair, I was two bottles deep into Sabine's pink wine." He chuckled and rubbed a hand up and down her arm. "I don't know if I'm relieved or annoyed that I couldn't get even that right."

"Why did you call?" she asked, watching him. Calm, curious, warm.

He tightened his arms around her a bit, feeling her nearness, letting it reassure him.

"To say sorry. To tell you I missed you." He inhaled, the old ache of missing her no longer present in his chest.

How about that?

It wasn't there. It had been there yesterday.

And today it was gone.

"You missed me?" she asked.

Her soft tone had him seeking her eyes.

"Yeah, I missed you. Every day. No matter where I was or what I was doing, the ache of missing you was always there."

He slid a finger under her chin and tipped her lips up towards him. He kissed her lightly and the return pressure from her lips sealed something in his soul. Something he hadn't known needed sealing.

This was it. This was the first day of their new beginning.

No second-guessing, no more running away.

"You need to know something," he said, holding her close. "I'm done running away. I'm going to show up for you every time. No matter what. Every single time I'll be there. I'm going to be the one you count on forever."

She stared into his eyes, then curved one of her hands around his neck and pressed her mouth to his. Her tongue slid inside, and he groaned at the wet heat. His arms tightened around her, and he deepened the kiss.

He pulled away long enough to take the coffee cup from her and set it on the table next to them. When he came back to her, she was shifting in his lap to straddle him. She draped her arms around his neck and shoulders and then she kissed the hell out of him.

Long, slow strokes of her tongue into his mouth. One of his hands curved around her hip and then over her ass while the other ran up her spine to cup the back of her head. The taste of her, the heat of her mouth, the feel of her soft body pressing into his, had him ready to go.

The honk of a horn startled them both and they stopped kissing and eyed each other. The horn had sounded like the kind clowns use and it was just odd enough to give them pause.

The horn sounded again a bit closer followed by Nikki's dad calling from up the path.

"Get yourselves decent and come up to the house. Breakfast in fifteen."

Nikki closed her eyes and her forehead dropped to André's chest.

"Oh my God," she groaned. "Did my dad just catch us making out?"

André's laugh grew until they were both shaking. It cooled his arousal immediately, but it was too funny to be upset about it.

"Did your dad just stop us from making out with a clown horn?"

Nikki's cry of embarrassment had him straight guffawing.

She scooted off his lap and stood. "Sure, you laugh, but if it was *your* dad, it wouldn't be as funny."

André shrugged and also stood. He followed her back into the cabin.

"No, your dad embarrasses you because he loves you. Mine does it because he's just an embarrassment." André pulled work pants and a fresh tee out of his bag along with his suspenders.

"You don't talk about your dad much," Nikki pointed out casually. She laid clothes out on the bed too.

"There's not much to say. He's a prick."

Nikki grimaced and he went to her, pulling her into a hug. She wrapped her arms around his middle and sank into his embrace.

He loved holding her.

In any and all capacity.

"You make that face because you don't know. You have a dad that loves you and has made that clear your entire life. It's okay for me to call mine a prick. He is one."

She stood back and ran her hands over the tops of his shoulders and then tugged at the hair at the nape of his neck. Her blue eyes bright and observant.

"When was the last time you saw him?" she asked.

His cheek twitched. "The night I was supposed to meet your parents."

Her eyebrows dipped and she looked so sweet and was so soft in his arms that for the first time he felt safe enough to say what he had never said out loud.

"He told me that I couldn't hope to keep someone else happy long term. That getting married was a waste of time and money. And as soon as you realized what a bore I was, you'd be gone. And some other things of that nature."

"André," she said, her eyes shone with compassion. "That's…wow. He really *is* a prick."

André chuckled and kissed her forehead. "Told you."

He let her go and started to get dressed.

"I know what that's like though," she said. Her tone reflective.

"Shelby used to tell Asa and me how bad we were at everything. That the only reason we were in her band was because she felt sorry for us."

That sounded like Shelby.

He hadn't known her for very long or very well. But he knew a bully when he saw one.

It had never made much sense to André why Shelby was considered the leader. She was mean and demanding but lacked the talent and drive of the other members. If anything, the pity went the other way.

Just thinking about how Shelby spoke to Nikki had his blood pressure rising.

"When was the last time you saw Shelby?" he asked, trying to keep disgust from permeating the question.

"You were there."

Now it was his turn to grimace. Winking Pete's last show had not gone well. Especially backstage.

Shelby had really lost it. She'd pushed Nikki offstage which led to Nik breaking her arm. And as they were trying to get Nikki to the hospital, Shelby accused her of breaking her arm on purpose to ruin the show.

Anger and guilt churned in André's chest. He tugged his shirt over his head and crossed to the other side of the bed where he gathered her in his arms.

"Oh." She dropped the clothes she'd picked out and instead wrapped her arms around his neck. "What's happening? I missed something."

He held her to his chest and buried his face in her neck, inhaling the sweet scent of her. "I'm sorry."

Her body relaxed into his and he kept going.

"I should have done more at the time. I have always regretted it."

"Oh, babe." Nikki pushed back so she could see his eyes. She frowned at him and shook her head. "No. That wasn't on you. Shelby's a dick. Please don't feel responsible for any of her stuff."

He ground his teeth together, knowing she was right but not being able to get rid of the feeling that he ought to have done something to protect her.

Nikki's expression shifted slightly, and a soft smile curved her lips. "Besides, it wasn't all bad. You took me to Paris, remember?"

"Yeah..." He nodded, and then a thought struck him. "You don't still think about what she said, do you?"

Her eyes drifted away and she worried her bottom lip.

"Nik," he prompted after a beat too long.

Her eyes came back to him, and they looked...guilty.

"Sometimes someone says the very thing you already think about yourself, you know?"

He nodded once, understanding and unease swirling in his gut.

"I know... *I know* that she only said it to hurt. But that doesn't mean it's not true." She tried to shrug but it was small and so unlike her. He could feel it, the pull inside of her that believed those twisted accusations.

"Nik." He shook her a little in his hold. Maybe there was nothing he could have done back then. But he could do something about it now. "None of what she said was true."

She rolled her pretty eyes at him like he didn't get it.

"I understand." He made sure he had her full attention before he went on. "Sometimes someone repeats the worst things we think about ourselves, and we convince ourselves that it's true. But it's not."

She blinked, her thoughts warring inside her head with what he'd just said.

"Try to believe the people who love you. Not the ones who hate you."

"That's exactly what Asa said."

"It's good advice."

Her gaze drifted over his shoulder and then came back. "I'm trying."

He could cry at her admission. It was small but more than he expected. He could work with that.

"Okay." He pressed a kiss to her forehead and then hugged her to his chest. "I'm right here to remind you when you forget," he said over the top of her head.

She responded by burrowing closer to him and, in doing so, became a permanent part of his heart.

They got dressed and walked up the path to the big house where Bob and Mary had more food than they needed. Eggs, sausages, bacon, toast, muffins, fruit, and various juices.

They asked about his childhood and his hobbies. They asked about his work and how that might look in the future.

And they made him feel welcome.

Part of a family.

At least that's how it felt. The only family he'd really ever been at peace with was Sabine. He didn't know how to have Sunday dinners and joke about the workweek. He had no experience with "shooting the shit" as Bob called it.

But this? He could do this. With these people.

And he was able to see a new layer to Nikki.

Some of the stories he'd heard before.

But it was different this time. Not the story, but him. He was different this time. More invested. Present.

It was like listening to a song that you'd fallen in love with when you were young, but not understanding it yet because of age or lack of experience. Then you hear it again later, and all the things you loved are still there, but there's a new layer to it that makes it mean more.

And then there were the stories he hadn't heard yet.

"Of course, when she came home in eighth grade with her head half-shaved, I thought I was going to have a heart attack," her mom said, pressing a hand to her chest like the heart attack could still happen with just the memory.

"You shaved your head?" André asked, eyebrows lifted. It wasn't exactly a surprising idea, but it was younger than he assumed her punk rock ideals began.

Nikki rolled her eyes. “It was just half.” She ran her fingers through her silky strands on the right side of her head. “This side.” Her lips quirked with the memory. “Asa said I wouldn’t do it.”

Asa being involved wasn’t a surprise.

“Did she get into trouble?” André asked Mary.

Mary and Bob exchanged a look that said his question was sweet but misplaced.

Bob sighed. “We learned early on that Nikki was gonna do what Nikki was gonna do. Shaved heads and safety pin piercings were the least of our worries.” He smiled at his daughter who was smiling at her plate. “She was a wild child. We tried to focus on the important things. Was she kind? Was she happy? Was she healthy?”

Nikki beamed at her dad. “Happy, healthy, and alive.”

That permanent place in André’s heart where Nikki now resided took up more space. He rubbed at the spot on his chest.

He had not adequately prepared himself for this trip up north.

But he didn’t regret a single minute.

After breakfast they got back to work.

The three of them made a good team. André carried the shingles up to the roof, one bundle at a time, Nikki placed them out, and Bob nailed them down.

They took a small break for lunch when Mary brought them out sandwiches and lemonade. They sat on the ground under the shade of a large oak tree.

André reclined back on his elbows and stretched his legs out in front of him.

Nikki’s blue eyes tracked up his legs, his chest, his face until she realized he had caught her looking. He smiled and shot her a wink full of promise of what was to come later that night.

This.

This was what he’d been missing out on for two and a half years. Thirty months’ worth of family dinners and hot looks under an oak tree. Thirty months of Bob and Mary. Thirty months of home improvement projects with the best partner he’d ever had (don’t tell Javier).

He wasn’t going to miss any more.

Whether Nikki realized it yet or not, what had started with that kiss in her office yesterday was just the beginning. Or rather, a continuation after an egregiously long intermission.

"You're going home tomorrow," Bob broke into André's peaceful thoughts.

André's head swiveled in Bob's direction, but Bob wasn't addressing him. He was scowling the gentlest scowl André had ever seen at his daughter.

"Don't think I'm so old that I can't see when you're using us as an excuse to avoid something."

Nikki's mouth fell open and she glanced between her dad and André.

André brought a hand up to cover the smile that he knew would not help the situation.

"Dad," Nikki started, trying to sound reasonable, but it came out slightly panicked. "There's still a lot of work to do."

"The hard part is done." Bob waved at the bunkhouse. "We have one bundle left thanks to Mr. Muscles, here."

André had to turn his head away at that one, his smile was too wide.

"Dad," Nikki huffed.

"Nicole Amelia Harry." Bob matched her tone. "Stop trying to pull one over on your old dad. What is it? What's she avoiding?" Bob asked.

It took a minute for André to realize Bob was speaking to *him*.

"Oh, I'm not getting in the middle of this." André shook his head.

Bob lifted his chin, a hint of mirth touching his gray eyes. "I thought she was avoiding you with the way she hollered when she saw your car pull up. But now I think you're trying to get her to come back with you."

André turned his gaze on Nikki, amused. "You were mad to see me?"

"Spitting," Bob confirmed.

Nikki was mad now from the way she was shooting daggers at both André and her dad.

But Bob held his ground, unconcerned with his daughter's ire.

"Just tell me what you're running from and let's see if it holds water." Bob waved a hand like he was offering the floor.

It was unlike anything André had ever experienced with a parent.

Discussion, compassion, conversation.

He had to quell the urge to laugh out loud. It would be an inappropriate reaction to what was happening but it was the way his emotions wanted to be expressed.

Nikki let out a disgruntled sigh. "Fine. I have the opportunity to produce an album."

Bob narrowed his eyes and waited.

"This…person thinks I'd be a good fit." Nikki scratched the side of her neck and looked away from the two of them.

Bob lifted an eyebrow at André and he felt compelled by the dad energy coming at him.

"Not just anyone. One of the biggest artists in the industry," André added.

She glared at him, but she didn't mean it.

He was pretty sure anyway.

"And?" Bob prodded.

"And I'm not qualified to do that, Dad." Nikki picked at the grass in front of her. "And any minute Zara is going to realize it and find someone better." She sighed, closing her eyes. "I'd rather she realize that before I get attached to a project I have no business being attached to."

André's heart squeezed with her words.

None of them were true.

But he couldn't just shake that information into her.

"Nikki," Bob said, his voice gruff and earnest. "You have always lived by one creed. What is it?"

She rolled her eyes and her lips twitched with an almost smile. "Chase your joy."

André had never heard that before.

Bob nodded slowly. "You will stand and fight for the weirdest of the weirdos to do what makes them happy. Even if no one else sees it as important or practical. Because you believe what?"

"Life is art. And art is subjective. So no one gets to decide if someone else's art is acceptable."

Chills raced over André's skin.

He'd never heard her say it so succinctly but that's exactly how she lived her life. That's how she treated everyone.

As far as lectures went, André was taking mental notes.

Bob had it down.

"Do you want to produce albums?" Bob asked.

She took a breath and her shoulders slumped. "Yes."

"Does it make you happy?" Bob asked.

"Yes."

"Are you sure?" Bob pressed.

She sent him a flat look.

"Maybe it's time you get real about what you want." Bob let his final words hang in the air for a beat. Then he patted his legs and stood up, giving Nikki a moment with her thoughts.

Nikki's eyes came to André, and he tried to convey to her all the things he'd said a thousand times. He couldn't make her believe it though. Her dad was right. She had to make the choice herself.

All at once she sucked in a breath and her eyes sharpened on him.

"Crap," she muttered.

She shoved to her feet and took her phone out of her pocket. She looked at André and he saw all the hope and vulnerability that meant she was getting ready to take a leap.

"You got this," he encouraged.

She nodded and inhaled sharply. "I have to make a call."

They finished the roof.

Had dinner, showered, and got naked again.

Being naked was André's favorite part of his entire trip up north.

She traced lines on his chest as they both caught their breath.

He ran his fingers through her hair, savoring the silk slide against his skin.

"Your name is Nicole Amelia Harry," he said. She stilled in his arms. He chuckled. "Your initials are NAH."

She flopped backwards onto her pillow. "I know, it's awful."

He followed her and moved a tendril of hair out of her face. "I love it."

She rolled her eyes but then she sobered and touched his cheek.

"Thank you for coming to get me," she whispered. Her blue eyes scanned his features and he saw a hesitancy there he'd seen before.

"What's going on in here?" he asked, grazing his fingertips over her temple.

"We have to leave in the morning," she said, a thread of sorrow in her voice.

"Yes." He wasn't worried though. Not this time.

"What happens back in the city?"

He tucked a strand of hair behind her ear. "What do you mean?"

"I mean with us." She moved to sit up and he let her. She tugged the covers around her chest and looked into her lap. "Was this just for here or…?"

"What? No." He sat up too. "Not for me."

She bit her lower lip and looked at him with those big blue eyes surrounded by dark lashes. "You want to be with me?" she asked.

That gorgeous vulnerability shone from her eyes, and he had to take a breath. He'd caused her to question him because of his past actions. Of course, she'd wonder what was on the horizon.

"At the risk of sounding too eager, yes. I want to be with you in every way I can imagine. I want to be with you naked. I want to be with you clothed. I want to be with you when work is hard, and I need someone to make me laugh. And I want to be with you when you're talking nonstop about things you love, and you make me love them too."

She smiled.

"I want that too," she said.

He cupped the back of her head and pressed a hard kiss to her lips. He rested his forehead against hers. "You had me worried for a minute. I thought you were only using me for my body."

She snorted and pushed him onto his back as she straddled him. His hands curved around her hips and a certain part of his anatomy came alive again.

"Oh, I'm doing that too," she said.

This woman.

She gave meaning to everything about his life.

He was going to do his best to make sure he contributed to hers just as much.

CHAPTER EIGHTEEN

KING OF MY HEART

NIKKI

She'd gone straight to the studio the moment they got back into town. She didn't want to waste any more time than she already had.

She and André had left the lake house just after sunrise. They had to drive their vehicles separately and she was grateful for the two hours of contemplation.

André was distracting in the best way.

But she hadn't had a moment to catch her breath since he'd showed up two days ago.

It was easy to believe that what they'd shared at the lake house was a singular event. But somehow, she knew it wasn't.

The André she knew three years ago would never have chased her down to make sure she was okay. He would have given her space and time because he was respectful. Also, because parents scared him.

But not only had he shown up, he'd *stayed.*

Her heart was still processing everything they'd shared over those two days. Their quiet conversations. Confessions. Adorations.

The way he touched her body felt new and reverent.

The way he held her like he couldn't and didn't want to get enough.

Never had she felt so cared for. So cherished.

So loved.

Her thoughts vacillated between everything she needed to get ready before the pop star arrived in Chicago, to the way André's hands felt in her hair.

Could she do this?

Could she really get everything she ever wanted? Could she make the art that she loved and love the man that made her life feel like art?

She pushed open the door to her new office and stopped.

It was even better than she remembered.

It was as if André had known exactly what she was going to need to do this thing with Zara.

She got to work, sorting the calendar, making arrangements with Zara's people. Johnny came in and she told him the news. He didn't look surprised but he did look proud. Of her.

Add one more warm fuzzy to the treasure box in her heart.

André had been right. The people around her supported her because they believed in her. Not because they pitied her.

She knew that—had known that the entire time—but she'd needed reminding.

After she'd spoken to Johnny, she went through what she had on hand and what she needed to procure so there wouldn't be any interruptions during the recording process.

"Do you have time to eat?"

She turned around from taking notes on the equipment in the second slide-out space André had built.

And there was the most handsome man in the world, holding a bag that smelled a lot like La Morena's.

She skip-hopped across the office and threw her arms around his neck. She kissed him on the lips. Just a quick, hard press, then leaned back and smiled at him.

"Hi," she said, happier than she could remember being in a very long time.

And happy was her baseline, so that was saying something.

"Hi," he returned, his free hand on her lower back, his smile warm and sweet.

"Have lunch with me?" she asked.

"Only if I'm not a distraction," he replied.

"No." She held his face in both hands. "Not a distraction. My inspiration."

He lowered his head to kiss her soft and slow. Her belly dipped and her heart sighed. She had missed this.

But no.

Not this.

Because it had never been quite like this.

He let her go and they made a small picnic on the floor of her office.

While they ate, she told him all she'd been working on that morning when something occurred to her.

"What about *our* schedule?" she asked.

André grabbed one of the many throw pillows from the couch and dropped it on the floor. He stretched out his long legs and rested his head on the pillow.

"What about it?" he asked.

"When do you go back to school?"

As far as she knew, the work on the lounge and her office was done. André had no reason to be at the studio every day anymore and that fact made her a bit sad. But he also had a full-time career—just like she did.

"I have to start getting things together. I go back in two weeks."

Right in the middle of her and Zara's time in the studio.

He folded his hands over his middle and closed his eyes like he could take a nap right there.

She wouldn't mind.

Fact was, with him being in her space nearly every day for weeks, she had grown accustomed to his presence. Even on the days she'd been avoiding him, knowing he was just down the hall or around the next corner, had given her a sense of security she wasn't looking forward to being without.

She didn't want to bring up things from when they were together before, because what they had started that week felt so new. But she couldn't just pretend that their lives were really all that different now.

Once the school year started, everything could change.

"Maybe we should have a scheduled date night, then," she suggested. "I hear responsible adults do things like that."

"That's an idea." He kept his eyes closed, his body relaxed and his breathing evened out.

"How about Wednesdays?" She threw a day out not knowing if that actually worked for her calendar. Just that today was Wednesday.

"I have therapy on Wednesdays. Early evening. I…" He took a breath. "I'm not the best company immediately after my appointment. I'd prefer a different day."

He had what?

"Okay, maybe Tuesday or Thursday?" she asked but she really wanted to know more about the therapy.

How long had he been going? Who was his therapist? Should *she* get therapy?

"Tuesdays and Thursdays I have polo with Tyrone until it starts to snow."

"Polo? You play polo?" And yeah, she didn't want to bring up things from before, but this seemed relevant. "I thought you hated organized sports."

A soft laugh puffed out of him. "That's still true. It's urban polo. We ride bikes and use a racket ball. There's no set field or anything. We usually meet in parking garages or empty lots."

"I have so many questions," she said after a beat. He laughed in response.

"Is *that* why you're so tan?" she asked. "Do you play this game shirtless? Can I watch? I'm sorry, I didn't mean that. But can I watch?"

His laughter grew but he wasn't answering any of her questions.

The sound of his happiness filled her heart in unexpected ways. It was one more thing about him that was different than before. Like he was finally *living*.

Maybe he shouldn't be wasting his newfound emotional freedom on an old girlfriend.

Especially if he was investing in himself with therapy. Maybe he'd only reached for her because she'd been there. A convenience, a familiarity.

Oh God, please don't let that be all it was.

But what if he would be better suited to another academic? Someone who didn't tell stories at swanky events that included the words, "Steinhoff's hairy butt."

"I can hear you thinking," he said, interrupting her unexpected emotional spiral.

She huffed a surprised laugh. "You cannot."

"I can and I also know what you're worried about."

"Oh, do you?" She sounded disinterested but she wished he really could know her thoughts. Because maybe then he could explain them back to her in a way that would help her understand them.

And help her realize she was being ridiculous.

It was new. That was all.

"Hey."

She slid her gaze his direction. He had turned his head to see her, eyes open and alert.

"You have the most important project of your life coming up," he said calmly. "I will do everything I can to help you achieve it."

"Should we wait to do this dating thing until our lives calm down?" she asked, hating every word as it came out of her mouth.

But it was like she had to suggest it so that she could hear it and then dismiss it.

André chuckled. It rippled through her and soothed her budding anxiety.

"No."

"No?" she asked around a surprised laugh. "Just no, huh?"

But the truth was, his quiet laugh and simple answer was exactly what she needed.

He sat up, tossed the pillow back where it went, and coaxed her to her feet.

His eyes danced over her face as a soft smile played on his lips. He took both of her hands in his and brought them up to his mouth where he kissed the back of her knuckles. First one hand, then the other.

"I have to wonder if we're just asking for trouble," she whispered and watched him for his response. Looking for any indication that he agreed with her fears.

"Dual dreams," he murmured running a thumb over her lower lip.

She tilted her head in question and his smile turned soft. "Neither one of our dreams takes precedence. We're both able to chase our ambitions as we see fit because it's what we want. And we chase each other—" He made another swipe of her lower lip and watched its movement, then came back to her eyes. "Because that's also what we want."

"I like that idea." She pushed his dark hair off his forehead. God, he was gorgeous.

"I enjoy what I do," he went on. "And I will continue on the path I've set because the work makes me happy and feel accomplished." He took a deep breath and his gaze turned ever so tender as he cradled her cheek. "But you, Nik, you're my heart. And when you're doing what you love, what makes you come alive, that brings me joy."

Tears burned her eyes in a good way and she pushed up on her toes to kiss him.

And what a kiss.

Long, slow, deep.

Pulling her heart into an embrace safer than she'd ever known.

They made it two days without seeing each other before she felt like she was dying.

Okay, that was a bit dramatic.

But working all day in the gorgeous space he'd created for her as she got ready for Zara Lorna's arrival had her thinking about him constantly.

She could see the care he'd put into every design he'd chosen. Could feel his dedication in the energy surrounding her.

Maybe that had been his goal the entire time. Maybe he knew that by creating such beauty in her workspace, she'd have no choice but to think of him.

Occasionally she'd drift off in thought, picture his hands sanding, and painting, and crafting. Then she'd inevitably picture his hands on her.

Whatever his goal had been when he'd designed her office, it had worked.

Not only was she thinking of him constantly, but she was highly motivated to finish her tasks so that she could get to him sooner.

By Friday, she was ready to show up on his doorstep naked.

If only she knew where he lived.

"Where are you?" she asked when he answered the phone.

"Just getting out of the shower. Where are you?" he asked. There was no mistaking the amusement in his voice.

They had texted earlier that day and had planned to meet at the Iggy in an hour because Asa was playing.

"I'm sitting in my car in the most ridiculous outfit hoping you'll give me your address."

"What are you wearing?" he asked, his tone low and sexy and teasing.

"Fishnets and dinosaur pasties."

Her phone beeped with an incoming text but she didn't look. She was waiting for his reply.

"André?" she asked when he hadn't said anything in almost a full minute.

"I sent you the address."

She looked at her phone then, and sure enough, the text had been from him.

"Be there in fifteen."

"Drive safe." His voice sounded strained. "Please."

She laughed. "I have no desire to get in an accident dressed like this." She was wearing an oversized hoody zipped up over it, but still.

His apartment wasn't too far from where he used to live but it was nicer than before. It had an elevator, for instance. The old place had unlit stairs that she never felt safe taking alone. Which was why they had usually gone to her place.

She stepped off the elevator and he was waiting for her at his open door.

In jeans and no shirt, his suspenders dangled by his side, and he was barefoot.

Why did that undo her so? She'd never cared about bare feet before in her life but something about André always being so well dressed and put together and then seeing him not so much…

She should have been ashamed of the whimper she made when she hop-skipped toward him but she just wasn't.

Unzipping the hoody as she went, he stepped back into the apartment, eyes molten. The door slammed behind her, she jumped, discarding the hoody, he caught her, she wrapped her legs around his waist, and it was on.

They never made it to the bedroom.

Suffice to say he really liked her Veloci-titties.

The next week was demanding for both of them.

Zara came to town which had Nikki flustered beyond belief.

Way more than she'd anticipated.

She was excitable and irritated and bouncing off every creative wall supplied to her.

André acted like she was fucking adorable even though she was pretty sure she was annoying as hell.

But he listened when she called to vent about things even though he would have no way of knowing what they were. Or when Asa was being weird. Or how Johnny said she was gifted and that had made her cry.

Sometimes she'd send him a naked picture to show her appreciation.

He was busy prepping for the school year. The weekdays were packed with responsibilities for both of them. But they managed to have a lot of sex.

Like, a *lot* of sex.

Nearly every single night she was texting him from outside his apartment. Sometimes at two in the morning.

She'd send the text and decide to wait five minutes before going home. If he was asleep, she didn't want to wake him.

She never waited longer than a minute before his reply.

And one time he stopped by the studio during lunch. Let's just say she was glad he had installed locks on her office door.

On Sunday, their scheduled day off, they had planned on doing "couple-y things." Like go dancing and try a new restaurant. Have a real date.

But Nikki was out of clean clothes.

"I have to do laundry," she said over the phone. Disappointment rolled through her. "I am legitimately out of clean anything. I am currently wearing polar bear pajama bottoms and a swimsuit top. They don't match."

André chuckled.

God, she loved that sound.

Ugh. She missed him.

"Bring your clothes over here. I have a full-size washer and dryer right in my apartment," André offered.

"You do?" She stopped picking up her clothes and stared at the wall in her room. He couldn't possibly be serious. Laundry wasn't a sexy date night activity.

"Yes. Bring your clothes over. I'll make us some food and we can watch a movie or something."

So simple.

"You're sure?" she asked, eyeing the basket of laundry she'd almost filled.

"Absolutely. I miss you. And doing laundry and talking about our week sounds like bliss to me. Hashtag goals."

A laugh bubbled out of her. "Did you just say *hashtag goals?*"

"Yes. What? Did I not use that correctly?" he asked.

"You're amazing." She laughed again. "I'll be there in a few minutes."

And that was how she found herself standing in André's apartment loading the washing machine while he cooked food for them.

She paused and let her eyes wander over her surroundings.

While they'd been spending a lot of time at his place, she hadn't really paid any attention to it. They were always busy with other things.

It wasn't extravagant but it was a spacious, open-concept loft. Clean, decorated with books and replica artifacts. A subtle masculine color scheme throughout in rich browns and cream and forest green.

She stopped when she felt his eyes on her.

"Can I ask you a weird question?" She closed the washer and selected a cycle.

"I'd be disappointed if you didn't." He crossed his arms and leaned a hip against the kitchen counter, watching her.

"We've had sex?" She came towards him.

He cleared his throat and rubbed his unshaven jaw with the back of his hand.

"I have to say that if you didn't know that's what we've been doing, I am very upset with myself."

"Shut up," she laughed, encircling his waist with her arms. "I'm trying to bring up something serious."

He wrapped his arms around her and gazed down at her like she was all he could see.

"Yes, we've had sex," he confirmed, trying to be serious and failing.

"I mean…" She took a breath as she tried to find the right words. "We had sex before, years ago…"

He lifted his chin as understanding dawned.

"But this time feels different," she said, softer than a moment before. Her eyes dropped to his chest. "Maybe it's just me."

She shrugged and moved to leave his embrace, but he tightened his hold, getting her eyes back.

"It's better," he confirmed.

"Yeah?" She leaned into him.

Because the sex had been great before. But now it was mind-blowing.

He pressed a kiss to her upturned lips. "Yeah."

"Why do you think that is?" she asked and then narrowed her eyes. "Did you read a book or something?"

He smiled but it was a different kind of a smile than she could ever remember seeing. Almost like he had a sad secret.

"It's because I'm all in this time," he said. He brushed her hair back, pressed his lips to her forehead and held for several beats. When he pulled back, she could see regret in his eyes like he was remembering something he wished he wasn't. He blinked and it cleared, bringing him back to the present. "I haven't hidden parts of myself from you. You're getting all of me. You will always have all of me."

Hours later, after they had eaten and watched a documentary on drummers; after the dishes were done and the laundry was folded and placed in her basket to take home, he convinced her to stay the night. To stay with him.

They both knew the next week was going to bring its own stresses and disruptions.

And truthfully, in the back of Nikki's mind she was waiting for the other shoe to drop.

What if they'd jumped back into this thing without taking into consideration all that their lives already held?

But even with those thoughts, she knew she didn't want to stop.

She wanted to be with him.

For as long as it lasted.

"What are you thinking?" he asked, threading his fingers through her hair.

She lay on her back, her head on his stomach. She thought he'd fallen asleep.

"How do you know I'm thinking?" she asked.

"Because I can feel it. You get too quiet."

"Hm. Maybe I just talk too much."

He reached for her hand and brought it to his mouth. "I like how much you talk. It's not too much," he said against her knuckles. His mouth moved along her fingers and he pressed a kiss to her wrist.

This was also new.

The constant contact.

Before—even though she knew it wasn't fair to compare the past to the present, it seemed to happen without her acknowledging it—he had been polite. Sweet, tender, but reserved.

Not now.

Now when they were in the same room, he was touching her in one way or another. Playing with her hair, his hand on her back, tangling his fingers with hers.

With every warm caress she grew more addicted to it. To him.

She never knew she wanted more physical contact in a relationship but now she would never be able to go without it.

Which was one of the things on her mind.

Was it sustainable? Surely it would burn out, right? Or at least mellow.

"Just tell me what's on your mind," he prodded gently.

"Are we being ridiculous?" she asked, surprised the words came out. She hadn't planned on saying anything.

"I hope so," he replied and then chuckled. "I have a feeling you mean something else though."

She chewed on her bottom lip and stared up at the ceiling fan above them. It turned slowly, blowing cool air on their heated skin. It was all so peaceful and perfect.

So why was she having these thoughts?

"I think I just need reassurance. One more time," she confessed.

"There are no limits on how many times you can ask me something. Tell me what you need to know," he said.

I need to know it's safe to love you. That you'll stay this time.

But she couldn't say that out loud.

Could she?

He sat up, pressed his back to the headboard and patted the space beside him. She scooted up to where he indicated, and he wrapped the sheets around her and tucked a strand of hair behind her ear as he looked at her with tender patience.

"Tell me what you're afraid of," he coaxed.

And there it was again. This sense of *right* that came with André looking in her eyes. It was so hard to remember all the things that worried her with his calm assurance holding her.

"This." She indicated the two of them. "This is good."

He cracked a smile. "Yeah. It's very good."

Having him say it too tied up a loose string in her heart she hadn't even noticed was floating in the breeze.

"I want you to stay," she said so softly she wasn't sure he heard her.

He ran a thumb along her cheek, his face serious. "Nicole," he said, voice rough. "I am never running away again. I am so sorry I introduced that fear to you. I will spend the rest of my life proving that no matter what, I am yours. I will always show up, and I will always be there."

"I love you, you know," she said. "I never stopped."

His lips came down on hers in a crushing kiss. His tongue thrust inside in a claiming, urgent move and she moaned in response. He pulled back, holding her face in both hands, his eyes wild and dark.

"I love you," he said, strong and sure. "I love you," he repeated. And then he was kissing her again. Their limbs and breaths tangled in the sheets. Urgency gave way to appreciation, and desperation turned to reverence.

And the last small drop of doubt in Nikki's mind disappeared forever.

ANDRÉ

The second week was a little more difficult for both of them.

He was very focused on making sure he was prepared for the upcoming semester, and she was hitting a wall with the recording process.

Apparently, creatives couldn't just turn it off and turn it back on again.

And when he'd suggested that as a joke, she'd stopped speaking to him for a full ten minutes.

Ten minutes in which he tried very hard not to find her reaction to his stupid joke hilarious.

He didn't hear from her at all on Friday.

Which wasn't unusual, sometimes she texted him late when she was on her way over. But when he went to bed that night and she'd only replied with a heart emoji, he knew something was wrong.

He couldn't sleep. Instead, he kept checking his phone every fifteen minutes.

He called her and it rang and rang.

Finally, he got out of bed, got dressed, and drove to Avondale.

Maybe she was exhausted and had gone home.

But he would still sleep better knowing she was okay.

He drove past her house, all the lights were off. Her car was parked in the street, but that wasn't unusual since she walked to work.

The similarities of what he was doing now, compared to the two and a half years when they hadn't been together, struck him.

He parked behind the studio and looked for any sign that someone was inside. He couldn't see any lights and there weren't any other vehicles in the parking lot.

There was only one way to know for sure.

He let himself into the back door and locked it behind him. If Johnny asked him tomorrow why he'd used his code to go in at two in the morning, he'd be honest.

He was looking for Nikki.

He found her in the control room of Studio X.

She was sitting at the board, headphones on, moving switches with her fingers.

He knocked on the doorframe, not wanting to startle her like he was prone to doing.

She turned towards him but didn't jump. Instead, her shoulders slumped and that's when he saw the tears.

It broke something inside him.

André came to her and sank to his knees at her feet.

She removed the headphones, tossing them on the board, and then wiped at her wet face with her fingertips.

"What's wrong?" he asked gently resting his hands on her knees if only to touch her, comfort her.

"I don't think I can do it," she said, her voice wobbling. Fresh tears spilled from her eyes, and she waved a hand at the soundboard. "It's like, I can hear in my head what it's supposed to be and it's not that. And I just..." She broke up as a soft sob interrupted her. Sucking in a breath, she looked at her lap and shrugged. "I'm not this person. I'm not made for this."

He cupped her face with both of his hands and carefully wiped the tears on her cheeks with his thumbs.

"Look at me," he whispered.

She didn't at first, but when she did, he could see it. And boy oh boy, did he understand it. That fear of having, of *knowing* exactly what you want and it being just out of reach.

"You are made for this," he said.

She shook her head and he smiled, undeterred.

"Listen to me, beautiful," he said, seeking her eyes again. "You are gifted. You are talented. The people around you see it and believe in it. They would not put this kind of thing in your hands if they didn't trust you to make the exact brand of beautiful you already are."

She swallowed and frowned at him. "You don't understand."

"Do I know how to make a record?" he asked and made a face. "Obviously not. Do I know what any of those buttons or switches do? No." He shook his head. "But I know you. I know your heart. I know how much care you put into the music you make."

"It's so hard," she said, fresh tears falling. "I don't know if I can do it."

These weren't words she was saying just to say. Her struggle was palpable, and he wished he could take away her doubt and fear. He would show her exactly how he saw her. And he would show her that the faith everyone had put into her talent wasn't in vain.

"C'mere," he said, standing up and holding his hand out to help her.

"I can't leave," she protested. "I have so much work to do."

"We're not leaving," he urged, keeping his voice soft. "Let me help you."

She huffed but took his hand and stood up.

He pulled her to the center of the control room and moved her arm to his shoulder. He put a hand on her waist, held their joined hands in between them at his heart, and pulled her close so her head rested on his chest beside their hands.

He swayed gently to the song in his mind until she relaxed into him.

And then he sang the only Billy Joel song he knew to her—"Vienna."

Somewhere in that small control room in the wee hours of the morning, he was able to reach her.

They held each other for a long time. Dancing, existing, breathing peace into one another.

Quietly she slipped away and went back to the soundboard. No more tears, just fresh determination.

And he lay down on the sofa and watched her work until he fell asleep.

CHAPTER NINETEEN

THIS LOVE

ANDRÉ

"And that is why..." He drew a line under his terrible illustration. It was supposed to be a cow, but it looked more like a hairy potato. Whatever. He wasn't an artist. "You always leave a note."

He smiled at the soft snickers behind him but schooled his expression before turning back around. He faced his class and capped the dry-erase marker.

"Any questions?"

One hand went up.

"Yes, Ms. Arias?"

The young woman, Mia Arias, was the most outspoken of the class. She asked a lot of questions, and it wasn't until about the second week that he realized she was asking questions given to her by her less confident peers.

But more than that, she was far and away the brightest student he'd ever had. She attacked each lesson with voracity. More than once he was certain she knew the information better than him. Definitely better than his TA.

But she also had certain expectations for her instructors. She'd established a theme over the past two weeks. He knew exactly where her line of questioning was leading and it wasn't about the lesson.

"Where did you *really* spend your fieldwork this summer?"

"I was in South Dakota. The Badlands." He'd already told them that of course. First day of classes, because it looked likely he would get to go back next year.

Mia shot a look to one of her friends and a sly smile spread over her face. "Are you sure you weren't in Egypt?"

A humorous murmur rippled through the room.

André suppressed a smile. "Quite sure."

"Would you tell us if you were?"

He cleared his throat and tossed the dry-erase marker onto the lectern. "Would I tell you if I was racing off to hopefully discover the lost tomb of Alexander the Great?" He took a thoughtful breath and tucked his hands in his pockets. "Would you?"

Mia's head jerked back slightly.

He let his eyes glance over the entire class. "Would any of you?"

"I would," Felipe spoke up.

A few other voices agreed.

"Wait, wait, wait." Mia waved a hand. "Does that mean you were in Egypt or you're going there now?"

"No." André shook his head. "It is very exciting that they think they've found such a promising lead. I do hope someone confirms it. As much as I appreciate how highly you all think of me, I am not Indiana Jones." He glanced at the clock on the back wall and then crossed the room to stand by the door. "I will leave the large discoveries for those more deserving."

The bell rang. The students gathered their things and filed out. He nodded to each of them as they passed, until Mia approached. She stopped and regarded him with suspicion in her dark eyes.

"You don't believe me, Ms. Arias?" he asked.

"You really like dinosaurs that much?" she asked skeptically.

"I really do." He tugged on his bowtie. A Christmas gift from his sister. It had little cartoon T. rexes on it.

Mia huffed. "I just find it really unfortunate that my professor isn't at all like what I had hoped." She waved a hand indicating his entire body. "All of this. The hair, the muscles, the dorky adorableness. Such a waste."

André arched an eyebrow but chose to ignore her inappropriate comments. He hinged forward slightly at the waist in challenge. "Why don't *you* do it?"

"What?" Her eyebrows dipped.

"Go be that person you look up to. You're very bright. Fearless. You have a passion for history that most don't and the kind of confidence that most aspire to. Go be it."

Mia sucked in a breath to argue but nothing happened. Her frown intensified and her gaze lost focus as her thoughts turned inward. "*I* could be Indiana Jones," she said under her breath.

He smiled to himself as she wandered from his room and out into the world.

Hopefully she'd take his words to heart. The world would be better for it.

Imagine the things she'd discover if she were turned loose on the planet.

He wasn't the adventurous type. Not in that way anyway.

But he did delight in watching others chase their dreams.

Speaking of.

He grabbed his bag and headed to his car. No office hours today. He had plans.

As soon as he hit the parking lot and the sunshine hit his face, his thoughts turned solely to Nikki.

He checked his phone and saw there was one text reminding him to be at the studio by six. That's when the party was due to start.

The wrap party.

Because she'd finished producing her first major album.

Johnny had suggested a party to commemorate the event and Zara Lorna had taken over from there.

It was intended to be a celebration for all of them; the musicians and engineers that had worked on the album.

But for André, it was a celebration for one woman alone.

And she had earned it.

She'd fought her personal demons again and again, and had worked until she couldn't think clearly. But she never stopped, even when she really *really* wanted to.

He was so damn proud of her.

He'd even gotten new suspenders for the occasion.

Unfortunately, the dryer at his apartment wasn't working and so he'd had to drop off his outfit for that night at a dry cleaner. He stopped there on his way, got his suit, and headed for home.

He glanced at the time again as the florist came into view.

It would be cutting it close but he wanted to bring her flowers.

To be honest, he wanted to bring her all kinds of gifts and trinkets and tokens of affection, but that would be annoying.

Maybe next time.

Or maybe when the album released.

He dashed inside, bought a single red rose, and *then* headed for home.

Rain began to splash the windshield as he parked his car.

The elevator opened and he was mentally running through his routine—eat a yogurt, shower, shave, get dressed, find the umbrella—so he definitely wasn't paying attention to anyone else in his hallway.

Though if he had been paying attention, would it have mattered?

Because there was no way to prepare for the gut punch that came with seeing his father waiting for him.

NIKKI

She still wasn't quite sure it was over.

And not *over* over—there was still a lot to do before the album was released—but she'd done all she could do.

She'd poured all of her ability and knowledge and know-how into this piece of art and now it was out of her hands.

Zara handed her a glass of sparkling grape juice—the studio was alcohol- and drug-free—and toasted her.

Her artist was happy.

And honestly, that was the best thing she could have hoped for.

"We did it," Zara said with a satisfied smile.

"How are you so calm about all of this?" Nikki asked.

Zara shrugged, her dark hair sliding over her shoulders like water. "I've been doing this since I was sixteen. I think this is the fourth time I've reinvented myself." She eyed Nikki with calm assurance. "I am prouder of this record than any I've ever done. And that's thanks to you."

"How?" Nikki scoffed.

Zara flashed a smile. "Our hearts recognize one another. We're meant to be, babe."

Oh, please let that be true.

Zara arched an elegant black eyebrow. "This won't be our last album together. I hope you know that."

Nikki shook her head, but she was smiling.

"Who knew a drunken phone call would lead to all this?" she joked.

Zara pursed her lips and narrowed one eye. Nikki knew that look. It was an idea forming.

"Can we enjoy this one for like five minutes?" Nikki asked.

Zara was nodding her head and backing away. "I just have to write something down."

Nikki checked her phone again.

It was half past six and she hadn't heard from André.

Hopefully he was okay. It had been raining pretty heavily last time she'd looked outside.

Hannah came over and offered her congratulations, which was surreal considering who she actually was.

Johnny made a small speech about being proud of Nikki and not being surprised at all that the record had turned out so well.

But André still wasn't there.

Nikki ducked into the hallway and tried to call him.

No answer.

The back door opened, and Sunshine and Sabine came in.

"Is it still raining?" she asked them.

"Not as much," Sunshine replied. "Sorry we're late. It was my fault."

Sabine slipped her hand into Sunshine's, and she asked, "Is André here?"

Nikki started to shake her head, and Sabine's expression shifted almost imperceptibly.

"What?" Nikki asked. "Is something wrong?"

Sabine glanced between Sunshine and Nikki. "It's probably nothing."

Nikki didn't move. Because Sabine clearly knew something she wasn't saying.

"Our…dad is in town." Sabine shook her head and looked down, disappointment clouding her features. She sucked in a breath and touched Nikki's arm. "It's probably nothing."

Yeah, she'd said that.

And it was probably nothing.

Although, the last time his dad had been in town, André had disappeared from her life without saying a word.

ANDRÉ

"I can't believe you're here." He sounded a lot more relaxed than he felt. André pushed a hand through his hair and turned to face his father.

A man he hadn't seen or spoken to since he'd made the worst decision of his life.

His eyes darted to the clock on the wall.

Shit.

He didn't have time for this.

"I was hoping we could get some dinner. Maybe catch up," the older man said.

André stared at him, truly not believing what he was seeing.

But there he was, in flesh and blood.

René Debois was in a charcoal suit (because he was always in a suit), with a white shirt. His gray hair was a little long but still stylish, slicked back in a way that older men could get away with, clean shaven.

And standing in my apartment?

"I still don't understand," André said. "You didn't tell me you were coming."

They hadn't spoken much since that night. A phone call a year seemed to be the new normal and André was okay with that. He didn't want to have anything to do with the man anymore. He just hadn't made an official announcement or anything.

Didn't think he needed to.

René let out a light, incredulous laugh. "I can't stop in and see my children every now and again?"

André's lip curled and his gut handed him another red flag.

"You live four thousand miles away. It's a little hard to believe you were in the neighborhood."

René jutted his chin out and put his hands on his hips. Indignant.

André crossed his arms, hugging them to his chest as he looked at him, *really* looked.

He wasn't wearing a tie. Which wasn't a huge clue except that he had also unbuttoned the top two buttons of his shirt.

He was upset.

"Shouldn't you be busy this time of year?" André asked. He hadn't followed the Premier League in years, for obvious reasons. But he was fairly certain that the season started again in August. His dad should not only *not* be in Chicago, but he should also be oblivious to the existence of anyone outside of his players.

René's jaw firmed and he looked away. He wandered over to the bookshelf in the living room and scanned the spines.

And that's when it clicked.

"They fired you," André said.

René stiffened and he cleared his throat. "Forced early retirement," he corrected, speaking down his nose.

Still.

He was standing in his estranged son's apartment having been fired from the one thing he had put above all else in his life and he was still too proud to admit it.

"Are you here for comfort?" André asked slowly.

René glanced André's direction but missed the hostility rolling off him.

"I thought we could go out, catch up."

"Now you want a relationship? Don't you think it's kind of late for that?" André asked in all seriousness.

René clicked his tongue. "Don't be so melodramatic. You're an adult for pity's sake."

André rubbed a hand over his mouth. He glanced at the clock again.

Shit.

"Dad, I actually have plans. Can we do this later?"

René screwed up his face and scoffed. "Change your plans. I'm in town."

André shook his head and rolled his eyes. Oh, Thomas was going to love this update on Wednesday. Sometimes he'd tell his therapist something his dad had said or done, and Thomas would look politely shocked. It was a fun game they played that André liked to call, "trick or trauma."

"No," André said firmly. "My plans cannot be moved. Do you have a place to stay in town?"

"I'm not a beggar," René said, disgusted.

"Great. I need to shower. I'm already late. Call me later in the week and we can…" Oh God, was he really offering to meet his dad later? "Discuss. Things. Sabine can join us. It'll be great."

René crossed the room, coming closer and putting his hands in his pockets. "I didn't want to see her. *You're* my son."

"Nice, Dad." André sighed.

"You misunderstand." René waved away his comments. "I already spoke with her today. But *you're* the one I wanted to see."

Like that was somehow better.

André's frustration was growing. It had been present from the beginning, but the longer his dad argued with him about leaving, the more it grew. And now it was starting to feel more like anxiety than frustration.

He looked at the clock.

Nikki was expecting him.

He had told her he'd be there.

Why did this moment feel so terrifyingly familiar?

"Dad. You have to go," he said, this time with more force.

"André," René replied, incredulous. "I haven't flown four thousand miles to be so disrespectfully dismissed."

He needed to leave the room before he did something he might actually regret.

"Whatever. I have to shower." André went into the bathroom and stripped off his clothes. Maybe his dad would take the hint and leave.

Fuck.

Nikki.

She was probably wondering where he was.

He needed to get there.

He'd told her he would always show up for her and here, on one of the most important nights of her life *again*, he wasn't there.

He hit the wall of the shower with the palm of his hand.

It wasn't fair to her and it damn sure wasn't fair to him. He didn't need this right now. He hadn't needed anything from that man in years.

When he got out of the shower, he didn't care to see if his dad was still there, he just continued to get ready.

He had to focus.

Shower, get dressed, get to Avondale.

He left the bathroom in a towel and grabbed his dry-cleaning from the kitchen counter where he'd left it.

His dad was watching football on his television.

Of course he was.

He got dressed, attached his suspenders, grabbed his jacket and headed back into the living room.

"I'm leaving," André said, slipping his jacket on. "Don't be here when I get back. The door locks automatically when you leave."

"André," René stopped him, standing up.

André stopped and faced his father. "What?"

"Where are you going? What's so important?"

André narrowed his eyes at the older man who once held so much weight in his words that André doubted in every single one of his choices. Not anymore. All he saw now was a man who never knew what he was doing and was now at a place in his life where he had no one and nothing to show for it.

"The woman I love is waiting for me."

René flinched.

"She's remarkable. Intelligent in a way that frightens me sometimes. Funny; kind; creative, and she loves me. I will always put her above everyone else. Every time. Without question. I didn't once before, and it was the worst mistake of my life." André looked René up and down. "Be gone when I get back. I will call you in a few days. If you answer, and if you're interested, we can discuss having something of a relationship."

He didn't wait for a reply and allowed the door to slam closed behind him.

The drive to Avondale felt like it took an eternity. He hit every light; traffic was diabolical. He saw why once he got close enough. The rain had washed out a section of the road and traffic had to be rerouted.

"You'd think they'd never had to detour before," he muttered as he navigated the clogged streets, trying to get to his destination.

Nikki.

He could only imagine what she must think of him at that moment. The biggest, most important thing in her career and he was ninety minutes late.

"Fucking hell," he hissed looking at the clock on the dash even though it had only been two minutes since he last looked.

"Please, please, please," he prayed out loud. He had no other words to add to his prayer, just emotion.

He hated himself in that moment. Hated that she would even have to doubt him. Hated that he'd introduced thoughts of him never being there for her. Hated that his father could still mess with his life without invitation. Hated that Nikki wondered where he was. She should never have to wonder. She should be able to count on him.

But he would apologize, and even though he was late, he was still coming.

He would never not show up.

Not again.

Never again.

The parking lot was full when he arrived, and he had to park in the street. He grabbed the rose and sprinted to the back of the building.

Pulling open the door, he raced down the hall to the lounge he'd built for her. It was full of people.

He heard his name come from a variety of directions but he only had one focus.

Nikki.

No one mattered but her.

He spotted her across the room. She was wearing an electric-blue dress that dipped in a deep V in the front and back. It hugged every curve of her body and was scandalously short.

And her shoes… Nikki and her fucking shoes.

Hot-pink, pencil-thin heels that looked like butterflies but with spikes on them.

She turned, spotted him, and smiled.

She smiled.

At him.

He took a breath for the first time in what felt like hours.

Every step her direction felt like climbing a mountain and she was the sunrise.

"I'm sorry I'm late," he said. "But I'm here now."

Her blue eyes, made more intense by the dress, took in his state and he could only imagine what she saw.

The next minute happened in slow motion.

She leaned in, a hand to his chest, and pressed a kiss to his cheek where she paused and said in his ear, "Sabine told me who's in town. Is everything all right?" Her voice soft. Concerned. Full of care.

He nodded and found her eyes, needing to anchor himself. Needing her to see the sincerity in his apology. Needing her to believe him.

"Nik," he said, his heart clenched in a fist. "I'm sorry. Please don't think this was something that it wasn't. I will never not show up for you."

Her expression softened and she tapped her finger on his chest. "I know. You've proven that to me again and again. I knew you'd be here. Even if it took you a few extra minutes."

He stared at her. Completely stunned.

She looked him over, a playful smile on those gorgeous lips. She took hold of his suspenders and gave them a little tug.

"Are these new? I like them." She beamed up at him, no anger, no disbelief.

It was already over. Like it hadn't even happened.

He didn't deserve her.

He knew that, of course, but it was so obvious in that moment.

"I love you," he said, wrapping his arms around her and crushing her lips with his own.

Her arms came around his neck and he lifted her up as he deepened the kiss. The room surrounding them grew loud with whistles and hollers.

He lowered her back to her feet but kept kissing her.

This incredible, amazing, excitable woman loved him. And it wasn't a normal kind of love. It was bright and boundless, just like her.

"This was for you," he said, remembering the rose. But it was all beat to hell and only had a few bruised petals left on it. He grimaced. "Sorry. It didn't start out like that."

She laughed as he chucked it onto a nearby table.

Then he gathered her in his arms and kissed her some more. Trying to pour all of his love and relief into it that he could.

"You made it."

André heard his sister, but he wasn't quite done kissing Nikki. He pressed one more kiss to her lips. Again. One more time. Nikki smiled and a small giggle rippled through her that he had the privilege of feeling in his arms and where her soft body was still pressed to his.

"Yes, he made it," Nikki said, soft and sweet, looking up at him the same way.

André took a deep, stabilizing breath, finding that solid ground in Nikki's eyes before turning his attention to Sabine and Sunshine.

Sabine's smile was of the all-knowing sister variety, and she waggled her eyebrows.

André had told Sabine via text that he and Nikki were together, but this was her first time seeing them together. And it was a lot better in person than in text alone.

"Did you see him?" Sabine asked, her mood shifting slightly.

She didn't need to specify to whom she was referring.

"He was at my place when I got there," André said. It still didn't feel real.

"What did he tell you?" Sabine asked.

"That he was 'in town' and wanted to chat." He narrowed his eyes at his sister. "What did he tell you?"

She rolled her eyes and curled a lip. "He wanted to know if Dave likes soccer."

André scrunched his nose. "That dodgy tosser."

Sabine snorted.

"He was fired," he told her. "Which means he's trying to use your rock star husband to get him back in with the owners. What a wanker."

Nikki gave him a squeeze and his irritation melted away again.

He didn't need to worry about his dad. The man could ruin his own life.

"Let's talk about you," he said, tipping Nikki's chin up towards him. "I am so proud of you."

She grinned and tugged on his suspender strap. "No, I think I want to hear you say more words like wanker."

Fucking hell.

"You can't flirt with me like that in public, Nicole," he said. She pressed her lips together and bounced a little on her toes. "I will embarrass us both."

"You could never embarrass me," she said, with a smile tempting him to be less than decent in her workplace.

"You'd embarrass me," Sabine said. "So please don't."

"You're always wearing suspenders. I like that." Sunshine spoke up.

Sabine chuckled in the way of a sister who was about to share something she maybe shouldn't. "He didn't have an ass to help hold up his pants when he was younger. Belts didn't work because he was so skinny."

"I guess I just got used to the suspenders. I tried converting to belts, but it didn't take. Too uncomfortable," André explained.

"Well, you always look great. Very sophisticated." Sunshine looked at Sabine. "Should I start wearing suspenders?"

Sabine screwed up her face. "Please, no."

Johnny and his partner, Hannah, came over and entered the conversation. They talked about the album and how proud Johnny was of Nikki. Hannah praised her talent and skill.

Sunshine concurred.

Zara joined them.

And Asa and Justin.

And after they had made Nikki sufficiently uncomfortable with their compliments and praise, Johnny and Hannah made her an offer.

"We'd like to offer you twenty-five percent," Hannah said.

The group grew quiet as everyone's eyes came to Nikki.

"What?" Nikki asked, a confused smile tilting her lips.

"Of the studio," Johnny continued. "No buy-in. Just yours. If you want it."

Nikki swallowed and her gaze cut to André. "What?" she asked him.

He squeezed her hand, his heart beating wildly for her. "Ownership," he said to her.

Nikki looked back at Johnny and Hannah. "What?" she repeated.

Johnny smiled and nodded. "But only if you want it."

"I want it," Nikki blurted. And then she hopped. "I really want it."

"I thought you might," Johnny said around a chuckle. "We'll do all the paperwork next week."

Nikki squealed and threw her arms around Johnny. And then Hannah. She spun around, grabbed André's suspenders and pulled him in for a triumphant kiss.

He laughed as he caught her, her joy infectious.

Another round of grape juice was poured and André held Nikki close, kissing her, hugging her, celebrating her.

He cradled her face in both hands and enjoyed the radiance shining out of her eyes.

"Are you happy?" he asked, knowing the answer.

But somehow her smile grew brighter. "I am so happy," she whispered. "I have everything I have ever wanted."

"So do I," he said, lowering his mouth.

"Tell me you love me," she said against his lips.

"I love you," he rumbled.

But he'd do more than tell her.

He would show her that he loved her every day for the rest of their lives.

Starting with this kiss.

CHAPTER TWENTY

GERONIMO

Two Months Later

ANDRÉ

"I'm not going to lie to her."

"Good. I don't want you to lie to her."

Asa narrowed his eyes in suspicion.

André remained still.

If this was going to work, Asa had to play this cool. Otherwise, he could throw all his plans out the window.

André's eyes cut back to the buzzing phone with Nikki's beautiful face on the screen.

"Are you going to answer?" André held his breath as Asa reached for his phone. He slid his thumb across the screen and put it to his ear.

"Hello?" Asa's dark eyes remained on André as he spoke to Nikki. "I'm at lunch."

True.

"With André."

Fuck.

"Because he asked me to lunch. Are you jealous?" Asa baited. "Ew. No. I'm sorry I asked." A light laugh trickled through the phone right before Asa hung up. "Instant regret."

André released his breath and sat back in the booth.

A moment later their server dropped off chips and salsa.

Asa crunched into the chips. André sipped his ice water. But neither of them spoke.

André had decided he would let Asa set the tone for this lunch. He didn't want to pressure him into anything. For this to work, it had to be natural. Easy.

This was fine.

They were fine.

Or they would be.

Eventually.

"So…" Asa said, dusting the salt from his hands and folding them on the table. "Nikki must have told you this was my favorite restaurant?"

"You told me once. I just remembered."

Asa lifted his chin and pursed his lips.

"What happens after lunch?" Asa asked.

"That depends on what happens during lunch," André replied.

Asa looked to the ceiling like he was praying for strength or patience, or possibly an alien invasion. "What am I doing here, André? We're not friends. We don't 'do lunch.' Just tell me what you want."

That was fair.

André drummed his fingers on the table and blew out a breath. Asa watched him, a crease forming between his brows.

"I'm going to ask Nikki to marry me."

Asa's expression shifted and he immediately looked bored. "Oh, are you?"

André held back a smile. He'd anticipated Asa's cynicism and it was nice to be right.

"Yes."

"I suppose you want my blessing or something?" Asa leaned back in the booth and rested his arm along the back of it.

"No." André shook his head. "Nothing quite so antiquated. I've already spoken to her parents, just to be respectful. But I don't require permission from anyone to ask her to spend the rest of our lives together."

Asa's mouth opened slightly and he blinked. He'd surprised him.

"You've already told her parents?"

André nodded. He'd called them yesterday. They were so excited that he knew he needed to speak to Asa before Bob and Mary spoiled the surprise.

Asa's gaze grew distant. He brought his arms off the back of the booth and rested them on the table.

The server returned with their order.

André added the house hot sauce to his tacos. Asa didn't touch his food. He just stared at the table.

"Who else knows?" Asa asked, voice terse.

"Just Bob and Mary and now you." André bit into his taco and closed his eyes. This place was awesome. Someday he'd tell Asa it was also his favorite restaurant. Not today. It was too soon for that.

But they'd get there.

"Why?" Asa asked, face stony.

"Because I love her," André answered matter of fact. Again, he'd anticipated this response.

Asa rolled his eyes. "You've said that before."

André sat back and sipped his ice water. That hot sauce was no joke.

"I know Nikki has forgiven you and all's well in your world," Asa continued. "But I was there when you broke her heart. I know what you did. I can't just forget that. I will never trust you."

André wagged his head back and forth, disagreeing. "Well, you trust me a little."

Asa jerked back, affronted. "I do not."

"You do a little."

"No, I don't."

André scrunched his nose. "A tiny bit you do."

Asa laughed despite himself and shook his head. "No."

"Asa." André leaned forward, serious. "It's okay that you hate me."

"I do hate you."

"I know." André waved a hand because he wasn't done. "But I love her and I'm going to marry her."

Asa sighed heavy and deep like the very idea was killing him. "Fine. What do you want from me?"

André grinned. "I need help picking the ring. And who better than her best friend?"

Asa tried to hate the suggestion. André could see it on his face as his irritation with André warred with the realization that it was an excellent idea.

"Fine." But he said it like he hated the very word.

"Great. Finish your food. I have an appointment for us in a half an hour."

"What? Today?" Asa asked, shocked.

"Yes." André nodded.

Asa finally started to eat his tacos.

André had already picked out three options before showing up with Asa. He didn't tell Asa that of course and was, again, very happy to be right.

But it was the square-cut pink diamond with a black diamond halo that they both kept going back to.

"It's small," André said.

"So is she," Asa murmured.

"I can afford something bigger," André pointed out.

"She's not that kind of person."

No, she wasn't.

None of the other options they had considered were very large either.

But this one was simple and almost classic, with just enough badass to it to be beautiful.

"That's the one," André said.

Asa nodded. "Yep."

The clerk ran his card and packaged up the ring.

"So when will this all take place? Did you have a ring last time?" Asa asked.

"I did have a ring. I still have it. Somewhere." André took the bag from the clerk, smiled his thanks. Asa followed him out of the store.

The chill of the October wind bit at his ears as he zipped his coat up.

"But I didn't want to propose with that. I wanted something new. Neither one of us is who we used to be."

They went north on Michigan Avenue toward the Water Tower Garage where André had parked.

"By that logic you should be buying her a new ring every few years," Asa pointed out.

"Maybe I will," André said, shooting the other man a grin.

Asa shoved his hands in his coat pockets and shook his head.

"What if you chicken out again?" he asked.

"Then I expect you to kick my ass and tell me to get back in there," André answered honestly.

"Oh, I'm gonna be there when it happens, huh?" Asa chuckled.

André nodded. "Where do you think we're headed?"

Asa twisted his neck to gape at André. "Now? You're asking her right now?"

André just smiled and kept walking.

Yes. He was asking her as soon as he saw her.

They reached André's car and got inside. He started it up along with the seat warmer and then turned slightly to face Asa.

"I have no reason to wait, Asa. I'm not afraid. I love her and she loves me. What else is there?"

Asa stared at him a beat. "All right, man. But if you hurt her…"

André smiled wide. "I fully expect you to ruin my life."

NIKKI

She pushed the shelf back into place and stood up.

Having that storage in the back wall of her office was the best thing that ever happened to her.

Okay, maybe not the *best* thing. But it had to be in the top five.

It saved her time and money and space… Three things that were so hard to come by most days.

"Nik."

And there was the real best thing that had ever happened to her. She smiled at the soft way he said her name, as if he didn't want to disturb her.

She turned around and her smile grew when she saw André standing in the doorway of her office. His coat was tucked under one arm and both hands were shoved in his pockets.

"Hey, you," she greeted. "How was lunch with Asa?"

He scanned her up and down and smiled. "Good. Are you busy?"

She waggled her eyebrows. "Not anymore."

He chuckled and crossed to the sofa, depositing his coat over the arm.

"Should I lock the door or…?" she asked, slowly making her way in his direction.

He held out a hand to her. "Come here."

She took it and he sat her down on the sofa while he remained standing.

She narrowed her eyes at him. "What's going on? You're being weird."

He flashed a smile and then schooled his features. "Stop being cute. I'm trying to be serious."

"Oh." She sat up straighter and rested her hands on her thighs. "Well, in that case."

Again, he fought his amusement and looked away from her.

When his hazel eyes came back to her, they were lit from within. And she knew that look. That was his "he has a secret" look.

She loved that look.

He licked his lips, swallowed, took a deep breath…and got down on one knee.

Her stomach flipped over and her heart began beating the samba.

"André?" she said so softly she wasn't sure the words made it out.

"I have to ask you a very important question," he said. "Possibly the most important question of my life."

She tried to keep her breathing steady. If this wasn't what she thought it was—

"I love you, Nicole. I love everything about you. I love your laugh and your joy. I love that you cry more when the hero gets it right than when everything goes wrong. I love that you show up to reroof a house when you should be sleeping. I love that you see people and appreciate them for all their differences. I love that you never stop hoping for better. I love that you're excitable and you have a lot to say because it's all things I want to know. I love listening to you, talking to you, sharing my heart with you."

He took her hand.

"And I was wondering if you'd mind, if you weren't too busy, would you consider spending the rest of your life letting me love you? Properly?"

She launched herself at him and he caught her. She rained kisses all over his stupid handsome face until he lost his balance and fell back. She went with him and continued to pummel him with a frenzy of kisses.

When she sat up straddling his waist, he was smiling.

"Is that a yes?" he asked with a short laugh.

He brought her hand to his heart, and she glanced down. Her gaze bounced back to him and then back to the ring that sat, inexplicably, on her finger.

"I will love you for the rest of my life, Nik," he said, serious again.

She realized he was waiting for her answer. Obviously, it was yes. But it suddenly felt like such a small word for such a large feeling.

"André?" She took a breath. The pink diamond glittered in the light. Or maybe those were her tears. "I will only say yes on one condition."

His eyebrows dipped and he nodded once.

So earnest.

So committed.

"You have to let me love you just as much as you love me."

He grinned, sat up, wrapped his arms around her, and rolled so she was now on her back.

"You can try, but I'm not sure you understand how much I love you. It's an enormous amount. Gargantuan, in fact."

She pushed his dark hair back where it had flopped messily onto his forehead. "I think you'd better show me."

EPILOGUE

CELEBX- OH BABY

As usual, the NMAs were filled with drama and excitement.

The biggest upset of the night was Zara Lorna winning Album of the Year for First Comes Love.

A passion project that focused on deeper tones and a rock and roll foundation. Zara's sixth studio album shook up the industry.

The surprise nomination wasn't expected to win.

Zara Lorna is a regular nominee for the NMAs. She's won Artist of the Year twice and Album of the Year four times. It seems that even switching up genres, she can do no wrong.

The album's producer, Nicole Harry, also won Producer of the Year.

Harry is the former guitar player for the now defunct alt rock band, Winking Pete. She had co-writing credits and mixing credits on an Ashton James album and a Sunshine Capone album. This was her first time being nominated.

Nicole Harry's friend and former bandmate, Asa Young, accepted the award on her behalf. She could not attend the event due to it being too close to her pregnancy due date.

Insiders close to the producer said her water broke right after she was announced the winner.

Sources say mom and baby are doing fine.

PLAYLIST/CHAPTER TITLES

1. Resolve…Foo Fighters
2. I Bet You Think About Me…Taylor Swift
3. Feel It All (And Nothing)…Eliza & The Delusionals
4. OH WELL…Christian French
5. Incinerate…Sonic Youth
6. Swimming Pool…Eliza & The Delusionals
7. Death By A Thousand Cuts…Taylor Swift
8. Pull Apart Heart…Eliza & The Delusionals
9. Oh!...Sleater-Kinney
10. Cruel Summer…Taylor Swift
11. Get a Hold of You…Eliza & The Delusionals
12. Favorite Crime…Olivia Rodrigo
13. What Do I Do With All This Faith?...Bleachers
14. Too Much Too Fast…311
15. Long Road To Ruin…Foo Fighters
16. Put Your Arms Around Me…Texas
17. Sugar Kane…Sonic Youth
18. King Of My Heart…Taylor Swift
19. This Love…Taylor Swift
20. Geronimo…Sheppard

ABOUT THE AUTHOR

Heidi writes stories that she hopes will inspire her readers to take their hearts on one more adventure.

She still lives in the Black Hills with her alarmingly handsome husband, their fearless child, and a rather large and spoiled dog.

She is fueled by her unwavering and perfectly normal devotion to Dave Grohl and coffee.

And a whole lotta love.

heidih.net

Email: heidih.writer@gmail.com

Find Smartypants Romance online:
Website: www.smartypantsromance.com
Facebook: www.facebook.com/smartypantsromance/
Goodreads: www.goodreads.com/smartypantsromance
Twitter: @smartypantsrom
Instagram: @smartypantsromance

OTHER TITLES BY HEIDI HUTCHINSON

Smartypants Romance Common Threads Series:

Key Change (#3-Ashton)

Lost Track (#5- Sunshine)

All Mixed Up (#7- Nikki)

Double Blind Study Rock Star Series:

(Interconnected standalones, Adult Contemporary, Romantic Comedy)

Learn to Fly (#1-Luke)

In Your Honor (#2-Blake)

Tectonic (#3-Shane)

Deepest Blues (#4-Mike)

The Hope That Starts (#5-Harrison)

Brand New Sky (#6-Sway)

Into the Night We Shine (Holiday Shorts #7)

Matter of Fact (holiday novella #8-Carl)

Soaring Bird Surf Series:

(Interconnected standalones, Adult Contemporary, Sports Romance, spinoff of Tectonic)

Tectonic (#0.5-Shane)

Like the Back of My Halo (#1-Brady)

Sushi and Sun Salutations (#2-Kip)

Puppy Love and Peanut Butter (#3-Bo)

Rope a Dope (#4-Steve)

Caught a Vibe (#5-Adam)

In Between Series:

In Between the Earth and Sky

In Cold Mud Series:

(Women's fiction)

Stubborn Hearts (prequel to Brand New Sky)

Crossover with Bria Quinlan in the Double Blind Study Rock Star World

Things That Shine

www.heidih.net

ALSO BY SMARTYPANTS ROMANCE

Green Valley Chronicles

The Love at First Sight Series

Baking Me Crazy by Karla Sorensen (#1)

Batter of Wits by Karla Sorensen (#2)

Steal My Magnolia by Karla Sorensen (#3)

Worth the Wait by Karla Sorensen (#4)

Fighting For Love Series

Stud Muffin by Jiffy Kate (#1)

Beef Cake by Jiffy Kate (#2)

Eye Candy by Jiffy Kate (#3)

Knock Out by Jiffy Kate (#4)

The Donner Bakery Series

No Whisk, No Reward by Ellie Kay (#1)

Dough You Love Me? By Stacy Travis (#2)

Tough Cookie by Talia Hunter (#3)

The Green Valley Library Series

Love in Due Time by L.B. Dunbar (#1)

Crime and Periodicals by Nora Everly (#2)

Prose Before Bros by Cathy Yardley (#3)

Shelf Awareness by Katie Ashley (#4)

Carpentry and Cocktails by Nora Everly (#5)

Love in Deed by L.B. Dunbar (#6)

Dewey Belong Together by Ann Whynot (#7)

Hotshot and Hospitality by Nora Everly (#8)

Love in a Pickle by L.B. Dunbar (#9)

Checking You Out by Ann Whynot (#10)

Architecture and Artistry by Nora Everly (#11)

Scorned Women's Society Series

My Bare Lady by Piper Sheldon (#1)

The Treble with Men by Piper Sheldon (#2)

The One That I Want by Piper Sheldon (#3)

Hopelessly Devoted by Piper Sheldon (#3.5)

It Takes a Woman by Piper Sheldon (#4)

Park Ranger Series

Happy Trail by Daisy Prescott (#1)

Stranger Ranger by Daisy Prescott (#2)

The Leffersbee Series

Been There Done That by Hope Ellis (#1)

Before and After You by Hope Ellis (#2)

The Higher Learning Series

Upsy Daisy by Chelsie Edwards (#1)

Green Valley Heroes Series

Forrest for the Trees by Kilby Blades (#1)

Parks and Provocation by Juliette Cross (#2)

Letter Late Than Never by Lauren Connolly (#3)

Peaches and Dreams by Juliette Cross (#4)

Story of Us Collection

My Story of Us: Zach by Chris Brinkley (#1)

My Story of Us: Thomas by Chris Brinkley (#2)

Seduction in the City

Cipher Security Series

Code of Conduct by April White (#1)

Code of Honor by April White (#2)

Code of Matrimony by April White (#2.5)

Code of Ethics by April White (#3)

Cipher Office Series

Weight Expectations by M.E. Carter (#1)

Sticking to the Script by Stella Weaver (#2)

Cutie and the Beast by M.E. Carter (#3)

Weights of Wrath by M.E. Carter (#4)

Common Threads Series

Mad About Ewe by Susannah Nix (#1)

Give Love a Chai by Nanxi Wen (#2)

Key Change by Heidi Hutchinson (#3)

Not Since Ewe by Susannah Nix (#4)

Lost Track by Heidi Hutchinson (#5)

Ewe Complete Me by Susannah Nix (#6)

Meet Your Matcha by Nanxi Wen (#7)

All Mixed Up by Heidi Hutchinson (#8)

Educated Romance

Work For It Series

Street Smart by Aly Stiles (#1)

Heart Smart by Emma Lee Jayne (#2)

Book Smart by Amanda Pennington (#3)

Smart Mouth by Emma Lee Jayne (#4)

Play Smart by Aly Stiles (#5)

Look Smart by Aly Stiles (#6)

Smart Move by Amanda Pennington (#7)

Lessons Learned Series

Under Pressure by Allie Winters (#1)

Not Fooling Anyone by Allie Winters (#2)

Can't Fight It by Allie Winters (#3)

The Vinyl Frontier by Lola West (#4)

Out of this World

London Ladies Embroidery Series

Neanderthal Seeks Duchess by Laney Hatcher (#1)

Well Acquainted by Laney Hatcher (#2)

Love Matched by Laney Hatcher (#3)

Milton Keynes UK
Ingram Content Group UK Ltd.
UKHW040829111023
430376UK00004B/224